Publisher: Ken Olive Publishing

ISBN-13: 978-0-615-39384-1
ISBN-10: 0-615-39384-5

First Edition: August 2010

10 9 8 7 6 5 4 3 2 1

Goldie's Garden

A Flowers Novel by Ken Olive

Goldie's Garden

A Dog's Tale of War, Hurricanes, and Heroism

Feb. 96...I Am Me

My first memories were of protected warmth, surrounded by little furry, squiggly things with cold noses, all wiggling around, under, and on top of me. Then, on a very nice schedule, I would feel an almost hairless, bulging rotation. I would find a little knob, and pulling it with my mouth, aaah…a sweet warm substance entered my body, making me stronger, and likely to sleep. I would awaken to a rough, wet caress very often. And as time went by, I would hear in the routine a small yip or squeak. It was then I knew that I was not alone. But, company also meant competition for the knobs and the sweet substance, so I learned to crawl over and squeeze closer, so as not be left out.

Then one day, after a blissful nap, a light appeared for the first time. I heard a voice; "her eyes are open, she's the first one." I looked at my world…the other little wigglers whose scent I knew so well, the belly of a bigger wiggler, who I named the "Large One," possessing the knobs, and sharing my space. A space where in a couple of more days, I would start to wrestle and cavort with my siblings. A space that had a blanket, a bowl of clear liquid, and bars of a hard substance which hurt my nose when I got too close. I liked to get close…to see down the hall. There were lots more spaces with bars. And from these spaces I heard loud voices communicating fear, anger, and confusion. I was not afraid. No one could harm me or my mates, as long as the "Large One" was there.

The next morning creatures foreign to me came to our space. "Daisy, what a beautiful group of young puppies you have, all five of them. I think it's time for the ribbons." A piece of something was tied around the neck of each of us small ones. "You were the first to open your eyes, so you'll get the red one," I heard.

They all looked the same to me. The creature was nice, but different. "Now we can tell you apart." From this, I learned the "Large One" was named Daisy. "Oh, How cute, they're just opening their eyes for the first time," said several small voices.

A little while later, what I know now to be adoption time at the shelter, other, similar creatures would come down the hall. They would look at us and make soft noises, sticking parts of themselves between the bars.

Daisy didn't mind, so I was not afraid. This went on for a couple of days. I kept hearing the words "they're not quite ready yet." What did that mean? And more creatures kept coming to see us. We were celebrities. Every creature who came made soothing noises and laughed at our antics.

Then one night I awakened to hear Daisy, whining, and furiously licking the one they called "Green" I went over to him, and snuggled up as close as I could. He wasn't warm anymore. The creatures came in the morning. I could tell they were sad, I didn't know why. They took little "Green" away. Daisy was sad. I was afraid, and confused. If Daisy couldn't warm him, who could? We all stayed closer together, now, huddled against the possibility of becoming cold.

One morning, a group of creatures came in and took all four of us small ones into another room. They handled us nicely, played with us, and after awhile, I heard " we'll take the two males, we've got plenty of room, and the twins love them."

When I got back to my space, it was just me, the "Pink one," and Daisy. This process continued for several more long periods of light and dark. Being fondled by strangers, getting to stretch my legs outside my space, being returned. I began to eat from a bowl, and drink water. I was getting to be me.

Then, one day, an amazing thing happened. Someone picked me! "The red one" the little creature called Josh said. "Definitely the red one."

He picked me up and looked at his larger creatures with him. He had a huge gap-toothed grin, and the others nodded, "Happy 13th Birthday Josh."

My world was changed forever. I looked back over Josh's shoulder and saw Daisy, and "Pink." I heard someone say that "Pink" would be fine. She would get a new space, for sure, but that Daisy, being older would be a problem, to place. Why was that, I wondered? She had been the warm, gentle "Large One" who gave us life.

I wanted to run back to them, to be safe and warm. I tried, but was not nearly strong enough, as Josh held me tight to his chest. I wondered if I would ever see her again. I still dream of Daisy at night. The warm beginnings of my life. The wet kisses of love. Maybe that was the first time I realized that, outside of the space I was born in, was a whole different world.

I was soon to find out. It would be an adventure.

4-96...My Journey Begins

What a space! As far as my eyes could see, there was no end to it. It was so different. Very bright, full of new scents and smells. Josh put me into the car, on his lap and let me look out the window. His parents were in front, and a smaller creature named "Jessica" sat beside Josh in the back. We started moving, and Josh rolled down a crank to let the air flow hit my face. This was fantastic! My tongue lapped out of my mouth, my tail wagged, my breathing grew heavy with excitement. After just a little while, it was nap time again, and I surrendered to it.

I felt the motion stop, and I perked up to see a huge space. Jessica got out of the car hurriedly, slamming the door. " I wanted a puppy too!" she exclaimed. "Jessica, you're not even 11 yet, and having a dog is a big responsibility. I'm sure when you are 13 you'll be ready for your own. You can practice by helping Josh with his." "I don't want anything to do with his dog. If he is big enough to take care of it, he doesn't need any help from me."

When the uproar subsided, Josh took me inside the big space...they called it "home." It was all on one floor, but Josh had his own space inside. He already had a smaller space for me beside his bed. A cardboard box, with a blanket, a small bowl of water, and guess what? No bars to look through...Wow!

Later, all the creatures, I now call them my new family, sat around a large table. The table was full of delicious smells. I was getting hungry. "Have you picked a name yet son?" the Largest creature said. The boy said, "Since she's a Yellow Labrador, I want to call her 'Goldie'." That's a perfect name for her he said.

"Not original, but very acceptable," said the largest one at the table. "I think Goldie is a wonderful name." "How about 'poopy', as in poop?" Jessica yelled, as she pointed to the floor. What was everyone staring at? I did nothing out of the ordinary.

"The house training begins early, I see," the large one spoke again, looking directly at me. Josh scooped me up and took me into the back yard. Another wonderful, open space. Wonderful but hot, as I found out later we were in southern Mississippi.

"At least it's not raining," Josh said. "Goldie, you stay out here, until you're finished." Finished with what, I wasn't sure.

After a few days of this type of drill, I realized they wanted me to do my "business" as they called it, out in the back yard. That was no problem.

I found out that this would be my home "space" while Josh was at school, unless it was raining. That was great for me. There was a large fence there, and this was a much larger space than even the house.

I stayed close to the fence in the shade of a large Magnolia tree. Josh's Mom would walk over to visit me, bring me water, and talk to me as she was beginning her Spring garden. We became great friends. She enjoyed talking, and I loved having another "Large One" as a protector.

She planted tomatoes, carrots, squash, herbs, and melon, that first year. She explained to me that one day part of my job would be to keep the rabbits and other varmints away. No problem, I was already getting bigger every day. To help, she put up a small "chicken wire fence with a little gate and buried the bottom of the fence slightly into the ground.

She put up a net on top of 6-foot poles, to keep the birds out, but it let in the sun and the rain. During the day, while I was on guard, she left the gate open, for her numerous trips in and out. She had a small shed in the back yard where she stored things. I was practicing my protection from about 50 feet away, in the cool shade, but was always alert.

The highlight of my day was the squealing of the air brakes on the school bus which brought Josh back to me. It was the second squealing of the afternoon, the first one brought Jessica home, and she mainly went inside and ignored me. But Jessica's bus arriving, let me know that Josh was not far behind, and I was excited. As excited as if he had been gone for weeks…every school day.

"Goldie, I'm home girl" he shouted. I ran to the fence gate at high speed. Nothing could have run that fast, and been that happy. Guess what? He was happy too. He wrestled me on the ground, rubbing my belly, cuffing my ears, till his Mom said "Josh, not in your school clothes." Josh hopped up and called me inside with him while he changed. I was beginning to feel like part of the family, an important part.

I maintained order in the back yard. Keeper of the garden. Even snoozing in the shade. I could hear if a squirrel or rabbit dared enter the yard, and I was in charge. I was enjoying life with my new family. I didn't dream so often of Daisy and "Pink," and hardly ever had nightmares about "Green"…just sometimes, and then I would cry.

8-96...An Unexpected Trip

One morning, it must have been in the Summer because Josh had been home everyday and it was hotter outside than ever, I heard Mom say "OK son, it's time for our visit to Doctor Yung's" Josh asked "do we have to?." "Now Josh, you know that was part of the adoption agreement for Goldie. In order to adopt, you have to agree to spay. That way there are fewer unwanted dogs in the world." I thought that sounded odd. But then I thought of Daisy, and my last look at her. And how the people at the shelter had said she would have a problem finding a good home.

Josh hung his head and nodded. But what did this have to do with me? I was barely out of puppyhood myself, 6 months old. In a few minutes I walked outside behind a slightly depressed Josh. He, Mom, and I got into her small car. It was much smaller than Dad's, Mom called it a "Bug." Mom drove a few minutes, then across a long bridge with lots of water underneath it (how do they do that, I thought?)

We pulled up in front of a square building, looking much like I remembered the shelter, and the three of us went inside. After waiting awhile a young girl escorted us into a smaller room with a high bench in the middle. Josh put me on the bench and said "It's going to be OK, don't be afraid." In walked a little woman, sort of frail looking, and not really taller than Josh. "Dr. Yung," Mom said. "It's so good to see you again. I believe the last time was when we found that bird with the broken wing, and brought it to you." "Oh yes, that was a brown pelican, an endangered species. I sent it to the Sanctuary in New Orleans. I still get reports on it. That bird has hatched 4 chicks since it recovered from her injuries. It was a very good thing you did."

"Now little one, let me look at you." I realized she meant me! "You'll do great, one night here for observation, then right back home." I was afraid.

But she was very gentle, making soft sounds, looking into my eyes and ears, putting an object on my tummy and chest, opening my mouth wide.

"She'll be fine" she assured all of us. "You didn't feed her last night or this morning?" I could answer that, I was hungry.

"What time should I pick her up tomorrow" asked Mom. "After lunch would be perfect." Mom looked at me. "I'll be here, I promise. Josh has chores to help Dad with, but I'll be here." The next thing I knew Josh and Mom gave me big hugs, and left through the swinging door. Oh no! What was going on?

A skinny young girl came in the room and took me to a different, larger room. "She's ready for prep," and another girl flipped me on my back and started shaving my belly. I had something put over my mouth and nose. It smelled different than anything I had encountered before. After a couple of breaths, I started feeling like I needed a nap. I was asleep before I knew it.

I started to wake up. It was nighttime. I heard others making different types of noises. Where was Josh? And then I saw it...the bars again. I didn't like it and I was afraid. I crawled back to the corner of my space, and went back to sleep, hoping it was only a bad dream.

Morning came, and I was still in the dream. After awhile, a young person brought me a tiny container of water. "Not too much now, drink slowly." I looked through the bars at my situation. How much worse could it get? What had I done to deserve this? It was much more noisy. I could tell that the others had been awake for a while. And they were making quite a lot of noise.

Doctor Yung came in to see me. She looked at my belly and nodded with approval.

She spoke with one of the girls and said, "You can take her out now, for a short walk, then up to the front. I went outside to do my business, as taught. It felt a little different, but not too bad. When I was finished, the girl guided me by my leash through the place with bars, through some more rooms, and out to a large room where I saw the most beautiful sight I had ever seen…Mom smiling, squatting down with her hands stretched out for me. "Come on girl, lets go home."

I started to dash off, but she pulled me back with the leash. "Dr. Yung says you have to take it easy for a few days. No running, wrestling, and only a little food today." I didn't care. I didn't feel hungry anymore, anyway. She helped me into the "bug" and I was curled up on the seat asleep before we got out of the parking lot.

Holidays 96…
I'm Growing and Learning

I was now becoming familiar with my surroundings, and I began to learn more about my family, and my rank in the pack.

We lived on 5 acres of what was once farmland in a rural part of Biloxi, Mississippi. Our house was on the north side of Biloxi's "Back Bay," in an area called De'Iberville, away from the casinos, hotels, and beaches only a few miles away on the Gulf of Mexico. This part of Biloxi was wooded with pine and live oak trees. Our front yard was dominated, and shaded, by two giant live oaks. The brick home was only 3 bedrooms plus a bonus room over the 1-car garage, which they used for storage. Our land reached all the way to the water on a peninsula of Back Bay. Dad had a small boat tied to a dock at the end of the property, but, he didn't use it very often. The waterline was muddy, as I saw on one of my infrequent early visits that far from home with Josh. The Bay water was dirty, so population here was sparse. My family had bought it for just that reason. The "Big Dog" of the pack, Dad, wanted to keep far away from the raucous atmosphere created on the Gulf Coast by the casinos, bars, and tourist traps. He wanted his family safe, with room to live without being crammed in by neighbors, like they were across the Bay.

It was also close to his work. I learned that he was a Captain in the U.S. Air Force, at Keesler Air Force Base. His first assignment had been at a place called "Eglin," but, I heard him say he liked Keesler better, except for the casinos. He was a weather instructor there. Some kind of long word starting with "meteor." I once got to ride with him there to pick up something he had forgotten, and it was only a 20 minute drive by car, most of it over the I-110 Back Bay Bridge, but when we got there it seemed so much larger. People walked faster, drove faster, but treated the Father like he was important, calling him "Captain Flowers.

Mom called him Tom. The only other thing I knew about the Base was that Josh had been born there, shortly after the family moved here.

Mom (Karen Flowers), I knew pretty well due to her gardening. At times she would talk about her two older sisters, one in San Antonio, Vicky, who had become a young widow, and one in Atlanta, Beth. Karen's mother also lived in San Antonio, and she used the word "senile" about her with both sisters. I got the idea that those places were huge, even larger than Biloxi. Both sisters also had a daughter.

She liked the sister in San Antonio better, I could tell the difference when they spoke over a device called a phone. She even let me listen once when Josh called from the school after a special study program. I could hear him in there, but how did he get that small? I'll have to think about that. My hero, Josh, the one who picked me. I knew him best of all. He was growing almost as fast as I was. I liked him because he had golden hair and big goofy feet like I did. He made good grades in school and because of that, they let him start playing a game called basketball.

The bad part of Josh's basketball was that he started coming home later from school, and his arrival was no longer announced with air brakes. Instead, I listened for Mom's little car coming into the oyster shell driveway. I was still ecstatic to see him, and the feeling was mutual. The good news was that this only happened part of the year, which he called the "season." The better news was that Dad built him a "court", in the back yard. It was cement, with a tall pole and hoop at the end. Josh would stay outside for hours throwing a ball at the hoop. Sometimes he stayed outside until dark, and I was there with him. I'd run down the ball when it got away from him. It was much too big to fit into my mouth. I liked throwing the tennis ball better because it was smaller and easier to retrieve, but I made the best of his basketball practice it by butting it with my head and shoulders back to Josh, just like I was part of the game. That made both of us happy. Josh started to have more friends call on the phone. I guess they got small somehow as well. He seemed to take an interest in a girl. Wendy was her name. He started sitting beside her on the morning bus. Oh well, I had him all to myself at home, why not share?

The weather outside had turned a little cooler. It was still hot, but cooler with some breezes from the south. We had a long weekend called Thanksgiving. I was going to meet some new people, I found out. Mom's Texas sister, Vicky, her niece, and their mother, was going to come visit us over the long holiday weekend.

Josh's Grandma had lived with Vicky since Vicky's husband had died several years earlier. They finally arrived Thursday morning, Thanksgiving Day, having left San Antonio, 640 miles away, the day before. They stayed Wednesday night just west of New Orleans. Her sister was very nice, and looked a lot like Mom. She came right over to me, the first thing. "So this is the little one I've been hearing so much about. You are such a beautiful girl." I felt warm inside. She was like mom's twin, though she was a little younger. "Looks like I have a new friend, thought Goldie." I tried to stay near Vicky, and make her feel welcome. It's not easy being the new one.

Josh's Grandma (Doris) walked into the house and said "Hi, Tom, how about a cocktail while I light up my stogie on the porch? My own daughter wouldn't let me smoke in the car. My own daughter."

Mom and Vicky looked at each other and just shook their heads. "Nothing's changed I see, she laughed." Mom's niece (Connie), was only a month older than Jessica, but wore lots of makeup on her face, and short shorts, with high heel shoes, that made Josh look twice. Because there were 3 of them, and our bedrooms were full, they stayed just down the road at a small motel for their visit. I was thankful that Josh was out of school for a few days. Dinnertime finally came. I was amazed.

There was so much food around everyone got stuffed…even me.

Dad and Josh let me stay in with them one day to watch a "TV" where large creatures slammed into each other. One side was called the Lions, and the other was the Saints. I couldn't tell what was going on, but they kept hitting into each other so much that it had to hurt. Dad was very agitated and excited…"Go Saints" he would yell. So whenever he yelled, I let out a little gruff bark, too. "Look Dad, Goldie is a Saints fan." "Never a doubt, she's a smart dog, and has class too," came from Dad. After a long time they had a halftime, at which point Dad's enthusiasm turned into a nap time. Being the loyal family friend, I joined him. "Just saving up energy for the second half," Josh grinned. The game ended, unfortunately with the Lions winning, Dad said the Saints were "robbed." I wasn't sure, but I tried to look saddened, in keeping with the mood.

On Sunday the relatives left. I was sorry to see Vicky go, we had bonded well. She was always giving me little doggie treats she had bought special for me from the store. But, they had to get back to Texas, as Vicky had a part-time job at a legal firm, and a full-time job keeping Connie and Grandma out of trouble.

A little longer into the season, I started noticing Mom putting up decorations all over the house, but mainly in the Family Room. Little bows, candles, statues of little people, things like that. One Sunday, Dad came home with an actual tree. It was taller than him. He and Josh put it in a stand in the living room. It didn't quite touch the ceiling. Mom and Jessica put sparkly things on it, strings, balls, stars, even what they called "popcorn."

Then I heard Dad say "ta-da," and lights came on everywhere. It was glorious. It was like when I went out at night time and looked into the sky seeing all those sparkly things. But, this was just closer, much closer.

Day by day, I saw boxes appear under the tree. Boxes of all shapes and sizes. I noticed all of them, even Dad, sneak in when they thought no one was looking and shake the boxes.

One morning everyone woke up excited. They stayed in their night clothes, and sat around the tree with the boxes. "Who's first?" Dad shouted. "Me,Me,Me," squealed Jessica, as she grabbed a box. She ripped into the paper and the box, like crazy. "Perfect, a CD player…and not just any CD player a portable 'Sony Discman'. Now I can take Pearl Jam and Hootie & the Blowfish with me everywhere I go. I knew Santa would come through for me, I've been good."

"Well, you can't take it to school, or in my boat, but you can listen to it while you do your homework" Dad proclaimed.

Josh was next. "Oh, my box sounds like shoes. I know I need some, but I hope I'm wrong." It was shoes, alright, "Nike Air Max! "Wow, Mom and Dad, I'm going to quit growing. I'm gonna wear these forever!

Wait till my friend Chase sees these, he'll be green with envy. I'll bet I can jump 6 inches higher than before." Chase was his best friend, but didn't play basketball. He was shorter and wider than Josh, and was crazy about playing football.

Mom and Dad exchanged little boxes and hugs. They made big smiles. Obviously they had a warm feeling for each other. There was one box left. The biggest box of all. "Well Goldie, I guess the last gift is for you." I couldn't believe it. Dad picked it up and read me the card, "To the newest member of our family. May all your dreams be sweet." He opened the box and removed a huge object. "It's your new bed, girl.

Wow, my own bed! What a good thing this Holiday Season is.

It has a big message stitched into the fabric which says "Goldie's Place." I knew now what it felt like when warmth was deep inside you.

Of course Jessica didn't let it go by without a comment…"I got the best present ever, and it wasn't you." I just decided to work a little harder at winning her over. Little did I know just how difficult that would be in the future. The now, 11 year old little girl, still had an attitude about me. I made up my mind to try harder to please Jessica. I wanted all of us to get along as a family.

The next couple of weeks were lots of fun. Josh was out of school, always playing basketball, except when it rained. Then he was inside watching basketball, or that other game football. I liked basketball better. It was a game with large men running, jumping, and throwing a ball just like the one Josh had. In the football game, it was huge creatures, still hitting each other. When they showed them up close on TV, it seemed like the creatures had eyes like people, and the ones not playing, standing on the side, had heads like people. It was very confusing. I was just glad Josh played basketball with other boys.

We had a party one night, for something called "New Year." The next morning Dad said, "We will see what 1997 brings us. Hopefully the best of everything, including health." I could tell no difference, other than a couple of days later Josh returned to school, and "the season resumed."

I can describe January and February in southern Mississippi in one word…"wet." It rained almost every other day. So I was inside a lot, and I could see Mom anxiously waiting to begin the garden. That was special for her, which meant it was special for me, too.

Spring-Summer 97
The Garden

March was the planting month in southern Mississippi. This year the garden was going to be larger than ever. Mom was planning on adding four more rows for new types of vegetables, including radishes, string beans, and 2 types of lettuce.

Mom borrowed Dad's car one Saturday, went to the store and came back with sacks of dirt. Why? We had plenty of dirt. She brought out the wheelbarrow, hoe, shovel, and her tough garden gloves and went to work. She hoed and filled in dirt for 3 days. I was out there with her, and glad for her sake that the heat had not yet fully returned. Then she started planting. In most cases, just seeds, but for the tomatoes she used little miniature plants which would give us lots of big red juicy fruit later in the year. It took her a week to get everything just as she liked it. She expanded the fence line, careful to bury it a couple of inches into the soil. When she was done, she looked at me with a big smile. "Well, this is your year to start protecting." I was ready.

This garden was her pride and joy. She seemed at ease whenever she was working in the dirt. I couldn't figure out what was so special about it, but it really made her happy, and that made me happy.

I stood by her side in the following weeks as she watered, fertilized, and nurtured her crop. I was as proud as she was to see the daily, then weekly progress. This was going to be her best one yet, and I was part of it. Things were sprouting well. We got lucky with a little rain in late April that seemed to boost the growing pace of everything. Things were great.

Before I knew it, the plants were taller than me. I stayed under the Magnolia tree when it was hot. But, now that I couldn't see over the garden, I made regular rounds inspecting the fence line and the gate.

I would be rewarded by Mom with praise, and treats. She acted like I was her assistant gardener, and was somehow responsible for the upcoming harvest the family would enjoy that summer and fall.

We bonded over a little patch of ground that was very special to her. It brought us together for a common cause. In June, she would pick the first of the tomatoes. I didn't know what they would be like, but the family loved them.

It was now, after the basketball season, so Josh was arriving home on the bus, again. He was still practicing his moves in his special Nike "Air Max". I was glad his basketball goal was near the garden so I could play with him and keep up with my duties with the garden. He was taller now, almost as tall as Dad. I was sure by this time next year, he would grow even taller, just like the plants in the garden. Once school was out for the summer, Josh started to take me for walks down to the water's edge. He would sit there in his "Air Max" shoes and look over Back Bay thinking, and talking to me. He would sit on the dock and point out little fish, turtles, and crabs to me.

"Some people work the water, 'watermen', they call themselves," he said. "They make a living selling crabs, oysters, shrimp, and the like. But not me. I'm going places, and I'm going to make a difference in this world." I knew that he would.

Late one night, I heard noise in the yard. An unusual noise. I left my special bed, next to a sleeping Josh. What was it? Is there someone, or something outside, in the back yard. I perched up on the window sill to observe. It was very dark. The porch light, which was usually left on, wasn't on. Finally my eyes adjusted to the darkness.

From the window I could see something standing by the back porch, a small figure. I waited, unmoving, until I could find out where the noise was coming from.

There it was! I was confused. I recognized a barefoot Jessica creeping toward the garden gate. She opened it a few inches, looked around to make sure no one had seen her, and scurried back inside the house. I knew we never left the gate open at night. The garden was unprotected, and there was nothing I could do.

The next day I was put outside while breakfast was eaten, I noticed that the gate was closed. I didn't know when it had been shut, but maybe it had all been a bad dream. I laid down beside the garden. I couldn't see anything amiss, but then, I had no idea of what to look for. The gate was closed, but something wasn't right.

Later when the Mom came out she was upset. Something had eaten part of her garden. She saw gnawed carrot, a ruined squash, and holes where digging had gone on. She was upset as she walked around the fence looking for holes or tunnels dug, but didn't find any. She looked at me in a disappointed way. "Did you sleep yesterday afternoon while this happened?

I didn't inspect the garden when I closed the gate last night, it was almost dark, and you were still outside." I wanted to hide. Mom thought I had let her down. Maybe I had.

A few minutes later Jessica came out. She never came in the backyard in the morning. She looked at me, leaned close and said "Even rabbits have to eat, you dumb dog. I guess you're not the protector everyone else here thinks you are." And she walked quickly away. For the second time that morning I wanted to hide. A member of my own "pack" betraying me. Why?

Mom came out and began to repair the damage. She didn't yell or scream at me, I wish she would have. She came over and held me close. Close like Daisy had. "We all make mistakes" she said. "It's part of what makes us stronger." I closed my eyes and covered her face with wet licks. I felt warm again. I belonged.

Redemption

I didn't sleep much the next few days. I didn't pace the floor, or make noise. I just watched and listened. Even lying on my bed, I had my ears peaked. On the 3rd night after the garden incident, I heard something, looked out and saw Jessica going out to the garden gate, barefoot again. She was intent on ruining my standing in the pack for some reason. As soon as she opened the garden gate I started barking and jumping at the window with all the volume I could muster.

She looked at me in the window with a frightful face and ran back inside to her room. I kept barking and awoke the entire pack, probably the rest of Biloxi as well. "What's wrong girl? Who's there? Is someone outside?" Josh let me out of his room and ran outside with me. I stood defiantly beside the open gate. Father and Mom were right behind us. Mom shook her head. " I know I closed that gate she said. I even double checked before going to bed, after that one time."

"Well" said Dad, "They say that raccoons are smart enough to open gates, trash cans, and the like. Looks like that may be the case here." Mom looked me in the face and said, "Goldie, I knew you didn't let me down. I just didn't know what else it could have been." I was happier than I had been in the car, that first day with the wind in my face. I slowly walked over to her and leaned against her leg. She petted me sweetly and began to cry. I was warm inside.

Then my hero, Josh, had an idea. "Dad, why don't we get a couple of those motion sensor lights for the back yard? The raccoons or whatever will be scared away, Mom's garden will be protected…" "And you'll be able to practice your silly basketball at night," squealed Jessica behind us, pretending she just woke up. "It's not fair, boys get everything."

"Good idea, son. Tomorrow's Saturday, and I can pick up some lights at the hardware store and install them this weekend. Until then, we'll just wrap some wire around the gate which the varmints can't untie. But son, easy on the night time basketball."

Jessica's little adventure had just come to an end. I smiled...big! Now I was back in the good graces of the family, except for Jessica, of course.

Oh, the return to normal. Mom working in the garden. She had now begun to expand it, her new enthusiasm bolstered by the belief that we would at least have the fruits of her labor undisturbed by small creatures.

As the days, weeks and months went by, I was becoming a much larger part of the "pack." I was trusted, confided with, and respected. My life was good, again, and I was respected.

Fall 97...Busted

Jessica and Josh were back in school. Jessica had been particularly distant since the garden incident, But I was still trying to be nice and get her on my side. One day after school, she and her friend, Emily went down to the dock, They locked me in the yard, but that was OK, I had to stay beside the garden.

I looked through a space in the fence and saw Jessica and Emily passing a cigarette back and forth and coughing. They saw it as being grown up. Dad would have punished her severely for that...Mom too. Josh would have never approved, but what was I to do? They were only 12 years old, almost 13, but they liked to act older. Why young people wished they were older, and older people wished they were younger, was always a puzzle to me. But like I heard Dad said a couple of times, "Youth is wasted on the young."

That Fall, Jessica and Emily saw a great deal of each other. As girls would do, they giggled over their private jokes, called their friends ugly names, and generally made fun of everyone.

One afternoon after school, they walked about a half mile down the road to a little "strip" shopping center. It had a pizza place, a drug store, and a small consignment store, appropriately named, "A Second Chance", which had second-hand clothes, costume jewelry, and some shoes.

Emily and Jessica liked to hang out at the drug store. They could read all the young fashion magazines, see the latest styles, and compare their "look" to that of the young movie stars. Soon they tired of the drug store, and Emily suggested they go Into the consignment store to look around. The place was pretty full of things for the season. Sweaters, jeans, raincoats, things which looked good, but not new. "Good afternoon, girls," came from a thirtyish woman wearing jeans and a pullover sweater behind the cash register.

"Hi," they both responded. Jessica thought she knew the woman from somewhere, but couldn't be sure. "Are you looking for anything special," she said in a polite way. She thought they were just in for looking around, but in retail, you could never be sure of their intentions, and they both had mothers, who the girls could send in to buy something.

"We're just looking around," said Emily. "Let me know if you need any help," the lady replied."

They dawdled around for a while. In just a couple of minutes, Emily whispered, "Jessica, look at this cool necklace. It's several shades of blue, and goes with both of our eyes, what do you think?" Jessica agreed that it was "cool" but didn't see the point. The girls didn't have any money.

"Jessica," Emily hissed again. "You go over there and try something on, get her attention, for a few minutes." Now Jessica knew exactly what was going on.

"Ma'm," she said, where are the sweaters? I'm looking for a sweater for my Mom to buy me."

"Just over here on the table," she said. "Let me try to help you find your size." Jessica went to the side of the table that would put the woman's back to Emily. "Maybe something in blue," Jessica said.

She looked up and saw Emily put the necklace in her pocket. After trying on a blue sweater, Jessica looked at her watch, and sounded alarmed, "Emily, we're going to be late getting home. I don't want us to get into trouble. Thanks for your help," she said. And they started to walk out of the store.

"That's fine dear, and please tell your Mother, Karen, that Mildred said hello." A cold chill ran up the backs of both girls, she knew who they were, or at least, who Jessica's Mom was.

Now, Jessica remembered Mildred, from a PTA meeting a while back.

Later that afternoon, the phone rang and Jessica's Mom answered. She seemed concerned, but didn't say anything but, "I see, thank you for telling me. I'll call you back tomorrow."

About an hour later, Dad came home from Keesler. They went out to the back yard for privacy. Jessica was looking through the window. She saw her Dad's face go "beet red" as he shouted, "Shoplifting? Bring her out here."

The inquisition was on. Finally, Jessica admitted to her role as an accomplice in the theft of the necklace. Her Dad said, "I'm so disappointed in you. You know better. We raised you to be better. Mildred is going to call Emily's parents, how they deal with her is their business. Your punishment will be determined tomorrow. We have to decide how you can repay the store."

Mom called Mildred the next day and apologized. She wanted Jessica to come in and apologize. She would also be bringing her $5 per week allowance to the store every Monday after school, for the next 4 weeks. Mom and Dad told her very seriously, that she should learn from this.

She promised she would. I had my doubts.

But, I was wrong. Jessica seemed humbled by the experience. She had let Emily talk her into something she knew was wrong. It wasn't the first time she had made that mistake. It probably wouldn't be the last.

I learned something out of that experience as well. Mom and Dad were fair minded, and not into harsh punishments. They were good parents.

Holidays...97

This Thanksgiving and Christmas, I knew what to expect. Food, presents, Josh out of school to play basketball with me and yes, football. After that, New Years Day, and lots more football.

This Holiday Mom had said that her sister Beth, and her husband, Brian, would be visiting from Atlanta. They had a child, I learned, a 14-month old daughter, named Lindsay, they would be bringing. Due to the distance, they would fly into Mobile, and drive a rental car the 50 miles to Biloxi.

Mom explained that since Her sister and brother-in-law had spent so much money on the airfare, Josh was going to sleep on the couch, and the visitors would use his room. Mom said she knew this was going to be a sacrifice for all of us, but we were going to make the best of the situation for 3 nights.

They arrived Thanksgiving Day, about noon. Beth was nice to all of us, even me. You couldn't help but notice a close resemblance to Mom. She had visited the family about 4 years ago, and she kept exclaiming how much Josh and Jessica "had grown like weeds, what are you feeding them?"

Brian had never met anyone in the family, (he and Beth had a whirlwind romance and marriage), so introductions were made all around. He was shorter than Dad, no, he was shorter than Josh, who claimed to be "5,5" whatever that meant. He was a very pale person, with a huge stomach. He said that he was an actuary, which Dad said meant he worked with numbers, figuring how long people would live. He came over to pet me. His hands were soft, like a pillow. "I brought a six-pack with me, it's imported, my favorite. I hope nobody minds." "Not at all Dad said, and they put the beer into the refrigerator.

Suddenly, the peace was upset with a wailing shriek, "Waaaaah, Waaaaah.

The little bundle Beth had been clutching was screaming at the top of her lungs. The ruckus caused by that little being was non-stop. My ears hurt. Dad looked at me and said, "Kids, I think Goldie has to go outside." I'll take her," Josh offered. "No, me," came from Jessica. She had never volunteered to take me out. Her ears must hurt too, I thought. "Both of you, out with Goldie, go," Mom said, and we hastily retreated to the relative calm of the back yard. Leaving I heard Beth explain, "It's just a stage she's been going through."

Dinner was at three. Mom had cooked a huge turkey, cornbread stuffing, tossed salad, rolls, and pumpkin pie for dessert...her standard Thanksgiving fare. The family was digging in (I was in my position, awaiting leftovers) when Lindsay started screaming again, even louder than before. Beth had left her sleeping on the bedroom floor in a blanket. That sleep didn't last long. Beth excused herself from the table and ran into the bedroom, trying to quiet the toddler. Nothing worked, so she closed the bedroom door to muffle the sound.

Brian said, "Don't worry, that's her job", as he kept stuffing his fat face. I caught a glimpse of Mom and Dad looking at each other in surprise, then they concentrated on her food. As the last fork hit the last plate on the dinner table, Lindsay took a "cease fire" on the squealing, and the home was eerily silent. Beth came out of the bedroom, and sat on the couch with the child. "I'm sorry for this," she apologized.

"Don't worry about it," Karen said. "Jessica, go over and hold Lindsay while I make Beth a plate." Jessica looked around for an exit to this dilemma, here was none. If Brian wasn't going to volunteer, Karen would make sure that Beth had her dinner. Jessica walked tentatively over to the couch, and Beth handed the girl to her. "Just hold her like this," Beth showed her. "I think she's calmed down now."

Beth went to the table, where Karen had fixed her a sample of everything, the turkey and stuffing reheated in the microwave.

It took a few minutes for Beth to calm down, and everyone else as well. Goldie noticed that Brian was still trying to eat everything which remained on the table.

He ate the last dinner roll, in 2 bites, the last of the turkey (we always had leftovers in the past), and surveyed the kitchen with his greedy little eyes searching for one last morsel.

Jessica seemed to be getting the hang of holding Lindsay. She was starting to smile and talk to the baby. Lindsay was sort of standing, while being held on Jessica's legs, when "Bloooop, a large orange stream exploded from the child's mouth, covering Jessica's front in an enormous "spit-up." "Phew, help, help, I'm drenched. OH, MY, GOD!! Get her off me, get her off me." Karen ran over and took the child, "Jessica, go to the bathroom, get those clothes off, and get in the shower," Karen shouted. "I'll bring you some clean clothes." Beth came over for the Lindsay hand-off. To top it off, Lindsay started wailing again, sounding like a fire engine was in the room.

Brian just smiled, chewing on another piece of pie. Dad and Josh went into the family room to watch the game. "Brian, you're more than welcome to sit in here with us," Dad said. "No, never got into football," he replied. "Just a brainless game, played by stupid men. I'm going to go out and sit on the back porch, and have a beer." Dad, as usual, fell asleep during the game. Josh and I saw the whole game, we might have dozed off, a little.

Mom and Beth had cleaned up the kitchen, Jessica sulking in her room due to the "throw-up", but somewhat satisfied that it got her out of cleanup assistance. Mom and her sister sat at the smaller kitchen table, and caught up on things that sisters talk about. Namely kids and husbands. They talked for a while, Karen sharing all the growing pains of her kids with her sister. "I have 2 great children," she said.

"Differently great, but still as good as I could hope for."

"Brian's not that bad," Beth assured Karen. "He lives in his own world. In that world, there's Brian, and numbers. He comes home every day, never asks how my day was, or about Lindsay, just tells me the latest actuarial estimates for people. I listen, because it's who he is. The only other thing he does is eat. He eats a lot." Karen pointed to the sleeping baby, "Well, he obviously does 'something else'," she said, and they both got a big laugh out of that.

Beth continued, "I'm glad we've got the condo, because it's zero maintenance. I could never, never, get him to do yard work, much less a garden like you have. He hates the outside, and is afraid of bugs. He says he's very sensitive to insect bites.

"My," Karen said, "it's 9 o'clock. We've been talking for 3 hours. Lets go pry the men away from the TV, and get ready for bed. I know you've had a long day."

They walked into the family room. Karen shook Josh, "Son it's past 9, it's been dark for 2 hours. Time to let Goldie out and get ready for bed." She looked over at Dad, as he was beginning to stir. "Where's Brian?" Beth asked. Dad replied, "He's outside." "Outside," Beth said, "He couldn't have been outside since 5, could he?" She walked out the door behind Josh, who was already letting Goldie out.

There sat Brian. Slouched asleep in the rocker, three empty beer bottles beside him. He seemed even more fat and swollen than before, but he had eaten more than any two others at the table. He was also covered in red splotches. "He's got red welts, everywhere," Dad said. Brian awoke from his stupor, scratching everywhere. "What happened?" he asked. "You fell asleep out here," Beth said. "It's hours past sunset, Brian complained. Why didn't you wake me up?. "Let me go inside." He slammed the screen door on his way in, Beth running after him.

Josh and Jessica were laughing out loud. "He looks like The Pillsbury Doughboy with pimentos all over," Jessica said, describing him perfectly. And they continued their hysterical laughing. "And he said football players are stupid," Josh said.

Dad gave them the "glare" and they settled down, only laughing now and then. They heard the bathroom door slam, and in answer to that, Lindsay cut loose with a barrage of screams which could be heard for miles.

"Waaaaaaaah," it was louder and longer than before. She squealed for about an hour, exhaustion finally had set in. Goldie could hear Beth and Brian arguing in their (Josh's) bedroom. So could everyone else for that matter. She was laying on the floor, next to Josh who was trying to sleep on the couch.

At 2 am, it sounded like "Chinese New Year" in the little house. Lindsay was bawling uncontrollably, Brian had locked himself in the bathroom as a refuge, and Mom was trying to console Beth. "No, that's my decision," Beth said. We're going back to Atlanta tomorrow. I can change the tickets. The baby won't stop crying, she hasn't stopped since she was born, and now Brian, and his attitude. It's more than I can ask you to handle. Brian came out of the bathroom in his t-shirt. He was covered in pink blotches of "Calamine Lotion" which Mom had given Beth for him to use. He went to get another beer, and returned to the bathroom.

Karen couldn't change Beth's mind. At breakfast the next morning, Lindsay threw egg on the floor (I didn't mind the clean up). Directly after the meal, where fat Brian had 3 helpings of french toast, scrambled eggs, bacon, biscuits with gravy, and coffee (with low-fat cream), the three of them drove their rental car away from the house, Lindsay's howls fading away with the distance.

Everyone sat at the kitchen table, I laid beside it. Dad was the first to speak, "I'm tired, he said," His wife and kids looked at him and nodded, all together.

"I'm going to bed," Josh commented. "Wake me on Monday."

Christmas 97 and New Years 1998, were very tame after that. Almost uneventful. I believe that this one, Thanksgiving episode, lasting less than 24 hours showed all of us how lucky we were to be in the Flowers family.

Josh and Jessica helped each other and Mom, all the rest of the Holidays. An unspoken truce had been called, and how long it would last was anyone's guess.

Crabby...Spring 98

It had been another wet winter. When March rolled around, signs of life began to appear naturally in the foliage, nesting birds, and warmer days, and also in Mom's garden. Her constant attention and improvements, made every year better than the one before.

This first weekend, there was lots of yard work to be done. The annual cleanup from winter started by removing dead branches which had fallen, heavy with rain, weeding, before the weeds really took root, and this year, adding some fresh crushed oyster shells to the front drive.

Once this was done, Josh's last project was to check out the boat and the dock. Make sure the lines were not loose, make sure it was tied so as not to hit against the dock with the wind and tides, see if the boat needed cleaning, etc. By now, he was taking Goldie down to the water with him whenever he went. She was delighted by the new scenery, and felt it was a special treat for her.

Josh and Goldie got down to the waters edge, and there was Jessica. "Oh here you are, dodging work again," Josh chided. He looked at the boat the way his Dad had taught him to inspect it. He walked all around the bank, keeping Goldie on a leash for safety.

The boat looked good, the lines were holding up, but he would retie them in the next few days. The dock was missing two boards, easy enough to fix. What about inside the boat he wondered. "Here, take her for a minute?" Josh asked, handing the leash to Jessica. "Don't want to," she answered. "OK," Josh said, "I'm going to ask Dad to come down here while I look into the boat. I can't bring Goldie on the dock because we have a couple of missing boards, and you refuse to help. I'll be right back."

"Oh, OK, give her to me," the girl whined, "but only for a minute." Josh handed the leash to Jessica, and walked up the dock, testing each board for security, as he went.

Just then, Goldie saw something flash by her on the bank. It was a funny looking creature, running sideways, with claws extended. Goldie woofed. When Jessica saw the crab, she started screaming. "EEEEEEEEK."

The crab ran for the safety of the water. Goldie dashed after it. The crab made the water and went in, so did Goldie and a still shrieking Jessica, she hadn't let go of the leash.

Goldie plodded through the muddy water, snapping at the crab. She sank into the mud, it was tougher now to run, but Goldie was determined, and Jessica was still screaming.

Finally, Goldie slipped and fell into the wet mud, dragging Jessica behind her.

The crab escaped, and Goldie returned to the muddy bank, dragging the girl on the leash behind her. It was a funny sight. Jessica was spitting out mud, and muddy water. Her whole body looked like she had been dipped in chocolate, her hair was mud caked. Goldie had chunks of mud in her coat as well, almost looking Rastafarian.

Josh was sitting on the dock laughing his head off, at the fiasco. "Just what are you laughing at?" Jessica asked.

"My kingdom for a camera," he answered. "If I only had a camera." His sister threw the leash down and stormed off into the yard. Josh grabbed the leash and caught up with her. "And where do you think you're going? You can't go inside like that." He yelled ahead, "Dad, Mom, we need a hand here." Mom and Dad were both in the backyard. They both dropped their lawn tools in a stunned silence.

"Hey," Josh said, "I have a chocolate covered sister, if it was only Easter." Jessica was storming toward the back porch, when her Dad said, "Stop right there."

You and Goldie, over in the corner. You hold her leash, I'll get the hose." It was like a scene out of those old prison movies, hosing down the inmates. Goldie liked it, snapping at the stream of water, and enjoying the wetness.

"Now turn around, let me get your backs. After about 5 minutes, they were clean enough for a bath. Mom had filled an old basin with soap and water. "Josh, go inside and give your sister some privacy. I'll call you when it's the dog's turn." He went inside and called his friend, Chase. He laughed all through telling him the story. As he hung up, Jessica marched straight for her bedroom, wrapped in a beach towel. "Oh, Jessica, Chase said to say Hi," he rubbed it in.

"Josh, get yourself out here," yelled his Dad, who himself was trying to stifle a laugh. Mom had refilled the basin, and Josh had to be the lead "bather" for his four-legged friend. Goldie thought it was all a game, and was continually jumping on Josh, soaking him as well. This was a story which would be retold at every family event for years, much to Jessica's embarrassment.

6-98...The Mad Catter

In a couple of months, Jess (as she liked to be called now), with her usual theatrical flair had stated that she had, attained the age, if not the maturity, of responsibility. She wanted what she was unfairly deprived of three years ago.

"Yes, a cat. I want a cat! You said when I was 13, I would be responsible enough to have my very own pet. Well now I want a cat. Emily has a cat and shows me pictures at school all the time. A cat is a better companion for a girl. Everyone knows that cats are way more delicate and proper!"

After much discussion, Mom and Dad relented. The next Saturday morning the 3 of them went back to the same shelter where I was from, and went "cat shopping." In a couple of hours they returned with an orange ball of fur I soon learned had been named "Princess." Josh said "how appropriate," but I didn't get it.

Mom introduced me, "Goldie this is our newest member of the family." She held the tiny creature in both hands and let me smell it. I gave it a kiss. I wanted it to feel safe. I remembered my first few days. "HISSSS" it said, and swatted at my nose. Boy that stung! "That's just it's way of claiming space" said Mom. I just walked over and laid on the dining room floor and let Princess have the show to herself for the rest of the afternoon.

Believe it or not, in the next few weeks and months the cat and I bonded pretty well. She could jump higher than me, but I was much stronger and larger. We had many side-by-side naps. Princess was good at those, and sometimes she would lay on me and we would both be warm. Jess would take her away to her room and sometimes close the door, but we always found a way to play with a ball or a small toy, part of the day, especially when school was in session. She felt safe with me, but Princess was a little "jumpy."

Goldie's Garden 39

She was quick to hide behind furniture, or run from sudden noises. I think she felt better laying next to me.

Princess' and my friendship grew the next few months in spite of Jess. The girl was becoming a little wilder, more rebellious than before. She talked on the telephone at night to her girlfriends in a kind of "code" no one else could understand. I saw her out at the dock one day with her friend Emily. Jess had Princess with her and the cat did not look happy at being so close to the water. She was out at the dock quite a bit, which didn't bother me. I think she thought of it as her escape place.

Mom kept telling Dad, and I overheard, that Jess was just going through the same phase all children did entering their teens. Yes, they thought they were smarter than anyone else. They all thought their parents were "un-cool." and they joined little circles of friends, who talked about all the other circles of friends, behind their backs.

After a while, Dad just sort of let Mom handle issues with Jess. It just seemed that Mom was able to handle her better when she became unruly or threw a tantrum.

One day Josh's friend, Chase came over. He had only a week left of free time, so they spent a great deal of it together. Chase had less summer than Josh, because he played football. His practices started three weeks before regular school. Chase, Josh, and I were out by the water when Jess and Emily walked through the back gate, not knowing the boys were sitting on the dock. They were whispering and giggling, until they were about 50 feet away, and Jess spotted the boys. The girls turned to leave, their sanctuary having been taken from them, when Chase yelled, "Jess." She turned to look at him with wonder in her eyes. He never spoke to her, unless he had to.

"Yes?" she asked. "Gone skin divin' for any crabs, lately? Crabs for dinner sure sounds good to me." And the boys hooted and howled hysterically.

"Mooooommm!" she screamed while running to the gate and the house beyond.

The rest of the 1998 proceeded very well.

The Holiday Season was routine. No relatives visiting, a real quiet time of family togetherness. The New Year of 1999, began the cycle of the garden, basketball season, and school's summer vacation. Josh starting to become a man, Jess sprouting, and my place in the pack very secure.

That summer of 1999 was the first time Josh got to drive himself anywhere by himself. He had taken a drivers education class at Dad's insistence and earned his license in April. Jess, of course was very jealous. What difference does a birth certificate make?" She would ask. "That doesn't make you a better driver. Emily's grandmother is 84, and she ran into the side of the house last week, oh, but she's of legal age."

In the summer, Dad had spoken of some "base downsizing" possibilities, but he saw that as years away. He really wasn't worried, or so he said. Things were good, but summer was almost over.

9-99, A Storm in the Gulf

I'll never forget the first time I heard the word "Hurricane." We were all eating our breakfast one Saturday morning, just a couple of weeks after school had started for Josh and Jess. Dad was reading the paper, and said absently to whoever was in the room, "They called from the base already this morning. The storm bounced off Cuba, and could turn our way. It shouldn't be anything like Camille, but it could be significant." "What was Camille like?," asked Josh.

Dad loved these types of questions. "Hurricanes are a mix of natural wonder and fear, at the same time. Of course we weren't here, but in August of 1969, the greatest storm of the past 100 years made landfall about 15 miles west of here in Long Beach.

"We clocked wind gusts at Keesler of 220 miles per hour, but the highest sustained winds were 190, with a storm surge of over 26 feet. Our storm shelter then was the same as it is now, D'Iberville High School. The surge there was over 16 feet, and the place held up. We lost all the coastal lighthouses except the Biloxi lighthouse, because it is made of cast iron. You know, a hurricane is basically just a low pressure center. Camille's barometric pressure of 26.7 is one of the ten lowest ever measured. The damage was unbelievable. But, Biloxi, Gulfport, and the rest of the Gulf Coast communities rebuilt. No handouts, just a lot of hard working neighbors working together. That's what makes this country what it is" he said as he looked straight at Josh. "People taking personal responsibility, helping others, standing up for what's right. It takes real courage. It's when you know you're behind before you begin, but you begin anyway and you see it through no matter what."

Josh thought that speech sounded like it could have come from Atticus Finch, in *To Kill a Mockingbird*, which he was reading now as a school assignment.

You could tell he was proud of Dad. Tom went off to work, calling Karen once he had seen the radar. Dad said, "We're going to get some bad weather, how bad, Karen, no one knows.

Karen listened intently, then looked around the house, gathering her thoughts into an action plan. "We're going to get hit," Mom said, putting down the telephone. Josh and Jess were just getting home from school, and she told them the news and the plan.

"Dad says it will probably side-swipe us tomorrow mid-day. Maybe 80 miles per hour. The real danger will be 6 inches of rain, and flooding, especially if it hits at high tide, which is very possible. They are making all the weather staff at his office stay at the Base, until the storm passes. He says we should be fine here at home."

Karen grabbed a legal pad and pen and started making a list of the precautions to take, and the various supplies they had to gather for a "worst case scenario." Right now, they had no idea if the power would remain on, the phones would work, or if the bridges and roads would flood out. Mom ran to the door and said "Josh come with me to the store, quickly, while they have anything left." She hoped they had gotten an early warning. They dashed out to the bug and were off.

The local Wal-Mart store looked promising. "Josh, you go get 6 gallons of distilled water, 40 pounds of ice, a gas can, and 2 more flashlights with extra batteries, and batteries for the radio too. Get some candles, and some matches. I'll take care of the food." They left there, then stopped at the gas station, filling the "bug" and the 5 gallon gas can up.

The family got home and on to the preparations for the storm. No lawn chairs or tools were to be left outside which could become deadly projectiles in the wind.

Anything can injure people or property, wind driven, at high speed.

Mom took the cover off the garden and removed the poles it had been tied to. Wheelbarrow, water hoses, and all loose impediments were put into the shed. We were lucky enough to have underground power and phone lines refitted back in the late 80s due to the regularity of storm damage. Next came the inside. Mom told us to always stay in the center of the house and away from the windows during the storm.

She said we should all take an early shower tomorrow, then we would fill the 2 bathtubs with water, and have a bucket by each. It helped for flushing toilets, if a water line broke.

The next morning was very exciting. People were scurrying about. Mom made breakfast. Everyone ate and the dishes were done. The clouds darkened, and the wind picked up, sometimes making a howling kind of noise. Princess seemed terrified, and I think I was close behind.

About 10 o'clock the bottom fell out of the sky. It rained so hard you couldn't see our mailbox at the end of the drive. We had thunder and lightning like I'd never seen before. The wind came through and blew pine cones, branches, and small limbs into the side of the home. Everything that wasn't secured was moving with the storm, from the north. The power flickered, but stayed on.

Jess was frantically searching for Princess. "I know she's trapped in the storm," she wailed, looking outside all the windows, with Mom pulling her back, "That's not safe, it's crazy. A limb could come through the glass."

And then about noon, everything stopped. The sky brightened, the wind was no more. I heard the screen door slam, but gave it no matter. Mom checked the phone. It still worked. She called Dad's direct line, and after a couple of rings he answered.

"We're OK, shouted Mom, we made it through just fine, it's all gone."

"No, Karen, the storm turned north, right at us. You're in the 'Eye', the worst is yet to come, from the south, and at high tide. You're 26 feet above sea level, so you're fine in the house. This should be past us by mid-afternoon." Mom hung up and passed on the news to us. All except for Jess and Princess.

Mom panicked. "She's gone looking for that darn scairdy-cat. Josh, you look through the house, I'll check the garage and yard." In 5 minutes Josh came back, "Found the cat, she was under your bed." Mom was frantic. "Jess thinks it's over, but it's going to get worse. I'll check every place I can think of she might go."

I knew where she was...and I was going to get her!

Thirty seconds later, Craaack, went a lightning bolt, and our power went out. The rain started coming down in buckets. The wind howled again from the opposite direction...directly from Back Bay toward our house. When Josh went outside on the front porch to see if anything was hit by the lightning bolt, I squeezed past him in a flash, and headed around the house, into the worst of the storm.

I could barely see, rain stinging my eyes, but Dad had told me about my heritage, I was two things. A water dog, and a retriever. It took me 5 minutes into the wind just to reach the water line, which was much higher up toward the house than I had ever seen it. I couldn't see the boat, and the dock was coming apart.

Down below, just a few feet from the water was a huge tree limb. It looked like the water was going to reach the limb and float it away. But beside the limb was a blond braid, with some red marks on it.

Yes, a head with a tiny body. It was Jess! I knew it! She came here searching for Princess. The water was lapping and waves were blowing ever closer to her. She would drown.

I started barking at her. Even more loudly than when I saw her at the garden gate. I pushed her with my nose, I licked her face, until she woke up. She raised her head to me and I could see we had a problem. Her eyes had been filled with blood and mud, but she knew it was me. She hung on to me for balance and she was able to stand on the third try.

I started walking toward the house, nudging her right or left when she would stray off course. Finally she grabbed my collar and let me guide her. It was slow going, but we were going to make it! We finally got to the front yard. Josh and Mom spotted us at the same time, Jess was still holding my collar, and letting me lead her home. Josh ran to gather us up, and carried Jess up to the porch. Mom took her to the bathroom to clean her up and inspect her for injuries. Josh grabbed some towels from inside and starting drying me off. As many times as I shook, and he wiped me down, I was still soaked to the bone. He let me inside and I collapsed on a blanket, dead tired.

Josh checked me over, constantly saying "good girl, you're a hero, what would we have done without you?" Mom put some ointment on a scrape on Jess's neck, inside the hairline. It bled, but Mom didn't think stitches were be required.

Jess was exhausted as well, sobbing and shaking until Mom got some dry clothes on her. She ate half of a pre-made turkey sandwich at the kitchen table, with a glass of iced tea. "Mom," Jess croaked, " Goldie saved me. I could never have found my way back here by myself. She woke me up and guided me back. I thought I was going to die...and after the way I've treated her."

"You're safe now honey, you just need a nap."

"No, I have something to tell you first. Something I've got to say. It was never Goldie who left the garden unattended."

"I snuck out and opened the gate because I was jealous," she said. "And she saved me anyway. Would it be OK if I took my nap lying on the blanket with her?" As I laid there, I felt a warm little arm around me. The wind and rain were still showing their strength outside, but I was not afraid.

I woke up, when Dad pulled into the driveway with a big crunch from his tires. After talking with Mom he examined the grounds, walking all the way back to the water. "Well, the dock and boat are gone, and it looks like the live oak on the bank lost a large limb, but it got swept away, too. The house lost a few shingles, but Josh and I can pull clean-up detail this weekend, you'll get the garden covered again, and everything will be back to normal."

"We did more than survive today, Tom," said Mom. "Your little girl just grew up today." And, she sat down and told him the story. Just as she finished, the electric power came back on. I took it as a good sign.

There was no loss of life due to the storm and damage was manageable. None of the hotels or casinos were flooded, and in a few days things were back to normal.

Transition

The rest of that year went along smoothly. I was basking in my new-found glory, and family-wide acceptance. Princess and I became even better friends, now that Jess had welcomed me into her inner circle. This fall and winter sailed by with school, Thanksgiving, Christmas, and then the New Year of 2000. Josh was now a junior on the D'Iberville High Warriors basketball team. In fact, he was the highest scorer on a less than average team, to hear him say it. Some people were worried about the world collapsing due to a "millennium bug", but I didn't think much about it.

One day in January (yes, it was raining), Dad came home early from work, even before Josh and Jess were out of school. I heard him and Mom talking at the kitchen table. His voice was shaking. "It just came down from the top, today," he said. "They're de-activating my unit, and plan to switch it to the Air National Guard." "Where are we moving to, now" Mom asked, "I don't want to move." "That's just it, Karen, I'm being retired at 25 years. One, July, 2000. Yes, I'll get some money to help with the separation, and also my retirement pay and benefits. But, we can't live on that. I'll have to find another job, so that the kids can go to college, and we can stay in this house."

Mom accepted this as a challenge. "This is a family, Tom, and we're all going to help. You know I've been wanting to work at the library. Sheila Moss tells me I'm welcome there anytime I want. It could be part-time at first. The kids are almost grown. Josh can get a summer job. I already told him that if he wanted to go on his senior class trip next year, he was going to have to earn the money for it. And yes, we can help with college, but they can help as well. We'll only have one year where they are both enrolled at the same time. And, how many times have you told me that you really appreciated your education because you worked you own way through with jobs, and some scholarship assistance.

Your father died when you were young, and you had to do it yourself. Tom, we have a strong family, with good kids. Together we'll make out just fine. You were getting bored, anyway."

I had never seen Dad cry before. But, he was laughing at the same time and he gave Mom the biggest hug ever.

When Josh and Jess got home they all four met at the same table, and were given the news. Actually, as Mom predicted, they were supportive. The family had turned into a real team. And I was a part of it. No one wanted to move away from life-long friends, school, and so forth. Do I have a great family, or what?

As the end of the school year approached, Josh was interviewing for summer jobs. Mom had been working at the library on Central Avenue 3 days a week for about 2 months. It was only about a mile from home. Dad was applying for weather jobs at the TV stations and the local newspapers, without much luck so far. And Jess, she was now in charge of the garden. Mom had enlarged it again, "To put more fresh food on the table," she said. And I was on guard duty as always, especially on the days Mom wasn't home. Sometimes Princess would help, so I made her my partner..

Josh struck it lucky and landed a job at the Burger King on D'Iberville Rd. It was only about a quarter mile past the Library, so it was close as well. He worked mainly weekends until school was out.

Some days he brought me home some "French fries." He was excited to be making his own money now, and the school had decided that the senior Class Trip next year would be to New York City, he was thrilled. Plus, Mom had let him use the "bug" (it was still running) for a couple of "dates" he had.

Lots of the time he "double dated" with Chase, and for that they used Chase's Mom's van, it was much larger. I think he was still friends with the girl from the bus, Wendy.

Dad wasn't having much luck with weather jobs. I heard him telling Mom one night, "The only people hiring are the casinos. And, you know how much I hate those places, but it looks like I will have to swallow my pride and investigate opportunities there." On 1, July, Dad came home with a box full of things from his office at the base. "A box of memories," he said.

The next day he went to the Biloxi "strip" to inquire about job possibilities. Dad was a realist.

They hired him at the first place he went. The "Beau Rivage" casino and hotel, owned by the same people who owned the "Bellagio" in Las Vegas. Because of his background in command, he was given a position in personnel management. It wasn't a lot of money to start, but he walked in thinking he would be lucky to get a job making change, he knew nothing about gambling. This hotel/casino was certainly the nicest on the coast, and it was located right at the southern edge of highway I-110, a 20 minute commute from home.

Dad came home that day and announced the news at dinner (I'm pretty sure that Mom already knew). He said, "I always thought I was in the weather business. My new boss said that I had been in the people business, all my career."

I'm going to give it a good shot. I think working with people, helping them to succeed, sounds like a lot of fun. I'll be learning new things, adapting things I did in the Air Force to a civilian environment shouldn't be that hard. Plus I don't have to work the weekends or nights, unless we have a special project."

Summer-Fall 2000

The days were lasting longer, and becoming hotter. Our home became a beehive of activity, constantly changing with 3 people having jobs, compared to only 1, in the past.

Mom had picked up a 4th day a week at the library, Dad's job was going smoothly, and Josh had already saved up and paid the $850 for his class trip next April. He was working full time, plus some overtime at Burger King, and had his eye toward getting a new (used) car. Dad had told him he would split the cost with him and match every dollar Josh made toward his purchase...Josh was motivated. Jess was having a great time with her friends, and doing very well with the garden when Mom was at work. We had beautiful tomatoes, fat green beans, carrots, lettuce, and much more. I guess Mom's "green thumb" was inherited by Jess.

When the start of school was a week away, Dad went to Josh. "I might have a good lead on a car for you. I was at the commissary, and saw a car for sale on the bulletin board there. One of the junior officers is being shipped out to Europe, and he's selling his car. It's a 92 Honda Accord with low mileage on it. He's asking $3,600 for it, he may take less. Here, he had some copies of a color photo attached. If you like it, I have an old buddy in the motor pool who will check it's condition for us." Josh was excited, the car looked almost new. "Dad, I only have $1,600 saved so far, so I need $200 more for my half." "We'll offer him a little less, and whatever you're short, you can pay me back. How does that sound?"

That afternoon, Dad called the car owner, seems they had many mutual friends. The car was still available, and Dad arranged for a test drive, and a visit to his mechanic friend, Lanny, at the motor pool. Before the day was up, Josh drove home in his first car.

The first thing he said when he got out was, "I'm taking my best girlfriend for a ride." I sat there and looked around until he opened the passenger door and said "Goldie, lets go."

I jumped in the front seat in about 1 second. Josh cranked the window down halfway so I could stick my head out and feel the breeze. I didn't know where we were going, and I didn't care. Neither did Josh.

As that summer went into fall I remember my family being happy, and all working together, doing his or her part to contribute. By the time Christmas and New Year's came I was an experienced pro at doing my part of the season. Watch the Saints on TV (usually, robbed again), watched Mom start to put up decorations, watched Princess climb the Christmas tree and topple it...oh no! But, after a couple of hours of repair and clean up, the tree was almost back to normal. She didn't get punished. After all, it scared her more than any of us.

Jess had grown up even more. She was 14, after all. She was taller than many of the boys in her classes she said. Mom had let her do away with the Braid look and Jess now wore her hair in a short, straight style. She said it was low-maintenance and more modern. It did make her look a lot less like a little girl, and more like a young adult, she said. She was also starting to wear jewelry, and was anticipating more of the same for Christmas. She was popular in school and was on the middle school cheerleading team.

To hear Dad tell it, neither the high school nor the middle school sports teams had much to cheer about, but it was good to be enthusiastic, and show unconditional support. My job was to show unconditional love for the family, it was easy, and I got paid well, in trade.

New Years Day was right around the corner, and I knew that meant more football on TV, followed by 2-3 months of rain. A lot of inside time for me, and I was fine with that.

4-2001...The Big Apple

One afternoon night in April, after he got out of school, Josh came to me. "Goldie, I'm going to be gone for a couple of days, starting tomorrow. I'm going on a class trip with some of my schoolmates. We're going to a magical, faraway place called New York. I'll be back to see you on Sunday night, I promise." I understood his leaving for a little while. As long as he came back, I was fine with it.

The next morning, was departure day. Josh, Chase, and 46 other students with 4 chaperones, from D'Iberville High School met at the Biloxi / Gulfport Regional Airport. Everyone was excited to be there, and looked forward to a tremendous 3-day adventure. Many of these Seniors had never flown in an airplane before. Josh had been to Atlanta and San Antonio via air, so he was the veteran. They boarded the small jet (their group comprised ½ of the passengers), for a quick 1-hour and 15 minute flight to Atlanta. They would change to a larger plane there, and land at LaGuardia Airport in a little over 2 hours.

The flights were uneventful, and the novices all tried to look casual and worldly. Their act worked pretty well until they were introduced to the huge Atlanta-Hartsfield airport, changing terminals with thousands of others. Then, at LaGuardia. It was like they had entered another world. The airport was teeming with people from multiple cultures. They saw turbans, kaftans, and colorful outfits from who knew where. All around them was a cacophony of speech in languages and dialects they could never guess the origin of. Even the announcements were in several languages. Josh recognized the Spanish and French accents from his classes, but even the English sounded different.

"Stop gawking, and acting like a rube" Josh suggested to one of his fellow travelers. "Act like you've been here before." He had to admit though, this was weird.

At baggage claim the chaperones kept saying "once your bag comes line up against the wall, and make sure it's your bag, not just one that looks like it." After what seemed like hours, Lilly Parker's bag showed up…the last one.

They were marched outside, to behold even more amazing sights. The cab lines, the shuttle buses, the parking garage. Everything was big, and going fast. And the weather was cooler than Josh thought it would be. The group marched onto their chartered bus, and began winding their way to Manhattan.

I can't believe my eyes, thought Josh… the enormity and scale of everything. They left the multiple airport structures behind and went south on the 278 beltway. The group moved closer and closer to the great City. They couldn't help it, they were all wide-eyed with mouths agape. It was like the "yellow brick road," and were approaching the wonderful world of OZ! Gleaming skyscrapers, and yellow cabs by the hundreds. They diverted to the 59th Street Bridge where they actually entered Manhattan, at 3:30 p.m., Friday April 14, 2001. Narrow streets, honking horns all around, millions of people, all in a rush.

After a couple of turns they found themselves on "Broadway," what a feeling. In just a few blocks they pulled up in front of the hotel. They stayed at a little place on west 45th street, just across the street from the luxurious Marriott Marquis on the corner of Broadway and 45th. The group exited the bus single file, and there wasn't anyone who didn't stop and look up at the imposing steel and glass structures surrounding us.

Fortunately, they were all pre-registered, each of us with a roommate (Josh's was Chase). They were told to go to their rooms which were located on the 2nd, 3rd, and 4th floors, and meet downstairs at 5:00 in a conference room our school had arranged to use. The chaperones had arranged for pizzas and soft drinks to be waiting for us. Since most hadn't eaten since breakfast, this was met with great enthusiasm.

The room was small but clean, with 2 beds and a bath. Josh opened the drapes to discover that the view was of an adjacent building. You can't have everything. They hustled downstairs at 4:45. During 30 minutes of ravenous feasting, the 4 leaders told the group what was in store for them.

At 6 p.m. they were to leave the hotel take a right on Broadway, a left on 34th, and at 5th Avenue encounter one of the wonders of the modern world, The Empire State Building. The class would have a 1 hour tour of the massive marvel. At 7:30 we would walk a few blocks to 214 W. 42nd Street, The New Amsterdam Theatre, where there were tickets to the Broadway Show, "The Lion King." A lot for 1 day, but the class could only afford 3 days and 2 nights for the trip, returning Sunday evening with school the next day. The students weren't going to be tired. No one group ever had as much adrenaline and energy. They could go on forever.

Josh and Chase sat there trading their wondrous observations of the "City That Never Sleeps." It seemed that they were in a foreign country, even after leaving La Guardia Airport. They had seen the real "melting pot" that New York was famous for. And, they were just beginning.

Right on time they left the hotel and within just a few minutes were at the massive steel and concrete wonder. It hurt your neck just to look up at the thing. In the lobby they received given the standard factoids about the building. Built in less than 9 months, not counting the excavation, the structure rose 4 and one half floors per week, much of it fabricated off site, and was completed November 13, 1930, although it wasn't open to the public until May 1, 1931. The building was 102 stories tall plus a 230 ft. tower, antenna, and lightning rod.

The group sprinted to the elevators to get to the 86th floor observatory…1050 feet above ground. It took several minutes to get there, but what a sight to behold. No wonder a B25 had crashed into it in 1945. Halfway to the heavens, they were on top of the world. "Look out there, Chase. When I talk about going places, this is what I'm talking about. You can go anywhere, do anything in this wonderful place." They looked around the deck looking at the magnificent skyline for miles around. From the Chrysler building, the Statue of Liberty, all the way down to the financial district, and saw what would be the last stop on Sunday, the Trade Towers. It gave a great sense of pride being an American. You were free to go build your own "Empire." And you could succeed or fail, based on your own merits. After what seemed like far too little time, the group was told to meet on the street outside, as it was time to get ready to go to the theatre.

The class paraded a few blocks and came to the "New Amsterdam Theatre", 214 W. 42nd St. The theatre had reserved a section of the seating area for the class to occupy. A theatre spokesman gave an overview of the production, the storyline, the costumes, and the music, some by Hans Zimmer. The length was 2 hours and 45 minutes with one intermission. Once the intermission lights came up, many naps were suddenly interrupted. This group wasn't comprised of "theatre people", and it had been a long, long day.

Over 1300 miles in distance, and "light-years" in environment and culture made Josh want to travel, and see the world. He would get his wish, in less than a year, in an unexpected way.

The next morning they were able to sleep in, not reporting to the conference room / headquarters on the first floor until 9:30 where a buffet breakfast was served with unlimited eggs, toast, home fries, bacon, and sausage topped off by O.J., and for those of us who chose "The New York Breakfast", coffee and bagels. "Where are the grits" whispered Chase. "They don't have them up north," Josh answered, "don't ask anyone else."

"OK, on your list of things to bring was an outdoor coat," announced the head chaperone.

"Here's where you need it. We'll be on the water for about 3 hours, and it will be cold. There is an inside observation area on the boat for those of you who choose to use it. Get changed and we'll meet outside at 10:30, leave at 10:45." At 10:45, sharp, they set out and a few minutes later approached Pier 83, right at west 42nd Street, and boarded a boat. "Circle Line Tours" had been in existence for decades, giving tourists a view of Manhattan Island from the water perspective.

At 11:30 the boat's horn blew loudly for departure southward. It circled the island in a counter-clockwise direction. The tour director repeated the landmarks by rote. The Statue of Liberty, Financial District, World Trade Center, Brooklyn Bridge, et cetera. Some of the mansions, facts about the bridges, the names of the bodies of water we were on, so much information. I guess if you say it enough times it becomes easy. They had a pre-made box lunch with a Coke, chips, and a choice of turkey or roast beef sandwich.

The boat slipped back into the pier at 2:30. The group bought some souvenirs, said goodbyes and departed back to the hotel, arriving around 3. From 3-5 they split into 2 groups. One, mainly the females, went north to go shopping along with a couple of the chaperones. Most of the guys went 2 blocks south to "Harry's Arcade and Game Town"", where they had every game and video competition imaginable. The guys had a great time, and I'm sure everyone enjoyed having a choice, for once.

The class all knew to meet in the lobby at 6:15. The school had reserved a section in an "authentic" Italian restaurant, a few blocks south in Greenwich Village. The group got there about 7 o'clock and sure enough, it looked authentic Italian.

The sign said "Luigi's Restaurante Italiano." Inside, the section reserved for them was in the back. The seating was picnic style with red and white vinyl tablecloths, and lots of paper napkins.

The waiter appeared and introduced himself, "My name is Dominick, you can call me Dom. We have for you a great choice Linguini with white or red sauce, or you can have spaghetti with meatballs. We serve a salad at the beginning, not at the end like in Italia."

"We also have for you fresh baked, Italian Bread, Coke, tea, or water to drink, sorry no wine for this group, and Italian gelato for desert. I have 2 assistants who will be helping me to take your orders and serve your meals. Buon appetito."

The meal was great, Most had two helpings of pasta with red sauce (you could get spaghetti at home), lots of bread, tea, and gelato. The salad was great also. Josh thought, man these Italians sure knew how to cook and eat. The Italian neighborhoods in Biloxi could learn a thing or two from Luigi's. Josh got up to go to the men's room and passed by the kitchen on the way. Among the staff, yelling, screaming, and swearing in many languages, seemed to be the thing to do. He never wanted to be in the restaurant business. On his way back to the table Josh noticed a framed business license from the City of New York. Beside "Owner of Record" it said "Marvin Silverstein." Oh well, it still seemed authentic to Josh, and if the ownership wasn't Italian, he wasn't going to spoil it for the others.

The next morning, Sunday, everyone had packed and the leaders had checked out of the hotel. A bus was waiting outside the hotel to take everyone to a "brunch." I learned later it was the famous weekly event held at "Windows on the World," located on the 106th and 107th floors of the north tower of the World Trade Center complex. This is why all the guys had to bring a sports coat. They were required, no exceptions. Once upstairs, the view from our reserved section was spectacular. The windows themselves were 2 stories tall. You couldn't help but to be awestruck. People walked over to the windows...but not too close.

When you looked down from these huge windows, Vertigo would almost always affect you, and you would jump back to the safety of the room as a conditioned reflex. They could have done that for a while, but the chaperones said we were acting like 3rd graders, and herded the group to the tables which had been reserved for us.

After we were seated. One of the hosts came over to welcome us. He was young, probably only 24 or 25. "My name is Mark Romero. I'm one of the managers here, and I want to welcome each and every one of you to our establishment. You might think we are all fancy people, but it's people like you, and your parents, who give me a job. My purpose is to make sure your meal and your experience here are unforgettable. If I can be of assistance, please let me know." Josh was impressed!

The meal, the views, and the hospitality were something to remember. This young man Mark Romero was going places too. You could see it in his eyes.

The Group all got on the bus which had been waiting 90 minutes, and headed back to La Guardia, Atlanta, and home, arriving around 6 p.m. Boy, did they have stories to tell.

High School is Over, 2001

Josh graduated #3 in a class of 218 students. This standing, and good scores on his ACT testing, allowed him to get some scholarship help from The University of Southern Mississippi in Hattiesburg, only 80 miles to the north. He would still probably need a part-time job, but the help was wonderful. He saw a couple of the school's basketball games, and had spoken to the coaches, but he didn't want to have too many things on his plate, especially during his first year. He didn't think he was good enough to be anything but a "back-up" player, anyway.

Chase was also attending USM, and had decided to try out for the football team. He had gone to the spring game recently, and was a big fan. The team had always been popular inside the state, but burst onto the national scene when they gave a little known kid named Brett Favre, his only scholarship offer, in 1987.

Graduation Day came and went. Dad and Mom were proud of their son. How he had dedicated himself to getting good grades, how he had a perfect attendance record, never got into fights, or came home drunk. About a week afterward I saw a picture of Josh and Chase in their "caps and gowns. Josh was about 6 inches taller than his friend, but Chase was built thick, like the magnolia tree.

I knew that this summer would fly by, and that after that I wouldn't be seeing as much of my best friend. So I decided to stick as close to him as his summer job would allow. "Don't worry, girl. I'm only 90 minutes away and I'll still be home most weekends, holidays, and the summer. How about tomorrow we take a ride to the beach?" There were very few words I understood, but "ride" and "beach" were at the top of my list.

I started jumping up and down and Josh wrestled with me on the floor. Life was good!

The next day, before Josh had to go to Burger King, he gave me the signal and I hopped in his car. We sped away, the wind flapping in my ears.

All the way over the Back Bay Bridge we sped closer and closer to the beach. The beach was one of my favorite places in the world, but so was most anywhere else where Josh was. When we got down to highway 90, and the beach, he parked the car and let me run with him in the sand. I could outrun him, but I always came back to his side.

I'll always remember the days in the sand.

Poor Judgment

Back at home, things were getting settled in for the summer routine. Josh, Mom, and Dad were working. Jess helping at home, and making sure the garden got watered.

Josh had been going out with Chase on weekend nights, and occasionally saw Wendy. Jess had her driver's license now that she was 16, and she would go to a mall, called Edgewater Plaza, with her schoolmate friends Emily or Cindy. Jess had a 10:00 curfew, which allowed them to get home after the stores closed at 9:30. sometimes they would just cruise by "Pizza Hut" or some other hangout place to see what cute boys they could find to look at.

One Friday night, she dressed up a little, and Emily picked her up at 6, for a little bit of freedom. Friday and Saturday nights were "their nights," which usually meant trying to act a little older than they were.

Emily, a striking brunette with perfect teeth, said "I've got someplace special to go tonight, that's why I wanted you to dress up a little." She drove over the I-110 Back Bay bridge, but instead of turning toward the mall, she drove over and parked on the strip, outside several of the casinos. Emily turned off the car ignition, and said, "I think it's time we see a casino."

"We can't go in there, "Jess said, "You have to be 18."

"I set it all up," Emily grinned. "One of the guys at the door is dating my older sister, Kathy. He said he would get us in at 6:30, and we could stroll around for a while. What's it going to hurt, and who's going to know? I think it's time for us to broaden our horizons, a bit."

"I just don't know." Jess hesitated. She looked up at the sign over the door.

It said "Beau Rivage." "My Dad works here. What would I do if he ever fond out. I'd be grounded until old age set in."

"You told me he gets off at 6. We probably passed him on the Bridge on his way home," Emily countered. "And, my friend said definitely not try to buy a drink, so it's not that bad, we just want to see. Don't be such a nerd."

Sure enough, at 6:30, a tall young man walked up, winked at Emily, and opened the door. They stepped through.

Jess had never seen such a chaos of lights, the jingle-jangle of slot machines, and people rolling dice, yelling "YO." "Blackjack" tables were spread across the casino floor. Everywhere she looked were strobes of lights, neon flashing signs, and "zombie like" people sitting at the slot machines, with plastic cups full of coins, feeding them money and pulling a lever. She and Emily kept moving around every 5 minutes or so, as to not draw unwanted attention. The one thing that kept Jess from panicking, was that thy both certainly looked 18.

They stayed about a half hour, and left going back to the car, and started driving toward the relatively peaceful, security of the mall. "Wasn't that a trip?" shouted Emily gleefully.

Jess had to admit to herself that the experience was amazing. Plus, "no harm, no foul" was one of Josh's favorite sayings. They left the mall at about 9, and drove into the parking lot at "Bennies," a popular local hang out with video games, ice cream, and lots of rampant hormones. The girls figured they could spend a few minutes checking things out.

The average age in the place was probably 17, but after the girls' earlier trip to the casino, it seemed like they were the oldest ones in the place. They had a Coke, and giggled the story to their friend Cindy. She had to watch her younger brother until 7, and couldn't make the casino trip, now she was really jealous, and they rubbed it in on Cindy.

Then, Emily and Jess went home, Jess arriving at 9:55...no problem.

That night, she had dreams of living in a "Casino World" with lots of mechanical things and lights everywhere. The next morning she woke with Princess curled up at her feet, and the phone ringing.

"Karen," Dad said, "they need me at work for a couple of hours. I'm going in about 10:30, be back after lunch." She replied, "Josh and I will be at work. Jess will hold down the fort here."

Jess got dressed and ate the simple breakfast of cantaloupe and berries with milk. Ah, the glory of having a garden. And now it was a very large garden.

Jess let me outside after breakfast, my second trip out this morning. I assumed my position under the magnolia tree and watched as she watered the rows of fruits and vegetables. When it was dry she tried to water twice daily, morning and afternoon, because our garden, even with the net, was exposed to full sun, 90% of the day.

At about noon, I heard Dad's car skid to a fast stop on the oyster shells, and his car door slammed louder than usual. Jess had just finished pulling some weeds (they grow quickly with water, also). Dad yelled out the back door, "Jess, I need to talk to you inside." Jess, washed off her hands, and scooted inside.

"Please go sit in the family room, I'll be right there." Dad came in and turned on the TV, Jess was puzzled. He put a VHS tape in the player, and hit "Play"

Jess watched in horror as she saw a screen with a digital timer in the upper left corner which displayed 6:32 p.m., Fri. 06/01/01. It was her and Emily coming in the "Beau Rivage." The door being held by a tall young man.

The tape lasted about 30 minutes. It showed her and Emily in several casino locations smiling, laughing, and smoking cigarettes while leaning on a stand-up table. Emily looked extremely flirtatious. It ended with Emily and Jess leaving the casino using the same door they entered through, with a little more "bounce in their step" than before.

"Any explanation, young lady?" "Do you have an evil twin I don't know about who pals around with Emily Perez? How many trips to casinos have you made when you were out shopping at the mall?"

The room was spinning. Emily was stuttering. Her face was as red as a beet.

"Your mother and I work very hard to help you. And I thought we had done a better job raising you to respect the law. Jess, you're both 16! You can't go to casinos and bars. You're endangering our casino license, The same license that gives me a job, a paycheck, so that I can help this family meet our goals. Jess, you have to think about your actions."

"Dad," she started "it was a surprise to me too. I didn't know when Emily picked me up that she had arranged to go to a casino. If I did, do you think I would have picked the one you work in? Honest, I've never been in a casino before, and when Emily pulled up outside, I was as surprised as you are now. But, I didn't want to look like a chicken. What could I do, wait in the car?"

"You could have gone to a phone and called home. One of us would have been there in 20 minutes, and I'd still have a daughter I could trust, and was proud of."

With this, the tears came pouring out. "I'm sooooo sorry Daddy, but I couldn't call you to come get me and let Emily think that I was a big weenie."

"Well she's in trouble. I owe it to Mr. Perez to call him and tell him what happened. Any responsible parent has to make that call. I would expect the same respect from him if the roles were reversed."

"But Dad, we didn't try to buy a drink. We didn't have fake I.D.s. We just wanted to see what it was like. You know what Josh always says…no harm, no foul."

"But there was harm Jess. Why do you think I had to go in today? I had to meet with the director of security for the casino. You put me in a very uncomfortable position with my employer. I'm not in trouble with them, but Jess, I had to go in and fire that young man who let you in. He cried and begged me to change my mind, but it's the law. He'll have that termination on his record all his life. I just hope he learns from his mistake and bounces back. I told him, to use me as a reference for his next job. Fortunately, they're building more casinos every day, and a good word wouldn't hurt. It's the least I can do."

"So," he asked, "what do I do about Jess? Any suggestions?"

"I don't know, Dad, Jess cried. I wasn't trying to be bad. I didn't set out to hurt people. I just thought it was an adventure." Her lips were quivering with distress.

"Jess, when you turn 18, I'll take you there, myself. But you have to give me your word that there will be no more of this, and no more cigarettes, for sure, those things killed your grandfather when he was 40 years old. Every time he sucked smoke out of those things, it was sucking the life right out of him."

"Do you feel like you've learned something, Jess?" "Yes, Dad. And I promise, no more cigarettes. It was only 1 or 2 a day anyway. I'm not addicted."

Then a big surprise. "Ok, Jess, here's your tape. I don't want to see any more tape of you unless it's in a "G" rated movie. Your mother and I don't keep secrets. But one of these days soon, you're going to be the one to tell her. Throw the tape away, but tell your Mom what happened, or I will. I'll know when you've done it. And I still have to call Mr. Perez."

It was like the clouds parted and sunshine beamed onto her face. She had been granted a "stay of execution." "Thanks, Daddy," as she gave him a hug. "I'll try to hold up my end of the family responsibility, and be a better daughter in the future."

Summer 01

Josh worked a full schedule that summer, trying to get a head start on his savings. He didn't have to be in Hattiesburg until late August. Chase and he would be staying in the dorm for their first year, and felt lucky to get in. Chase, however had to report to school in early July, in order to try to "walk on" with the Golden Eagles football team. Chase would stay with friends who lived only about 10 miles away from the campus until the school year was close to beginning.

Josh was still at Burger King, and the district manager had been so impressed with Josh over the years, he had given him an open invitation to join their management training team whether he finished school or not. People just seemed to be taken by him. Always smiling, polite, and respectful. Not to mention, smart.

Even though he was working more, with Chase gone I got to see more of Josh than in previous summers. Also his "sort of girlfriend" Wendy, was going to "Ole Miss" (The University of Mississippi) in Oxford for her first year of college, so she and Josh didn't see that much of each other any more.

The summer went by quickly, as expected. It was hot outside, so when Josh was working, I stayed in my sentinel position in the shade of the magnolia tree. When he was off, if it was too hot for basketball, he let me stay inside and lay at his feet while he watched sports on TV or read a book. He had already received some of his college textbooks, and typical Josh, he wanted a head start on the rest of the kids.

The phone rang one day, Jess answered but, then gave it to Josh. "It's Chase," she said, "he sounds funny." I found out later when he talked to Mom and Dad about it, that Chase had broken or torn some things called an ACL and an MCL. His football days were over before they began.

Even worse, he would have surgery, and be in a cast and on crutches for at least 90 days. Josh said that he had never heard his friend so disappointed.

Tom said, we had a guy at the base who did the same thing to his knee. He just fell off the roof of his house, and snap, there began a 6-month rehab. He wasn't milking it either. This involves almost a total knee re-construction. He came back to work in 60 days, He was using crutches, and but couldn't walk without assistance for several months.

Two weeks later, the last Saturday in August, Josh had the Accord packed to the brim with all the things he was bring with him to school. The family stood on the front porch to say our goodbyes. "I'm proud of you son," from Dad, a tearful embrace from Mom, sneaking him an envelope with extra money in it. Even Jess, knowing that she had moved up a notch at home, was respectful, and gave him a big hug, while holding Princess. She knew her turn was only 3 years away. I was the last to say goodbye. "Saving the best for last" he said. "Don't worry, I'll be back, maybe next weekend. I think the Saints are on TV." I was hurting, but just as I grew from a little ball of fur in the shelter, to what I had now become, Josh had grown from a 13 year old boy into a fine young man. More importantly, someone I truly loved.

Once he was out of sight, the tears started rolling. It was the second time I'd seen it from Dad. But, that turned out alright, so would this.

Josh did come home the next weekend. His part time job didn't start for 2 more weeks, so I was part of the expectant, happy family awaiting his late Friday afternoon arrival. "Tell us all about it" squealed Jess. They all sat at the kitchen table and it seemed everyone spoke at once. Even Princess was laying beside me, and seemed unusually interested.

Josh proceeded to tell them about his dorm, the orientation, his classes, and the update on how Chase was coping with his crutches. Josh said he thought he was using his injury to impress the girls, but that's Chase.

Chase had ridden home with Josh, since he couldn't drive. Chase's father called Dad and offered to pay for the gas. Dad thanked him and said he wouldn't hear of it.

"Those two have been together more times than I can count," he said. "Friends don't keep score of who's done more driving. I'm just glad we can be of help to your family."

That weekend was blissful, the temperature was down into the high 70s (cool for Biloxi at this time of year) during the day, but only a few degrees cooler at night. We played some hoops, took a ride, watched the Saints, and had lots of "together time." When Josh left after the Saints game on Sunday, we all felt better about things. Our strength had been renewed.

Josh couldn't come home the next weekend, September 8. But our world was about to change, in a big way.

The Catalyst

At 9:30 on Tuesday, September 11, 2001, Dad had just let me out for the second time that day, as he was preparing to go to work, a little later than usual. In only an instant a high pitched siren started whining, getting louder and louder. I was afraid. "Goldie, come back inside, it's the warning alarm at the base. Something's terribly wrong." They hadn't used the old emergency signal the entire time I was at Keesler. He got on the phone, trying to reach his friends, but the lines were all jammed. He turned on the TV, and He, Mom, & I beheld a nightmare.

Two very tall buildings were on fire, there was yelling and screaming from people on the ground with smoke everywhere. I didn't know where this was, but I was happy I was here, and hoped that Josh wasn't there. Mom got in her car "I'm going to get Jess from school," she yelled. I guess there wasn't going to be any school that day.

Dad went into work, and volunteered to work whatever hours were needed. As it turned out he came home early. The casino business was slow that day, and they ran things with a skeleton crew. We heard all the reports of people called al-Qaeda who ran 3 airplanes into buildings. They had tried to smash a plane into another building, but were overwhelmed by the passengers. Yes, everyone on that plane still died that day, but the courage of the people onboard kept it from being an even greater tragedy.

On Tuesday night Josh called to check in with everyone. He said that he would definitely be home this weekend. He would be bringing Chase home to his family as well. At 5:00 Friday afternoon.

I heard the crunch of the oyster shell driveway, and my best friend jumped from his car. He came back to see me first. It was just me and Jess home, and I was just inside the gate when he opened it.

After a quick wrestling match (I let him win), we went inside and he gave Jess a hug. It was great to see him home, with the family again. My world was complete.

By this time we knew that 2,976 people had just died in a horrible, cowardly attack on our nation. As happy as Mom and Dad were to see Josh, it was a different time than before. They tried to pretend, but I could sense something was changing.

Dad said, "This country had suffered an attack, not from another country, or a hostile government who declared war on us. It had been because of a religion. An intolerant group of people who want to kill everyone who doesn't believe like they do." He continued, "Throughout history, more people have been killed in the name of religion, than for any other reason, and here we are again."

On Saturday night Josh said "I want to have a family talk tomorrow morning. I've made a decision."

The next morning came quickly..."The Marines?" Dad shouted. "What about your education, your plans, how hard you've worked to get where you are? You can't just throw all that away!"

"Mark Romero," Josh answered, "his name was on the list of the dead from the towers being bombed. Our class met him at "Windows." He wasn't much older than me. Now he's gone. I want to help bring justice to those people who attacked us. School will still be here when I get back, and the military will help pay for it."

"You're acting too impulsively," Mom said. "Absolutely," Dad added.

"I made a 2nd appointment with a recruiter for Tuesday, he said."

"I've thought it through, just like you've both taught me to do all my life. Dad, it was you who told me about standing up for what's right. You and characters like Atticus Finch. And look at what the military has given you in your life. It allowed you to raise a family, taught you rules, respect, and standards."

"Son, this is different. Going to war is too terrible to comprehend. You could do your part in the Air Force or Coast Guard. Somewhere a little safer than the Marine Corps," Dad pleaded.

"Dad, no offense, but I thing the Marine Corps offers the most challenging way for me to contribute. You've even said the few retired Marines you know say there's no such thing as an ex-Marine. They hold their heads a little higher, and have a genuine sense of pride in where they've been, what they've done, and a real sense of membership in something exclusive. Is that right?"

After hours of talking, negotiating, pleading, and harassment, Josh's decision was unchanged.

"I'm taking Chase back to school with me on Monday. I'll go through all the proper procedures withdrawing from school. I've only paid for the 1st semester, and the recruiter said I could possibly get most of that back. I'm sorry if you feel like I've let you down, but this is what I think is the right thing to do."

"Mom, Dad, the world is changing." Josh said. "We can't stick our heads in the sand and pretend different. There are people out there who want to kill us because of our freedom and beliefs. We talked about it all the way down here on Friday."

"Chase would go too, if he could, but he's going to need those crutches for at least another 3 months, and after that, the orthopedic doctor said there would be a lengthy rehab, probably 6-8 months."

"I'm going for a ride, down to see the beach…take a couple of hours to focus. Goldie, you ready?"

Boy, was I. I had never seen Josh like this. He invited Jess, too, and she came with us. That meant I had to sit in the back, but she rolled my window down half way, the breeze was great. We took the 110 over Back Bay, and once we got down to highway 90, Josh turned right, so we could get out of the hubbub of the casino empire, and in a few miles he made a U-Turn and pulled into one of the parking bays on the beach side of the highway.

"You know what this means," he said to Jess, "You've got to be the one to look after the house, and especially my girl friend in the back seat. Promise you'll watch over her, and our parents. They're all going to need you."

"You've got my word," said the sixteen year old. "Especially with Goldie, she saved my life, I owe her big-time."

"Well, I'm going to buy you that cell-phone you've been wanting, I'll clear it with Mom and Dad," he said as her eyes got larger. "It's partially for selfish reasons. I'll won't know their schedules, so I can always call you to check in on everyone, and give them a report. I think they'll like that. Also, if I get orders right out of "boot camp." I'll loan you my car while I'm gone. You got your license a few months ago, and this is a great car, but, just like Goldie, you've got to take care of it."

Jess started crying, and Josh gave he a big hug and said, "You're going to have to play grown up, while I'm gone. Let's us three take a walk on the beach, maybe even get our feet wet."

"Goldie, you heard what I told Jess. I'm depending on you, too."

Goldie hoped it wouldn't be as long as the trip to New York.

Parris, But Not France

In a little less than 3 weeks, Josh was on a Greyhound bus to Mobile, Alabama. From there he would Connect to Savannah, Ga. From Savannah he would take a military transport bus the final 45 miles to Parris Island, South Carolina, the Marine Corps Recruit Depot. Over 8000 acres, just outside Beaufort, S.C.

The first day, he saw all types of people, tall, short, skinny, heavy, black, white, Hispanic, long hair, short hair, you name it. They were told to "fall in" for a welcoming speech. It was the beginning of making these individuals, all the same, all U.S. Marines. We lined up and were welcomed to "The Corps." We were told with great enthusiasm, that we were lucky to be here. That it was going to be the most difficult 13 weeks of our lives, and some would not make it. The first week is for the issuing of clothing and equipment, medical screening, and "Initial Strength Test." Day 1, You get a buzz, "high and tight" hair cut, and assigned to a barracks which you share with 65 others, plus you get introduced to your Drill Instructor.

Our Drill Instructor was Sergeant Rawls. He was not in a good mood that day. You will address me by saying "Sir, Yes Sir or Sir, No Sir." I am your Drill Instructor and you will address me that way, not Sergeant Rawls. You will not ask questions. I am not here to answer your stupid questions. I am here to turn this group of misfits into United States Marines, and I must have done something to make somebody in heaven mad, because this group will be an impossible task."

For the next 3 hours we were shown how to pack a footlocker, make a bed, shine shoes…all the Marine way, the only way. The first day you also get to call home to let family know you are OK. There is a script which must be adhered to, or you will be cut-off. You don't want that, because it will be your last phone call allowed for 13 weeks. Of course we lined up to take turns on the pink (really) phone. The script posted by the phone reads:

(1) This is recruit (last name)

(2) I have arrived safely at Parris Island

(3) Please do not send me any food or bulky items in the mail

(4) I will contact you in 5 days by postcard, with my new address

(5) Thank you for your support, goodbye for now

I dialed our home number, held my breath, and Mom answered. I was happy she was there. I recited my speech, and hung up.

The night was welcomed. After we had chow, we watched 2 introductory videos on the workings of the camp, and it was lights out at 20 hundred hours (8 pm).

Three hours later, the lights came on and Sergeant Rawls came into the barracks banging two cymbals and yelling "Fall in, fall in, if I were the enemy you'd all be dead." We all lined up at the foot of our bunks, at attention.

"Starting right now, there will be one of you on guard from twenty hundred hours until five hundred hours, on three hour shifts, every night. If I catch your sentry sleeping, we'll all be going on a little 5-mile run, starting then. What's your name tall boy," he yelled at me.

"Sir, Recruit Flowers, Drill Instructor, Sir."

"You're pretty quick, Flowers. I like you even though you have a pansy name." I heard someone smirk a laugh, trying to disguise it as a cough. The D.I. was on him in a heartbeat. "What's your name funny boy?"

"Recruit Samms, Drill Instructor, Sir."

"Well boys, you can thank comedian Samms here…every one of you drop and give me 20." We all did as ordered, though a couple of the group had trouble, but finished out of fear and adrenaline.

"Now, Flowers, here, is the barracks leader, until one of you can take it from him" the D.I. said. "Samms is going to take the first sentry shift tonight. Flowers, who will take the next? It will be your decision tonight, and going forward."

"Sir, I will take the second shift tonight, Sir. Sir, tomorrow we will draw numbers, 1 through 66, for the sequence in the future, Sir"

"Smart, Flowers. It's good to be thinking ahead. Just remember, I hate a suck-up."

"Sir, Yes Sir, Drill Instructor, Sir," I replied. But I thought I had gotten off to a good start with the D.I. and, more importantly, with the other 65 recruits Over the next few weeks, Josh learned a great deal about the Corps, and developed a friendship with a few of the recruits, particularly, Privates Chet Perry, and Alonzo Brown.

These three, Josh included, seemed to be the best of the barracks at just about everything. They always led in runs, marksmanship, hand-to hand, you name it. It developed into a friendly competition between the young men, making them better Marines because of the challenges they posed, trying to best the others.

Josh had only one close friend Chase, before joining the Marines. Now he had new friends, and a huge support group, the entire Marine Corps.

A Tragedy...November 01

Winter was coming, such as it was in the deep south. Jess was back in school. She was a junior this year. Mom and Dad had been watching the news. American and British forces had been bombing people called the Taliban and al-Qaeda in a place called Afghanistan for about a month. The speculation was that we were getting "boots on the ground," and some of those boots had U.S. Marine feet in them. Josh still had several weeks of training ahead, so Mom and Dad were hoping for a quick resolution to this "Operation Enduring Freedom."

One morning about 8:30, the phone rang, we knew it couldn't be Josh, no phone calls allowed. Dad handed the phone to Mom, "Karen it's for you, a minister from San Antonio." Her face went white. She took the phone with a pause, added a deep breath, smiled and said, "This is Karen Flowers, how can I help you?"

"Ms. Flowers, This is Father Stevens. I hate to make this call, but your sister, Vicky Robbins, has died. She was a member of our parish. It just happened last night. The reports aren't in, but the coroner said it looks like some type of aneurism. If that turns out to be true, it was a sudden, painless rupture of a blood vessel, which could not have been foreseen or prevented. I only know because a member of my family died the same way. I'm so terribly sorry. Ms. Flowers, what can I do to help you, here?" Mom was speechless and struggling for answers, to age-old questions. Why didn't I call or visit more often? How could I have done better to show her the love I have for her?

"Ms. Flowers, are you still there?""Yes, I'm here," she said tears welling in her eyes. Please give me your phone number. I'll be there tomorrow." Her head was swimming...what to do,? Who to call? "Father Stevens, I have so many things to do, I don't know where to start." Father Stevens said, Ms. Flowers, the only call you must make today are to the coroner or a funeral home. State laws say that the body must be moved to a funeral home, unless there is a question of unnatural death, and in this case there is none. Many in our Parish use O'Neal Mortuaries, I can give you their number."

"That's fine, I'll call the funeral home. She wanted cremation, anyway. I know your faith doesn't support cremation, necessarily, but it is her wishes in the will," Karen said with tears running down her face. "She only had the will because her husband died early and left no will, resulting in excessive court costs and attorney's fees."

"Cremation is not forbidden, just not encouraged," replied Father Stevens. I'll be happy to help with a gathering of friends at the funeral home, if that is your wishes. Just bring a photograph of your sister with you, to place by the urn. I will get the word out to any of her friends who miss the obituary in the paper."

"Thank you for that, Father Stevens. I will definitely stay in touch. I finally got a cell phone this fall, here is the number if you need me after today."

She turned to her husband, who was holding her hand. "Tom, I'm going tomorrow, and I want to take Jess with me, for support. Southwest flies straight into San Antonio from New Orleans, and is faster and cheaper than the others. We'll drive to New Orleans tomorrow morning. Today is Wednesday, We'll stay at Vicky's...her heart ached when she said that. We'll stay with Connie and Mom. I'll plan on us returning Sunday, so Jess will only miss 2 days of school. I need her with me."

"Would you mind calling the principal at De'Iberville High? Tell him I'm coming to pick Jess up at 1:00."

"Tell the principal to be sure and tell her that it has nothing to do with her brother. I want to be the one to tell her about Vicky."

Goldie's mood saddened. A wonderful person, gone cold, like "Green." Why? She was my friend. I promised myself, I'd never forget Vicky.

Mom had many things to do, she told Dad. "I have to call my sister, Beth, then the funeral home, the airline, how can I get this all done?," she said with panic in her voice. Dad held Mom as he said, "I'll do my part to help. I suggest you take Josh's car. It's larger and in better shape than the bug."

"I'll take it today and drop it off at the Exxon, get the oil changed, tire check, etc. It would make me feel that you two are safer."

"Thanks, Tom," said Mom," I just feel so bad." She got Beth on the phone, and broke the horrible news. Vicky had been the oldest, then Beth, with Karen the youngest. Karen and Beth had really looked up to their "big sister." This was heart wrenching for them.

They both had many regrets, and self-incrimination, but all the tears couldn't console them, or bring Vicky back. They agreed to touch base tomorrow. Beth would check the airlines and book a flight for tomorrow, too.

After 3 hours of making plans, Mom drove the few minutes to school, and met Jess in the business office. She told her the news, and the plan. Jess shed tears in sympathy, but she was proud to be needed by Mom at this time in her life.

They went home, and started packing. "Don't forget, the new airline rules. No scissors or sharp objects, like pins, or nail clippers."

Jess thought that this was an overreaction. Like she would hijack the plane with nail clippers? But then she thought about all those innocent victims. Over reaction is better than no reaction, she reasoned.

San Antonio

Mom and Jess drove off at 6 a.m., sharp, for a 8:55 flight to San Antonio. New Orleans was only 70 miles away, but the airport was at least 15 miles west of the city, and Mom didn't want to take any chances with the early morning traffic there. She had heard that they had clogs of cars at all times of day, but rush hours were definitely the worst. She took I-10 west, which went straight to the airport exit.

She and Jess didn't talk much on the trip. Mom's mind was focused on the road, and the mission ahead. "How did aunt Beth handle the news?" Jess asked. "About as well as I did, I suppose. Blaming herself for not being closer, for not calling or visiting as often as she should have. You know Jess, life is fragile. This has taught me a lesson to be close to all my family," she said, a tear running down her cheek.

"You already do great," Jess comforted. In no time they crossed the Lake Pontchartrain Causeway-Bridge, at a length of almost 24 miles, reputed to be the longest bridge in the world.

They drove through New Orleans, Jess gaping at the skyline and especially the Superdome. Once they passed the Claiborne Avenue exit, they were headed out of town and traffic thinned out a lot. Twenty five minutes later, they pulled into long term parking, and caught the shuttle bus to the airport terminal.

Two hours and fifteen minutes after boarding the plane they landed in San Antonio. Once they collected their bags, they went outside and saw Connie and Grandma Doris waiting in Vicky's car, a 5-year old blue mini-van. Doris was in the driver's seat. It was obvious the old woman had been drinking. It was a sad day, but Karen had a feeling that this was the norm, not the exception. "Mom, are you OK?" Karen asked. "Doris answered, "My daughter just died. What do you expect?"

"Mom, let me drive, you've been drinking, please," she said.

"You don't know your way around here, Karen, you'll get us lost," Doris responded. "Mom, I don't have time to argue. Please, lets all try to cooperate and get through this together, as a family."

"Connie knows this place, and Vicky said Connie has her driver's license, if we need her to drive somewhere. The last thing we need is a DUI or an accident, so now, please, again, get in the back with Jess. Connie can give me directions from the passenger seat." "Are you OK with that, Connie?" Karen knew the girl had to be in shock. Losing her Mom just a few years after her Dad. Maybe giving her some responsibility, might help, for a while.

The old woman grumbled something about not being appreciated, but she got in the back of the van.

"We call this van the 'blue whale'," Connie joked, looking for a little levity at a tense time.

"Well, give me directions to where you park your "whale." We're going to drop off your grandmother. You and Jess can come with me on my appointments, along with aunt Beth. Your grandmother isn't going to be of any help today."

Vicky had lived in a little "patio home" of about 1800 square feet in a community called Castle Hills, just north of I-410 off Blanco Road. It was an easy 10 minute trip. Jess had only been there once before (why?, she thought)

They pulled in the driveway, and everyone emptied out. Karen said to Doris, "Mom, you're going to bed to sleep it off. Connie put on some respectable clothes.

"Those tight jeans with holes in the knees are going to raise eyebrows at the appointments I've made for today, and I want you with us. Put on some leather shoes, and wash 90% of that makeup off your face. We're leaving in an hour to go back to the airport and get up Beth. Let's talk about sleeping arrangements."

Connie said, "Well, my room's sort of a disaster, and pretty small. I did clean Mom's room and changed the sheets, and all." "That's OK Connie, Jess will bunk with you. Beth will sleep with me." Karen stated.

That afternoon, Karen, Beth, Jess, and Connie sat in the office of the attorney who had prepared Vicky's will, Dave Fenton. Karen produced the original copy of the will, which had named her the executor (on the flip of a coin), and sole beneficiary, and a general power of attorney, which had been notarized. In Texas, it was simpler with one beneficiary. That way they wouldn't have to go to Probate Court. Beth and Mom had agreed when the will was drawn, that after accounting for Connie's education, any remaining assets would be divided evenly between the sisters. Vicky had not been trying to play favorites, but the attorney said, the simpler the better.

"I'd like to have your sister sign off on this," Fenton said. "No problem," Beth said, "I'm right here." "Well, thanks, just give my paralegal some ID she can copy, and it will be so much smoother."

"I don't want to get into this yet," Karen said, "but I know your firm does real estate work as well. Can you give me the names of a couple of real estate agents who work in Castle Hills?"

Fenton left the office and came back with two names and phone numbers, and handed them to Karen. "My real estate partner says these are the two best in that area. He does business with both."

They got back in the car, and Connie said, "You're like, going to sell the house? Where will Grandma and I live?"

"That's for later," Karen explained. "We'll have to discuss things after the service. But, the more things I can look into now, will allow us to do make the best decisions later." Beth added, "We want to mourn for your Mom, but we promised her we would provide for you. That's a promise Karen and I intend to keep." Then emotionally, " I can't let her down now, she was a big part of us growing up." Karen assured Connie, "We'll talk as a family later, after the service."

Karen had followed Father Stevens advice an had already called O'Neal's. They arrived a couple of minutes early and waited in a somber room, with even more somber music playing. But, what did she expect, Jimmy Buffett music and drinks with little parasols?

Right away, Jim O'Neal entered, wearing a black suit. Karen thought they must have a rule book for funeral directors. Jim gave his practiced condolence speech, and then it got down to contracts and money, as always. They eventually arranged for a Saturday, 11 am visitation for friends and family.

There would be a beautiful urn containing the ashes placed next to a photo of Vicky in younger days. There would be a book for visitors to sign, and cookies, coffee, and soft drinks provided by the funeral home (at well marked-up prices, but Karen didn't have time to fool with it). An announcement would be in the paper tomorrow morning. Neither of the girls had said a word. They were there for support. It went both ways. They felt like a part of the process. Grieving, yes. But there was another side of death, also, a business side.

The last stop of the day was at First Mid-Texas Bank, where Vicky had done all her banking.

Attorney Fenton had already called the Bank President and explained that Karen had access to all of Vicky's accounts and records. Today, she just wanted an accounting of the estate. Mr. Ashton, the President of the Bank, was most gracious.

He had prepared a spread sheet of the family's assets and liabilities. Vicky had about $80,000 in the bank, mostly from her late husband's life insurance when he died several years ago. There was a small mortgage on the house of only about $25,000. The latest bank appraisal had shown a value of the house at $175,000.

Karen and Beth were relieved to see that, as suspected, Vicky had been frugal, had not bought the latest BMW every year, and had kept things in good shape. She took a copy of everything, and promised Mr. Ashton she would be in touch with him tomorrow.

Lastly, Karen used her cell phone to call the 2 real estate agents who Fenton had recommended. She would meet them on Sunday at the house, one at 10, the other at 11.

They got back to the house at 5:30. Karen wanted to collapse on the bed for a few minutes, so did Beth, and they did, for an hour. When they woke up, Karen realized 2 things. Jess had cleaned out one of the two closets, and the bathroom of her aunt's things. "I thought it would be easier for me, than for you or Beth," Jess said. "I know most of her clothes will go to charity, but I didn't want you to have to deal with it today." Karen hugged her daughter and thanked her. "You're a huge help, just being here."

Then she heard a ruckus in the kitchen, the old woman was cursing, and throwing things into the dishwasher. Karen and Beth washed up, and decided to drop the first shoe. "Sit around the table, everyone, you too Connie, we need to talk."

"What's with this BS of selling the house. I'm not going into an old folks home, just so you two can live high on the hog," stated Doris emphatically. Some more drinking had obviously occurred that afternoon. Karen explained. "We're just keeping all options open, until we know all the facts. No decision has been made, and won't be, until we have a better picture of the situation."

Beth added, "Now, what we'd really like to do is order some delivered dinner, and get to know each other better." She was buying time until the adults could work out a plan. She couldn't see leaving a wildcat like Connie appeared to be, with her senile, drunk grandmother guiding her in life. The situation would melt down within 6 months.

The girls loved the dinner option, and immediately agreed on pizza. Karen or Beth didn't care, and Doris probably just need some food in her system no matter what it was.

Connie got on the phone and called Domino's. "I always order from there because they have the cutest delivery boys."

The order would take 30 minutes, so Karen said, "I've got to report in to Tom, and your aunt has to check in too. Beth and I will be in the bedroom on the phone. Jess, here's $30, that should cover it.

After speaking with Beth, Karen called Tom. She explained her dilemma to him. "I just know if we leave them here, they will self-destruct. But we don't have room for 2 more people, I am at a dead end."

Tom had a suggestion, "Have you thought about finishing the bonus room?" he asked. "You said we would have a little money left after putting aside funds for Connie's college. We might have enough left to finish it out, and add a full bath to the bonus room, also."

"The 2 girls can stay up there," Tom said. "Your Mom can't climb stairs, so she'll have to take Jess's room, or Josh's, whatever. I know it's not a perfect arrangement, but it's family."

"I like it," said Karen, "I'll talk to Beth, and Jess, I want her to be a part of the decision.

Karen turned to her sister. "Tom wants to add on to the house, and bring them there. What do you think?"

"It may be the only alternative we have," Beth said. "Our condo in Atlanta is only a 2-bedroom, they'd never fit there. But, we have to sell this house, first. We'll do our share to help pay for the remodel. I'll take care of any objections from Brian, it's not his family."

Selling The Plan

Friday afternoon, they had only a few chores to do, and wound up shopping for a couple of items they needed for the ceremony, at the huge "North Star Mall." It was a giant complex, with a 40 ft. tall pair of cowboy boots right in the middle of the parking lot. That said it all.

That evening, they all took the "whale" to a local Mexican restaurant, properly named, "South of the Border." They ate simple, but great food, fajitas, tacos con carne, tamales, enchiladas, and Grandma had a giant margarita. This cooking really interested Jess. She had never seen Mexican, or as they called it here, Tex-Mex, food outside of Taco Bell. She asked the waitress if she could have a souvenir menu, and she said "Si, senorita, that is a compliment." They all went home and got in bed early. Tomorrow was a big day. Only Beth and Karen knew how big.

The next morning, early, Karen asked Jess to take a walk with her. Beth was making breakfast which would take 30 minutes. After half a block Karen said "There's something I need to tell you that you can't repeat, OK?" "Sure," Jess said, puzzled

"After the ceremony, tomorrow, we're going to have a family meeting. We've decided, with your father's, and Beth's husband's approval, to have Grandma and Connie come live with us, in Biloxi. We can't leave them here. Grandma would drink herself to death in no time and there's no telling what Connie would be up to. We can't afford to keep the house up, and pay for their living expenses. We have to provide Connie a chance at college. We promised that to Vicky."

"Dad will convert the bonus room into a suite with a full bath, you and Connie will share that. Grandma will take one of the downstairs bedrooms."

"I know it would be giving up your own room, but you'll actually have more space than now, and more privacy. I'll talk to your father about installing a phone for you girls, what do you think?"

Jess thought for a minute and said, "Mom, whatever you and Dad decide is best for the family is fine by me. I think Grandma is a bitter old woman, no offense, who drinks way too much. Connie is "out there." She might calm down some in a good environment, but maybe not. I'll do my part. Aunt Vicky was special to me. But most importantly, she was special to you and aunt Beth. Besides, there's something I have to tell you. It's about a mistake I made. A couple of weeks ago."

At 8:30, Jess and Connie had on their nicest dresses, and they all used the "blue whale" to go to O'Neal's.

Everyone entered the parlor. They walked back to see Mr. O'Neal to make sure everything was set. In a few minutes, no one could find Grandma. She had taken her coffee into another room, and was adding some "cough medicine" into it. Her daughters decided not to make a scene, and while she wasn't looking, Karen took everyone's purse into Mr. O'Neal's office for safekeeping, including Grandma's. No one had heard any coughing, before or after.

The ceremony was simple. Everyone got to meet Father Stevens, and there were dozens of people who came by to pay their respects. Some came from the law firm where Vicky had worked. Mr. Ashton came by from the bank. Karen and Beth slipped off to a little corner to talk. "Beth and I want to thank you for looking after Vicky," Karen began. "I know it was difficult it was after her husband died, it's never easy."

Mr. Ashton looked at her. "I came to pay my respects to Vicky. She has been good to all of us too, making Christmas cookies for my employees, always volunteering whenever we needed help with a special event, and was there whenever needed.

"I can also understand if you and Beth want to deal with your local banks, if that what you decide. I'll do whatever I can to expedite things on my end. Call me personally."

Besides business associates, many of the charities she was involved in sent people to pay their last respects. And then there were some who just called themselves, friends.

After the ceremony, at about 1:00, the family sat around the kitchen table. They had cold cuts, and chicken salad they had bought on Friday, for a little buffet luncheon, for the 5 of them.

Now the process began. Karen spoke first, "We spent most of the past few days tying up loose ends, and today celebrating Vicky's life. Now it's time to discuss and make some decisions about the future." Jess was amazed. Mom was making it seem like it was going to be a choice. That Grandma and Connie had a vote. And they didn't.

Karen continued, "One scenario is for Beth, Jess, and I to go home, tomorrow. Grandma still gets her Social Security check, and the house is mostly paid for. The reality is that you can't live on a little less than $1,000 a month. It would slowly drain all your resources to stay in the house. In six months you'd be broke.

"Or, you can try to use Vicky's savings along with Grandma's monthly check to pay the mortgage, keep the "whale" going, buy food, medical, pay for groceries, the electric, telephone, cable, taxes, insurance, laundry, Connie's school and clothes…it goes on and on. Those are just the basics, no pizza, no emergencies, no wine. (That got the old woman's attention). We figure you would last about 12 months, then have nothing, and be on the street. Grandma would be put in a 'home', and Connie won't have the opportunity to go to college. How does that sound?" Connie started crying, "Both of those are dead ends. It's not fair, I deserve better. Why did she have to die?"

"I agree," said Karen. "We have an alternative. Beth, Tom, and I think it would be best for Connie and Grandma, to come live in Biloxi with us. We can sell this house, and expand ours to meet the needs of an extended family. It won't be perfect, especially at first, but we can do it. You know our options, what do you think?"

Grandma looked up and said, "Anything's better than a home. Too many old people in there. No liquor allowed, and I hear they wouldn't cotton up to me and my stogies. No ma'm, no retirement home for this old gal."

"Mississippi is for rednecks." Connie shouted. "I like Texas."

Jess started selling, "We've got a beach only 20 minutes away, loaded with hunky boys, Connie. Boys that love girls from Texas." This girl is good, Beth thought, and caught a glance from Karen, acknowledging the same thing. "And I think we can talk Mom and Dad into letting us share a big room with a private phone."

This was another story entirely for Connie, and she asked Jess, "You think?" Karen replied, "I'm pretty sure we can work it out. Not on week 1, and not until this house sells, but I think we can do it. Grandma can use the 3rd bed room, downstairs. Connie and Jess will share a room until we can expand the house."

Karen added, "If we're agreed, Jess will return tomorrow without me. I'll stay here and get the house on the market, arrange Connie's school transfer, etc."

Karen continued, "Jess will give my return ticket to Tom, who will trade it in for a one-way back here next Friday, all the way from Gulfport. Then we will caravan it back to Biloxi early Saturday morning. It will be tight, in the 'whale' until we get to New Orleans to pick up the Accord from the airport, there. Jess will be fine at home by herself for a day or two."

Home, At Last

The drive home was boring. Tom and Karen took turns driving to New Orleans. When it seemed everyone was dozing Tom looked at Karen and asked, "How are you holding up?"

"I'm fine, I think the worst is over. We just have to make this work. Jess was a big comfort."Tom asked, "She told you about her adventure at the casino, didn't she?" Karen nodded, "Yes, and by the way, I think she really appreciates the way you handled the situation. So do I."

The next couple of months were hectic. Settling into a house too small was never easy.

Well, Goldie thought, new friends to make, and lots of chatter. She liked that. She liked the additions. She had met them one Thanksgiving, and really liked the girl. She was full of spark and energy. The old lady sometimes poured a dollop of a sweet smelling liquid in her coffee. She had liked the one called Vicky, too. But she had gone cold, like "Green" did at the shelter, years ago.

The house in Texas had sold in 5 weeks, sooner than anyone thought. Karen had picked the agent who lived in the area. Now they were beginning to finalize house expansion and other plans. This Spring, they would finish the bonus room, add a bath there, and expand the back porch, putting a screen around it so Grandma Doris could have her after-dinner smoke. On the horizon, Goldie heard, was Josh's graduation, becoming a full-fledged Marine. She couldn't wait to see him.

Thanksgiving was hectic, because the family was just back from San Antonio, and no routine had been developed. Christmas was closing upon us, and I was glad to see my old stocking hanging over the fireplace mantel. I was still a part of the pack, and did my best to make the new members feel welcome. Grandma was home all the time.

I was diligent in my garden sentry duty, except when it was raining.

One afternoon, it started pouring when Grandma was the only one home. I went to the small back porch and "woofed", hoping she would hear me. The main door was open, but the screen door was closed. I heard snoring sounds from inside, and saw Princess through the window. I watched over the garden from the porch, and everything was OK, except that I was cold. I stayed on the porch and finally got in when Jess and Connie got home from school.

Tom's biggest concern these days was that the girls had started dating. This was only for weekend nights, except for a special occasion, and the girls had an 11 pm curfew, which Connie regularly broke. Tom was staying awake on Friday and Saturday nights, until they both got home.

Jess usually was out only 1 weekend night a week, with a computer nerd named Milo. Connie, predictably, was dating a graduated Senior named Jimmy, who would be going to Tulane in the fall. She was out every weekend night, without exception. She regularly broke curfew, but not by much.

On Saturday night, Jess had come home at 10:30, Tom thought Milo was a pretty safe date, but at 11, no Connie. Then, at midnight, still no Connie. Tom was worried. Tom dropped off to sleep, but suddenly awoke at 2 am. He went to the girl's room and peeked in. Still, no Connie. Tom was frantic. He looked on the couch in the Family room, no Connie.

He decided against calling the police. What would he say, "Connie broke curfew?" He was sure there were other parents who went through this. He wanted to go out looking for her, but where?

As a last resort, he looked at the back screen porch, which was empty.

He walked around through the fence gate to look in the front yard. Right there, in a chair on the front porch was Connie, snoring, with a Budweiser can on the floor beside her. You could only see her because he had left the porch light on.

Tom was relieved, but also mad. She had a key, why hadn't she come to bed, inside? Then, I would have known what time she got in," he answered himself. His best guess was that she had been drinking (duh), and had passed out in the chair. She had probably not been capable of a stealthy entry, so she decided to "sleep it off" in the chair on the porch.

He opened the front door, scooped her 100 pounds of dead weight up, and took her to her room. He laid her on the bed, fully clothed, put a light blanket on her, and went back to his bed. Now, he could sleep?

Tom spent a few hours in a tossing attempt to sleep, finally resigning himself to the fact that it wasn't going to happen. He got out of bed at 5:30, let Goldie outside, and put on a pot of coffee.

Karen had joined him at the kitchen table about 8 am. Tom told her about what had happened in the wee hours of Sunday morning. They were talking in whispers, so as to not awaken the rest of the family

Karen seemed alarmed, but not surprised. "I'll have a talk with her," said Karen. "No, we'll both have that talk," Tom countered. "I've been thinking a lot about how to deal with this. I want her to understand that this behavior is unacceptable. But, she has to know we care. That we **both** know, and we **both** care."

"I think," Tom began, "that it has to be a 'win-win' agreement. We have to tell her that she put herself at risk doing this. I'm sure the boy she was with was drinking.

We see teens and alcohol involved in car wrecks at least once a week in the paper. Some of those wrecks the kids don't walk away from. Just as bad is the sexual side of having too much to drink, clouding your judgment. We explain that this concern is out of love for her, not some arbitrary rule that's been broken."

"If we get her to accept that, then we win," Tom explained. "How does she win?" Karen asked. Tom whispered to his wife, "We tell her that this is only strike one."

"That means no dating next weekend, but that we trust that she has learned her lesson from this mistake. That way, there is no long-term punishment, only recognition of a mistake."

Karen thought about that for a while. Tom said, "Put yourself in her shoes, Karen. She lost her Father a few years ago, now her Mother dies unexpectedly. She gets tossed into a completely new environment, having to make all new friends, in a new school."

"And at 16 years old, as well," Karen added. "We have a plan, but we have to tell her it's between us three, only." Tom nodded, "Absolutely, we agree. We'll talk to her this after breakfast, maybe outside, away from other ears."

Tom had a thought, and went to the front door. The Budweiser can was gone. He smiled. A little too late to hide the evidence.

They had a nice Sunday breakfast about 10. It was Jess's turn to clean up the dishes, and Doris was in her room. Karen caught Connie alone and said, "Let's you, Tom, and I take a walk with Goldie, down to the water." And the three of them left the house, trailed by their four-legged friend.

The discussion went as planned. Connie seemed to grasp the importance of maturity, but at 16, sometimes it takes more than one lesson.

Graduation...January, 2002

Josh made it through Boot Camp easily. He remained "Barracks Leader" for all 13 weeks. His training after week 1 consisted of:

Weeks 2-4: Instruction on military customs, courtesies, and history. Also they received training in hand-to-hand combat and Marine Corps Martial Arts. "Pugil Stick" combat was a core part of this training, as well.

Week 5: Swimming and water survival techniques. They had a couple of recruits not pass this course, it was difficult.

Week 6: Written testing, drills, plus the Rappel Tower and Gas Chamber training.

Weeks 7-8: Rifle training, M-16, 5.56mm. Weapon familiarity and maintenance, marksmanship grading, and qualification.

Week 9: Team building week. Recruits were broken up into smaller units, and performed various duties, including practicing for the final drill.

Week 10: Basic warrior training, field exercises, firing at multiple targets, combat shooting, combat endurance course.

Week 11-12: Practical application evaluation. Final Drills and grading.

Josh was highly regarded as a soldier, and a natural leader by those who evaluated him. Chet and Alonzo, had placed right beside him.

Week 13: Ceremony practices, Liberty Day (on the base 10-3) and Family Day on Thursday, with Graduation Event on Friday. On Thursday, Josh saw his parents for the first time in 3 months. Karen shed tears of joy, and Tom was proud.

Yes, he'd put on 10 pounds of muscle. He had been transformed into a man, a United States Marine. He proudly showed them his barracks, "leatherneck square", and other parts of the facility. At 3 pm, Josh had to go back to the barracks, his parents left for their motel room.

The next day, Friday, the parents attended the Graduation Ceremony, which began at 9 am on the Depot's Peatross Parade Deck. An hour later Josh was graduated.

Josh, and his parents had a chance to visit. "I couldn't tell you yesterday, but I've been assigned to Camp LeJune, North Carolina with the rank of Lance Corporal. I'll be part of The Marine Special Operations Command, there. I've been given 14 days to report, so I'm coming home with you, until I have to report for duty. We can have dinner tonight and leave tomorrow morning, I can bunk here, and meet you early tomorrow, say 0 five hundred?" Tom and Karen looked at each other. He was a Marine, 5 am?

That night the 3 of them had dinner at a modest little family-run restaurant a few miles from the base. It was Josh's first look at the outside world in 13 weeks. He sat up straight, and seemed to notice everything he had taken for granted, just a short time ago. They talked about the Marine experience for most of the meal. Tom and Karen had decided to tell him about his aunt Vicky on the way home, tomorrow. Today was a day for celebration, after all. They did discuss Jess, Goldie, and even Princess. "I can't wait to see Goldie," he said. "She's doing great," Karen replied, "and I'm sure she will love seeing you too."

The next morning (at 6 am, the parents had bargained), they took the short drive from Parris Island to I-95 South. In a few hours, at Jacksonville, they picked up I-10 West and headed home. They crossed the Florida Panhandle, and went through Mobile. Josh was getting excited. He was saddened by the news of Vicky's death, but anxious to see everyone.

At 5 pm (CST) they pulled into the shell driveway. 630 miles, with 2 stops, but it was all interstate highway, so they could drive 65-70 almost the whole way. Twelve hours, total. Everyone was waiting on the front porch, especially Goldie.

Karen had called home with her cell phone when they entered Mississippi, to give an ETA. I was a great reunion! Josh got hugs from everyone, even a few tears from Jess, and was literally "slimed" by Goldie, as he wrestled with her.

Wow, Goldie thought, he's so much bigger and stronger than when he left. They all talked for awhile, but having shared the trip with his parents, and talked the whole way, there wasn't much else to say.

"Dinner is at 7," Karen said. Jess and Connie went to the store and got some T-bones for tonight. We'll do them on the grill." They had taken Grandma along, and she bought 2 bottles of red wine to top off the evening. She probably hoped they wouldn't drink it all. Grandma liked these types of leftovers.

"I'm going for a walk around the property, and maybe go down to the water," said Josh, "I've missed it so much, It will be like seeing it for the first time again. Ready for a walk, Goldie?" Boy, was she. She hopped out the door and did her version of a jumping kangaroo, for at least 5 minutes. She brought him her old yellow tennis ball, and played "fetch" for a while. Josh remarked, "The garden looks great. Looks like you and Jess have done a great job." They went down to the waters edge. They had never rebuilt the dock which had been destroyed in the storm. Josh had to blink his eyes to remember it. That seemed like a lifetime ago.

"Well girl, it's just you and me now out here. I'm going to tell you some things, because you can't tell anyone what I've said. It's certain that I'll be at Camp LeJune just long enough to get my orders. I'll be shipping out to Afghanistan. There are men there called the 'Taliban' who were responsible for the attacks in New York."

"Now, they're trying to control the entire country by fear. They blow up churches and religious symbols, like the Buddhist shrines, just for believing in a different God," Josh explained.

"They even make non-believers wear clothing symbols which tell them apart. It all sounds like what Hitler did in Europe, 65 years ago. They also persecute women, and punish them, if they are attacked by a violent man."

He continued, "I really believe in what the world community is trying to do there. But, between you and me, I'm really scared too. From what I've heard it is stuck back in the time of the middle ages, or worse." Josh seemed to slip into a place far away, "The country is barren, cold, and unforgiving. Anyway, I'm not going to let shipping out, stop us from having a great two weeks. I'll tell the family before I leave, not about my fears, just about the probability of shipping out. No need for them to worry until they have to."

They walked through the yard going back inside. You could just tell the T-bones were almost done, by the smell. They had baked potatoes, gravy, and fresh corn on the cob. Dad poured a little wine for everyone, even a little taste for Jess and Connie. "Here's to a big welcome home for Josh. He's made his family proud, cheers." Everyone took a sip of the wine, Doris knocked hers back and poured herself another. After dinner, dessert was pecan pie, requested by Josh, with milk or coffee, depending on your taste. Grandma Doris, had more wine with her pie.

"I did a little recon on the sleeping situation. Since you're not beginning the bonus room conversion for another couple of weeks, I figured I'd bunk on the couch with Goldie by my side. It's still better than what I had the last few months." After discussion, there was the garage, which was cold in January, the bonus room wood floor, or the couch, so it was decided. "I'll be up before any of you anyway. It's a tough habit to break."

Twelve days flew by quickly. It would be an 18-hour bus ride to Camp Lejune, 750 miles away. So he would have to leave on the morning of day 13. He sat the adult family down, minus a snoozing Grandma that twelfth night, and explained to them most of what he had told Goldie, down by the water. Dad was a military man, so he knew it would do no good to complain or express his fears, he was very supportive (on the exterior). Mom was less calm, and asked if he was sure this would happen.

"Unless they settle this before I get there, it will be a 8 to12 month assignment," he replied. "But it's not as bad as it was at the beginning."

"From what I've seen on the news the Taliban have basically been routed in the north and are fleeing south. An international peacekeeping team has been assembled, and a new government is being formed. A secular, non-religious government. The hard work has been done."

Well, his Dad remembered reading about all the optimism and misinformation which had come out of Viet Nam just before he had joined the Air Force in 1975. He never had to go, but he had heard plenty from the returning veterans, especially about over-optimism, government incompetence, and micro-management. He kept this to himself, though. Maybe this would be different. Maybe the Pentagon, and Congressional Oversight Committees had learned their lesson, but he doubted it.

The next morning, Tom drove him to the bus station, Goldie was in the back seat. Mom couldn't bear to go. She stayed home, cried, and prayed for the best.

"I'll be back before you know it," Josh said. "and now I'll be able to make phone calls, write letters, and stay in contact more than

I could in boot camp. We were told in Camp that their time is 10.5 hours ahead of us. Where that half-hour comes from, I don't know."

"Son, your family is proud of you. Always remember that." after a big hug, they parted.

Another chapter was beginning in Josh's life. He already knew that after he checked in at Camp Lejune, The Middle East was not far away on the time horizon.

Baghram Base, Feb. 02

The plane skidded on the tarmac, which only a few months ago had been hardscrabble ground at a mile high. Boy it was cold, and hard to breath. Josh had lived all his life at sea level. Not only was Baghram (also spelled Bagram by the U.S. press) north of Biloxi's latitude by 4 degrees, the 4900 feet of elevation, made it one of the most inhospitable places in the world. Thin air, rocky soil, bitter cold…great! After checking in with the duty officer, Josh and most of the one hundred Marines from his flight, were distributed into 3 different companies of Marines. Josh knew 4 or 5 of the new men in his platoon, from Parris Island, and was especially happy to see Chet Perry was among them.

The mission of his Marine Special Operational Command, was to work with British and "Northern Alliance" troops to continue pushing the Taliban southward, by attacking them in the north. His platoon consisted of 32 Marines. They broke that down into 3 squads, and while they deployed as a platoon, they operated as a squad. Josh was 3rd in command of his 10-man squad. Their leader was a sergeant named Sykes, with 5 months experience "in-country," Josh listened to him very closely.

Only 4 days after arriving, Josh's first mission with his platoon was to search out Taliban strongholds, and communicate their positions for possible air strikes. This meant that if they encountered the enemy in the open, the Marines would be severely outnumbered. This mission was given a time of 6 days, in which the platoon would be split into the three squads, in a position to support the total if attacked, but still spread out enough to maximize the potential search area. At 0600, taking advantage of flying with the blinding sunrise behind them, they were choppered about 25 miles northwest to an area called Barfak. The 3 UH-60 Black Hawks stayed low to the ground and dropped them into an area at the base the first of 3 parallel mountain ridges.

The middle ridge was already controlled by Special forces and Northern Alliance troops. It was called "Base Camp Echo."

They hoped to "squeeze" the first ridge until they could identify the enemy, and could call in help from Baghram or the adjacent ridge which had a well-established position.

The choppers hovered about 6 feet off the ground, time enough for the men to deploy, and dusted out. After a couple of miles, they would climb to an elevation much safer from ground fire. In just this 25 miles, 15 minutes in a Black Hawk, the elevation was 50% greater than in Baghram

The 3 squads deployed into the base of the ridge, and immediately began seeking higher ground. You didn't want to be looking up at Taliban RPGs or AK-47s. It took until 0900 to reach the spine of their ridge, where they set up 2-man lookout and sniper teams in the highest possible locations. They communicated their arrival and location to Base Control at Baghram, and to the fire group on the next ridge. From that point, the squads set out at 200 meter spreads and moved north on the ridge. Josh was gulping in the thin mountain air, as were all the newer men, but he didn't want to show it.

After about 20 minutes Sykes shouted, "RPG, get down," as the whistle of a rocket propelled grenade flew over their heads, landing some 50 meters behind them. "Sandy, Sandy, Sandy," he screamed into the radio, "Eyes up ahead." but Sandy Taylor, one of the 2 snipers, was ahead of the game. His spotter had seen the RPG smoke trail from the beginning, and only seconds later his M40 A3 sniper weapon propelled a 7.62 round into the head of the Taliban attacker.

Sykes said, "Flowers, you and Kendall, come with me, stay down" They approached the presumed site of the attacker in a "leapfrog approach."

Two men covering the leader at 10 second intervals. They arrived to see a large pool of blood in the rocky soil, and an almost headless, man dressed in flowing robes, still clutching his weapon. "I think we got lucky," Sykes said, "no other footprints, he was a lone scout. Josh stared at the dead man.

"Don't worry about him, Flowers, he would have cut your throat in a heartbeat, if he had the chance. Let's get some cover until the others get here."

The platoon continued to push north along the spine of the hills. They were being careful about their spacing, and were always in contact with the spotter/sniper positions, to make sure they didn't get flanked.

Josh noticed that he was getting more accustomed to the thin air, but they still moved slowly so as not to attract unwanted attention. After about 5 miles of slow progress, they found a place to camp for the night, and assigned rotating, 3-hour sentry duty, in all 4 directions.

The temperature was dropping fast. After a quick MRE, Josh crawled into his modular sleeping bag.

His sentry duty began at midnight. He closed his eyes, but his sleep was filled with images of the bloody scene witnessed earlier.

The night was uneventful, Josh had returned to camp at 0300, looking forward to a 3-hour sleep. The sleeping bag quickly warmed with his body heat, and he slept much more peacefully. When he awoke at 0530, he realized he had just crossed an important point in his military life. He fretted no more about the dead Taliban scout. It was kill or be killed, out here.

They set out at 0600, in the same way as before. They encountered no one for the first 2 hours. Sgt. Sykes rounded a corner and froze, holding his fist up as a sign to stop. He edged back to his squad, and reached for the radio to signal the remainder of the platoon. "About 50 hostiles around the next bend," he shared. "Recommend calling 'wings in'," he advised Lt. Sheppard, platoon leader. "Roger that," Sheppard replied.

"I'll leave my laser tracking beacon 50 meters south of their current position, we'll bug out now," Sgt. Sykes replied. "Affirmative...two F-14s inbound, ETA, 6 minutes," warned Sheppard.

In about 5 minutes the entire hill was shaking from withering missile and machine gun fire. Josh's squad had hunkered down behind a rock formation about 200 meters back from the beacon. Even that was too close for comfort, as rounds spiked the dirt only a few feet away from the huddled men. The attack was swift and deadly.

"Time to earn our pay," shouted Sykes, "stay alert, these guys like to play possum, there's still a lot of danger out there." Josh's was the middle squad, the tip of the spear. They advanced, staying about 30 meters in front of the 2 flanking support squads.

The encampment had been left in ruins, but the distinct fire of AK 47s began almost immediately as they started to approach.

Josh and a team mate broke right and took some higher ground, in order to cover the advance. Josh fired his M16 in short controlled burst, and only at targets he could identify. "Aim small...miss small," he remembered from his training.

He went through the first clip and inserted another. The spotter/sniper teams had advanced and were picking off Taliban fighters at a regular clip. In another 10 minutes, the firefight ended. Two bearded Taliban fighters threw out their weapons, and held their hands up in surrender.

"Careful, men," admonished Sykes. "This could be a trick." Josh's squad searched around the remains of the encampment, while Sykes called the platoon leader, asking for their interpreter to be sent up for interrogation. Josh and his team found 26 bodies, lots of automatic weapons, and a blood trail heading north.

In Pashtu, the interpreter asked the men where the others went. There had to be another 20, or so remaining. "They say they don't know. They say they are innocent goat herders."

"Get Echo on the radio and ask for the Northern Alliance leader" said Lt. Sheppard. As they called the camp on the adjacent ridge, Sheppard said to the interpreter, "Tell them since they can't help us I'm going to release them into custody of their friends on the next ridge." As the interpreter told them this, the Northern alliance leader come on the radio. Sheppard smiled, and handed the radio to the taller of the 2 survivors. The big man's face went white with fear as he heard the Northern Alliance fighter speak to him.

He began shaking and speaking Pashtu, wildly. "He says maybe they can help us find the others who escaped," said the interpreter. "He says there is a large Taliban contingent a half day's walk away. If we find them before they get there, we can capture them, also."

"Tell them any tricks, or if we don't pick up a trail by noon, we give their friends on the next ridge what they want. He'll understand that," said Sheppard. The interpreter passed along the warning to the captives.

The platoon split up again, in the same squad configuration as before. The prisoners, wove them through rocky passes which they would have never seen. "Be ambush ready," shouted Sykes. "See anything, Sandy, or Baker?" (Baker being the other sniper).

The spotter/sniper teams were moving on the highest ground, but struggling to keep up and maintain visual contact ahead of the group. "That's a negative," came back.

The center squad kept moving through hidden switchbacks, the other 2 squads falling further behind, due to the prisoners familiarity with the terrain. "Call back to platoon leader, ask them to double-time, or we'll have to slow down. I don't want to get too far apart," said Sykes.

"Lieutenant says affirmative to double-time, for squads 1 and 3," said the radio man. After conferring with the lieutenant, and Main Base Baghram, a different strategy was developed. They were to follow the contingent of survivors, but not apprehend or engage. The larger Taliban stronghold had just become the main prize. They would have air and drone support. Fortunately, the terrain gave them good cover so the hunted could not see them coming.

In another hour, the spotter/sniper teams began to see a dust trail, headed north. "We're getting close," said Sykes, and then just below he could see a group of men running into a group of large rock formations, then virtually disappearing into the mountain.

The interpreter ran up to the sergeant and said, "The prisoners are panicked. They say that this is the stronghold. It was not their fault we could not catch the escaping survivors."

"Tell them, we believe them. I'm going to tie them up, and leave a guard with them. The Marines from the next ridge will collect them, not the Alliance. They've done better than they know."

Sgt. Sykes relayed this to the lieutenant. "Affirmative, said Sheppard, I'm calling in the support now. Spotters, can you paint a laser target on the entrance?" "Affirmative," came back from both spotters. "Will update in 5," replied Sheppard.

Back in Baghram, different groups had been scrambling in preparation for the past hour. Four, AH-64 Apache helicopters had been assigned to the task, along with four "MQ-1A Predator drones, armed with Hellfire missiles," plus a two platoon (about 65 men) assault team with mortars and RPGs. Add to this, two F-14s from the U.S.S Enterprise. All together, this had the makings of a pretty big party.

Sheppard came on the radio, "F-14s in 5 minutes, Drones in 7, attack choppers in 10, troops in 20, acknowledge, keep the target painted." Sandy on the north entrance, Baker on the south." "Affirmative" came back from the 2 spotter/sniper teams.

The F-14s came screaming out of their patrol from the north. Three "sidewinder" rockets hit the mark, the fourth missed harmlessly to the east. The deadly 20mm cannon strafed the target, and the planes climbed into the westward sky to be out of the range of any incoming friendly fire.

Almost immediately the drones fired their Hellfire missiles on the painted targets creating rockslides, and most revealingly, secondary explosions from the Taliban weapons cache.

Then the Apache's came in fired A6M 114 missiles followed by hundreds of rounds from their 30mm cannon. The craft would rise over the rocky wall of the Taliban camp, then duck down as cover from return fire. This offered a blistering attack and also covered the two platoons of Marines landing from the transport helicopters. The Marines scurried up the face of the hill, setting up mortars and establishing areas of cover.

Meanwhile, Josh's platoon had secured the highest ground in the area. Along with the snipers, they were inflicting casualties on the rapidly diminishing enemy. In about 30 minutes, it was over. A Taliban fighter threw a white flag tied to a rock out of the southern entrance.

He then stepped out of the entrance with another white flag, this time fastened to a stick.

The attack had been hugely successful. Over 120 enemy combatants killed, another 75 captured, and a huge stash of weapons destroyed. Most importantly the swiftness and efficiency of the attack would lend credibility to the entire operation.

As the cleanup commenced without further hostility Sykes said, "I watched you close, Flowers. You did well. You remembered your training, and didn't freeze up. I'm putting you up for Full Corporal." "Thanks," said Josh. "Just earning my Marine payday."

Home Redo...March 02

Back in Biloxi, the redo of the Flowers' home was underway. Tom and Karen had reviewed and approved a final set of building plans. They had decided to hire a General Contractor (GC) to orchestrate the remodel. His name was George Ponder. It cost them a couple of thousand dollars more, but could save much more in time and money. The trades involved were carpenters, sheet rockers, plumbers, electricians, and carpet–tile layers, lighting and plumbing suppliers, not to forget dealing with the city and county permit departments and building code inspectors. With both of them working, neither Tom nor Karen had the time to learn "on the job."

Once the job was completed, the Girls would move upstairs into the bonus room, and Josh's room would be vacant for him, when he returned. As March began, Jess and Connie were in the last two months of their junior year in High School. Tom had received a good review and small promotion at the Casino. Karen was working 5 days a week at the library, Grandma was constantly complaining, but had started going to the weekly Bingo games at St. Helena Parish Senior Community Center. It was less than two miles away. Usually a family member drove her there, but the last couple of weeks a friend named Max, had picked her up and brought her home. The rest of the family put that behavior in the "cute" category. Of course seeing your Grandmother in a wine-induced sleep with her false teeth in a glass by the bed, sort of erased Jess's idea of anything being "cute" from Grandma.

After the first 3 weeks, Tom and Karen held a scheduled progress meeting with Mr. Ponder. "Well," Ponder began "we're a few days behind, already." The carpenters, the Broussard twins, had been 'sick' the first two days, and since they represented the beginning of the project, everyone else had to be pushed back. They finally finished up on Tuesday of the second week.

George had been unable to get the Electricians and plumbers in until Friday. The electrician finished up his first phase, even coming in for a half day on Saturday.

The plumbers finished the "rough-in" on Wednesday of the 3rd week. The city inspector didn't show up to OK the plumbing and electrical until 4 o'clock on Thursday, so that day was shot. Once he gave them the "go," the sheet rockers began on Friday, and finished about ½ the job. So here they were, Saturday morning, 3 weeks into the project, with very little progress made, especially to the untrained eye. Karen, uncharacteristically, was becoming more and more impatient,

"I don't understand," said Karen. "Three weeks, and it looks worse than the beginning. What's the problem?" Ponder replied, "Ms. Flowers, we've made a great deal of progress. Most of the important work is what's behind the sheetrock." "Yes," said Karen. "I just found a half-eaten Whopper with cheese and some fries behind one wall which was almost finished. Luckily, the dog and the cat sniffed it out."

"Well, ma'm, the trades are not known for their thoughtfulness or for being neat," he replied. I think by this time next week, you will both be very happy." "You've got a date." said Tom. "I'm sure it will get better he said," squeezing Karen's arm to help calm her down. "She picked out the plumbing and lighting fixtures, and the carpet and tile this past week, and you said that you ordered them." He was pressing her point.

"Yes, I did," he replied. Ponder left the house, got into his pickup truck, and wheeled away.

Tom looked at Karen, "The last thing we need right now, is for him to quit," Tom explained. "This is a critical time. He knows the subs, we don't. Yes they let him down, but he gives his crew lots of work. Imagine how non-responsive they would be with us in charge." "You're right, Tom," Karen replied.

"I'm just getting tired of having these people in our house. They track dirt in, rain or shine, and they don't clean up after themselves. They must think their mother works here, and comes in to tend to the mess they leave. But," she promised, "I'll try to do better." Right," said Tom. "In a week or 2, we could finish the job ourselves, if we had to."

Work resumed the next week, and much more visual progress was made. The sheet rock was finished, the painters only took one day. The bathroom tile was laid, and by Friday, the shower-tub insert, and toilet were installed, as the plumber returned to finish up.

The next Saturday, Ponder expected congratulations at the meeting. He was sorely disappointed.

"The hot water barely leaks out of the faucet," yelled Karen. "That's because there's a leak in the hot water line that's left a big stain on the sheetrock and the floor in the bedroom. There's also a stain on the garage ceiling." I had to turn the hot water off for the entire house, an hour ago. Ponder was stunned. He accompanied the Flowers upstairs to review the problem. Grandma started follow, but swiftly retreated with Karen's "not now," glare.

"It looks like the sheet rockers nicked a water line with a nail, and a couple of days later it burst." He fetched his toolbox and opened up the wall.

"A scream came from downstairs, " The shower's cold."

"I think that's Jess," Tom said, "I'm sure Connie isn't out of bed at 10 am." 'I'll take care of her," Karen said. "You handle this."

Ponder saw the leak in the pvc line, and was able to temporarily seal the leak. Then he drained the hot water lines, and spliced a permanent fix to the pipe.

"That will take care of the leak. You can turn the hot water back on. I'll have the sheet rock repaired here and painted, along with the garage ceiling, first thing Monday. I'm glad the carpet wasn't in yet, this floor will dry. Carpet is something we always save for last," he mumbled. The repair people were there at 8 am Monday. A sheet rocker, a painter, and Mr. Ponder for extra emphasis. By Thursday, the carpet was installed and the project was complete.

That weekend, Jess and Connie moved into their "girl-world" suite. The Flowers had planned well. Beds on opposite walls, bathroom in the center. The bathroom is what they call a "Jack and Jill" bath. So, each girl had their own sink and dressing table, with the shower-tub and toilet in the middle with doors on both sides. Best of all, 2 huge closets, each the exact same size. The cordless telephone, on a table in the center of the room surrounded by 2 chairs, was to be in working order on Monday. Goldie's bed had been moved by the window on Jess's side of the room. Goldie was fascinated, looking down on the garden from above. She had not been this high off the ground before. She resolved to be vigilant in her duties, and the motion activated lights were a big help at night.

Later that night Tom and Karen called Connie outside, they walked out to the yard, past the old basketball goal post. Connie was confused. She didn't know what to expect. Tom began, "Connie, I want you to know that Karen, Beth, Jess, Josh, (yes, he answered their letter) and I, have come to a decision." The girl looked afraid.

Karen continued, "What he's trying to say, Connie, is that Tom and I would like to adopt you. You're already a big part of the family. For lots of reasons, we want you to become an official family member, if you'll have us. You don't have to change your name, you can make that decision later. Adoption just means that if something were to happen to Tom and I, you would be on equal footing, legally, with Josh and Jess."

The girl broke down, completely in tears. "Of course, yes, yes. This is the nicest," she said with a quivering voice, "thing anyone has ever done for me, except for my Mom. I know I'll always have her in my heart, but could I start calling you Mom and Dad?" "We would be proud if you did," said Karen.

Tom went to the back screen door and yelled, "Jess, come out and meet your new sister, she wants to give you a hug. And they all wept, as a new family.

Tipsy...4-02

That Sunday, Jess and Connie went cruising in the Accord, along with Jess's longtime friend, Emily. They would listen to the latest music, go to Edgewater Plaza, and went to "Bennies" to see who was hanging out. It was the same girl weekend adventure, but they all enjoyed being together.

Tom had decided to rebuild the dock. After waiting 3 months for the Wetlands Board, Army Corps of Engineers, and The City Planning Commission, he got a license to repair a damaged dock. He knew it "only" took 90 days because there were still two existing pilings, so it was officially a "repair". Approval for a "new" dock could take a year, if you could get an OK at all. He decided to be involved with the re-do, along with a friend, Jim, who was in the Seabees (naval **C**onstruction **B**attalion) in neighboring Gulfport, and another person, Earl, who was an engineer he had known at Keesler. Earl was very familiar with docks and their design and had built pontoon bridges and the like, all over the world. Tom was the laborer with no knowledge, working right beside them. They had started yesterday, Saturday, and were looking at a 3-weekend project, if luck and the weather held out.

Karen was gone to get groceries, a trip to Wal-Mart, and was running other errands. She had gotten a new car last month, finally trading in the bug on a used, 4-door 1998 Nissan Maxima. It was a big step up.

Goldie was laying in the yard under the Magnolia Tree, when, **Boom! Crash!**, she heard from inside the house. She ran to the door, and everything was quiet again, but something wasn't right, she could sense it. The kitchen door was open, but the screen was closed. She pawed the screen door, whining to get in. Nothing doing. Finally one of her big paws pushed the screen inward, just a little. But it was enough, to give her the idea that it was working. Frantically, she pushed on the lower panel of the screen door until it gave way.

She ran through the opening, and then the open kitchen door. Grandma was laying on the floor, not moving. Goldie ran over to her.

Grandma had fallen, and broken the glass end table in the family room. There was red liquid everywhere. Some of it was wine. Most of it wasn't. There was a large piece of glass sticking out of Grandma's neck, her ankle was at an odd position, and her left arm was underneath her. In her right, she was holding a wine glass which still had about an inch of wine left in it. Goldie whimpered, gruffed, and tried to lick her to wake her up. Grandma was non responsive to all efforts, and it seemed to Goldie, she was getting cold.

Goldie knew what that meant. She had to do something to help, and she had to do it now. Goldie raced out the kitchen door, jumped through the broken screen door, and ran as fast as she could toward the dock. Dad had left the back gate open, knowing that Goldie liked to watch the men work.

Jim yelled, "Is that your dog running at us like a bat out of hell?" The other men looked up to see a barking, almost howling dog on the nearby bank. Tom said, "What's up, girl?" And Goldie barked even louder. "Let me go check," he said. "It could be that something got into the garden, and if that's so, I may have to chase it out."

Tom waded the 10 feet to the bank, and started walking toward the house. Goldie was running back and forth on the path in front of him. About 300 feet later they were close enough to see the garden, and the house. Tom walked toward the garden, but he saw the broken screen door out of the corner of his eye, Goldie jumping through it. He walked inside and saw the problem, immediately. "Jim, Earl, come quick he yelled.

They ran up and Jim said, "Call an ambulance, she's cut bad."

"No Tom replied, "I can get her to the walk-in care emergency center, one exit down on I-10, before they could get here from the hospital. Earl, we'll use your pickup, I'll ride in the back, remove the glass, and keep pressure on the wound."

They all piled in, and Earl peeled out in a shower of broken oyster shells. In less than 10 minutes they pulled in front of the walk-in facility, Jim hopped out while the truck was still moving. In just a few seconds, a doctor and nurse hustled out with a gurney, took Grandma from Tom, and rushed her inside. "Her name is Doris Baine, and she's 75 years old," Tom yelled after them.

"Thanks friends," Tom said, after a couple of minutes of slowing their own pulses down. "I think we did the best we could do for her. Please take the rest of the day off, and I'll let you know the status tonight. I've got to call Karen on her cell phone, and I'm sure she will be here in minutes, but thanks from both of us."

"The dog saved her, if she makes it" Jim said. "She was bleedin' bad. I just hope we got to her in time. Yeah, and you told me she saved Jess, during that last storm." "You're right," Tom acknowledged. "She's a blessing, Tom agreed." "She's always been there to help us when we needed her."

Tom reached Karen, thankfully, as she was headed home. She changed directions and arrived at the clinic about 15 minutes later. "Oh Tom, how is she?" "The doctor said he'd tell us the situation, as soon as he knew more."

Karen had answered in a few questions, and replied "no, she wasn't allergic to any medications." She knew this from Doris' last stint in the hospital, in Texas, with gallstones.

"I'll call Jess, so she won't worry." Karen commented. "I'll tell her that Grandma had taken a fall, but downplay the mishap."

But, Tom knew once his daughter saw all the blood, there would be no "downplaying the accident." "Karen, I'd rather warn her what to expect," he said. "She's a big girl, now. Let me call her, and warn her about the blood, broken glass, and all so she doesn't freak out," he asked. Tom called Jess's mobile, and described the scene.

He told her not to go into the family room, or let Connie or Goldie in there, because there was broken glass which was very dangerous, especially to someone without shoes, like Goldie. He also told her there was a lot of blood, but not to be panicked by that.

They'd been there almost an hour when doctor Neff, a young, intern, called them back to his office. "We pumped a lot of plasma and blood in her. The cut is nasty, but her foot is only sprained, not broken. We had to type and cross for the blood, lucky she's O positive."

We ran a tox screen to make sure there were no drugs involved, and it appears that drugs were involved. "Drugs?" They both sad at once. "That's impossible," said Karen. My mother doesn't do drugs!"

"Well," said Dr. Neff, "her blood alcohol level was .14%, and the State standard for DUI is .08%. So she was 75% over the limit. I know she wasn't driving from what your husband said when he got here, but drunk is drunk, and I'm sure that contributed to the fall. However, let's deal with one problem at a time."

He continued, "Doris seems to have an ornery constitution, which is good. I think you got her here just in time. A large shard of glass in the neck is never easy to deal with, but she missed the Carotid artery by about an inch. We put 15 stitches in her. Another 5 minutes, and she wouldn't have made it, for sure. She's in critical condition, but stabilized." "What's the next step?" asked Tom. "Rest, and sleep," came back from the doctor."

Dr. Neff added, "We don't have overnight patients here, we just don't have the facilities, but in her case, I don't want to risk moving her, even in an ambulance. I've sedated her for the evening on a drip. If, you are willing to sign a waiver, I have 2 nurses who said they would split the 10 hours between when we close, and when we open," he said. "You'll have to pay them. They have my cell number, and I only live 5 minutes away. If she gets through the night, I think she'll make it."

"But, there is still a chance she could develop a clot, or have a stroke. Please, there is nothing more you can do, here. I can meet you, here at the clinic, tomorrow morning at 8 am, an hour before we open."

Karen started to shed tears. She couldn't lose a sister, and a mother in a 6-month span. It just couldn't happen. She stood up and said, "I'm calling Beth on our way home." In 5 minutes they were talking, "She got drunk and fell, breaking a glass table, and seriously cutting herself. I should know better than to leave her alone, but at this time of the year the girls are in school. They couldn't stop her from drinking, though. If I can't, what chance do they have?" "Beth, the doctor thinks she's got a good chance, but there's nothing anyone can do until morning. We're meeting at the Clinic at 8, which is 9, your time. I'll call you in the morning, right after we get an update. Oh, we're home now, and I see Jess's car, so I have to go speak to her and Connie."

"Wait," Tom said, "give me two minutes, before you go in." And he told her the story about Goldie saving Grandma. Karen was impressed, but not surprised.

"She saved Jess, now Mom, maybe. I think she's a saint, reincarnated. She has held us together in all kind of situations. She'll get her due, I believe in Karma."

Once inside, Karen found that Jess had cleaned up the entire family room. "It wasn't fun, Mom, but even hardwood floors stain after awhile."

I threw up, but I'm OK now. Even Connie helped for a little while." The room had been reassembled, sans glass end table, and smelled like Pine Sol. Tom told the girls their Grandmother's status, and the events leading up to it. Tom went out to the back porch, removed the hanging screen from the bottom panel, and rolled it up like a map. "I'll get this fixed in the next few days. I'll just take this up to the store to match it's color, and it won't take 30 minutes to re-screen. We'll just have to leave the kitchen screen door closed until then to keep the bugs and critters out.

"You know, Jess was great, and Connie, for all her wild nature, helped out as well. But we almost forgot the hero of this entire event." Tom went to the back yard, and called Goldie inside. She leapt through the door, excited to be included.

"How's our hero?," Tom yelled, and the family had a 10-minute "group hug" with her on the floor. "Life is good," thought Goldie."

The next morning, Tom and Karen were at the clinic at 7:45 sharp. They left the girls to go to school rather than accompany them, in case of bad news. They had seen a couple of cars parked on the side, and assumed one belonged to Dr. Neff. But, the meeting was set for 8 am, and he was probably checking on Grandma, now. They knocked on the door and a tired eyed nurse let them in. They searched, but could not read anything into her demeanor. "Dr. Neff will be with you in a moment."

In about 10 minutes, Dr. Neff, came out of the back, and while approaching them said, "It looks much better this morning, no seepage from the wound. I would like for you to make sure she gets plenty of bed rest for the next 3 days. I'll give you a prescription for some antibiotics, which you can begin tomorrow. She's got plenty in her for today due to the drip," he said. "I would like for your family physician to see her at the end of the week, to monitor progress, and discuss the drinking problem. We did an X-Ray, and there are no glass fragments remaining, so that's good news, as well."

But she's got to stay in bed, no stairs, and definitely no alcohol. I'll help bring her to your car in a wheelchair. Get her home, and put her to bed. You can return the wheelchair in a few days."

They drove home at no more than 45 mph, all the way. Cars screamed by them on I-10, but Tom didn't want to jostle her. Karen called Beth during the trip. "It looks like we're out of the woods, if, she does her part and stays in bed. I'll tie her down if I have to. No, Beth, I don't think it's necessary for you to come down. Tom and I will arrange our schedule so that someone is here with her at all times. We have the girls as back-up, but I don't want to use them for more than 15 minutes at a time. You know how ornery Doris is. The girls have been traumatized enough, just cleaning up after the accident."

Karen continued, "The doctor said we had to do something about her drinking, but we'll fight that battle when she's back on her feet for awhile."

They got Grandma home, and Tom carried the old woman up the front stairs, and into her bedroom. They had prepared the bed this morning, thinking that a little positive attitude was a good thing. They had let her keep her "hospital gown" from the clinic. The doctor said she would probably sleep most of the day, and to just leave her alone, as long as she was breathing OK, and there was no seepage through the bandage. Lots of bed rest was the best thing for her.

"Looks like the girls got off to school alright," Karen noted. "I'll make us some coffee, and some toast. I know we didn't eat much last night, but I don't think we're hungry right now." Tom agreed. In just a few minutes, they both nodded off, on the couch. The girls got home at 2 pm. Tom had gone to work at noon, and Karen let them peek in on Grandma, as evidence of her survival.

She was still resting peacefully. Karen was worried about her mother's attitude. Now she was going to be bedridden for at least 3 days, with a sprained ankle, even helping her to the bathroom was going to be a project.

About 4:30 Karen heard a wailing scream, "Wine...I want my wine.

Karen rushed in and calmed her mother down. "You've had an accident, but you're going to be OK. You have to stay in bed a minimum of 3 days."

Karen explained, "I can help you to the toilet when you need to go, but otherwise, you'll have to stay here in bed. See, it's good we got you that TV and remote control last Christmas. You can watch the *Home Shopping Network* all day now." She continued, "But, definitely no wine. Some chicken soup today, a little solid food tomorrow, if you feel like it."

Karen sat with her and recounted the events surrounding the accident. She particularly emphasized that it had been a group effort, with plenty of thanks to be given to all those involved, beginning with Goldie.

"Well," Doris said, "you can't make an omelet without breaking a few eggs." This infuriated Karen! "Mom, you're no omelet, you're a scrambled egg. Always have been, always will be! The worry, expense, and extra work you just put this family through is bad enough. And here you go trying to make light of it." The old woman turned her head toward the wall and said, "I'm going to take another nap." You could tell she was sulking.

Thursday of that week, Doris was able to walk a little, using the walker Tom had bought for her at the medical supply store. The atmosphere was somewhat subdued. Karen had found all the liquor in the house and locked it in the shed outside.

She told Doris that she threw it away, but sometimes, after Doris went to bed for the evening, she and Tom liked to have a little nightcap to end the day.

The weekend came and went, with Tom and his friends working some more on the dock. It was going according to plan, and they thought they'd finish up next Saturday.

The weather had stayed dry, and Tom was putting in a little extra time on the project during the week. He continued leaving the back fence gate open on weekends, so that Goldie could check the garden, and come down to the waters edge to watch the activity there. Goldie really enjoyed this extra bit of freedom.

Max

That night, Karen was cooking a country ham, sweet potatoes, string beans, and bread, for dinner. Doris came in the kitchen, and said, "My friend Max, called me today, while you were in the garden." Karen had come home from the library at 3, and had put on her garden clothes, a navy blue t-shirt and bib overalls, sneakers, and as always, gardening gloves. "Max who? Karen asked, she didn't remember.

"Max Bergeron," replied Doris, "He was taking me to Bingo on Wednesday nights at St. Helena, before my accident." "Oh yes," remembered Karen, "I never did meet him, you always waited for him on the porch."

"Well, I was wondering if he might be able to pay me a visit, It's nice having someone your own age to talk to. We could just visit in the family room, nothing improper." Karen blushed. "Well Mom, I knew it would be proper, you taught your daughters well."

"Well, he is hung like a bull, at least that's what he says, but I'd have to get to know him a little better, before pulling his pants down. You know with these new drugs, now, there's no age limit on a good sex life"

Karen got the "vapors" like Aunt Pitty Pat in *Gone With The Wind*. She was so shocked, it was impossible to hide her embarrassment. She recovered quickly, "Well I would hope so, Mom. You have to set an example for the girls."

"Well Jess is sort of timid, she'll be fine. Connie is a wildcat, she'll do what she wants no matter what."

Karen said, "I think you're selling Connie short, but I'll talk to Tom after dinner, about Mr. Bergeron."

"Tom, I think Mom is starting to 'get it'. She's been more pleasant around Jess and Connie, and I overheard her talking to Goldie, thanking her for being there when she needed her."
"Maybe so," replied Tom, "we'll see, and hope for the best."

The next morning the Girls drove to school at 8, they were both 17 now, as they often reminded Karen. Tom left early for work at 8:45, and Karen wasn't due at the library until noon. She called Doris to the kitchen. Karen started, "Tom and I think it would be a good thing for you to start having your own friends."
"Mr. Bergeron is welcome to visit you here, and when your foot gets better, you can start going back to Bingo, and other activities they have at the Senior Center. Just remember, no drinking, not here. What you do outside the house is your own business."

Doris gave her that "who me?" shocked look, but was instantly as happy as a 5-year old with a new toy. "He'll be over tomorrow, for a few minutes on his way to Bingo. Since the girls will be home, we'll sit on the front porch."

Wednesday, at 6 o'clock sharp, there was a knock on the front door. Karen opened it to a diminutive man, with a straw hat in his hand. His head had about 6 wispy hairs on it, all combed over. He had light blue, and white striped "Sans-a-Belt" polyester slacks on, pulled up almost to his chest, a brown checked, short sleeve shirt, and a green bow tie. He bowed and said, "Madame, I present myself, Max Bergeron, of the Thibodeaux, Bergeron's (like that meant anything to Karen). Our family moved from Louisiana to Mississippi, before the war, and both states were better off." Karen did a double take, and invited him in.

Doris came immediately into the family room. She had been primping all afternoon. Her cheeks had a big, golf ball sized, rouge application, too much lipstick, her hair was ratted, and she was using her cane, instead of the walker, for the first time Karen had seen.

"Oh, Doris, it's a thing of great joy in my heart to see you again. It has been far too long since that dreadful accident interrupted our visits. You look stunning."

"Max, what a charmer. You know flattery will get you everywhere." She looked suddenly at Karen, only a slip of the tongue, Doris thought. "Lets retire to the front porch. This time of the day we get lots of shade, and usually a breeze from the water."

The rest of the family had stayed out of sight, Tom down at the dock, the girls in their room. Karen was left to wonder exactly "which" war, Max was alluding to. Did he charge San Juan Hill with Teddy Roosevelt? And who had picked out his clothes, Ray Charles?

Tom came in after a while...Karen looked stunned. "What's wrong," he asked, "is everything alright? Is your Mom sick again, are the girls OK? You look like you've seen a ghost, you're pale.

"I think I did see a ghost," she replied. "No, everyone is fine, by that I mean healthy."

"But, whatever you do," Karen mumbled softly, "don't go on the front porch. We've gone back in time. I'm getting the wine out tonight, or maybe I'll just kill myself. It would be quicker, and less painful."

After about an hour, Doris came inside, hopping a little with the cane. "Damned cane, she said, but it's better than the walker, got to dump that, ruins any chance I've got to"...

She looked up and her voice faded. "Max said he enjoyed meeting you, Karen." "I hope I'll be able to go back to the Senior Center in a week or two." "I think you're making good progress, Mom," her daughter said.

Later that night, when it was just Tom, Karen, and a glass of wine, she observed, "You think about raising your children, the birth, colic, measles, school…and when you get to the point you can relax, and put only 1 hand on the steering wheel, BAM, you've got a parent, who acts like a child, to raise, all over again."

Tom put his hand on top of hers. "It'll be OK. I'll do my part."

"Tom, that's just it, you shouldn't have to do any part. You've worked all your life, and your parents aren't with us anymore. I'm sure you wish they were, but you can't have this piled on you too." "For better, or for worse," Tom said, and gave her hand a big squeeze.

The next Wednesday, Max and Doris met on the front porch again. Tom had finished the dock, and after checking on his new, but used, 12 ft' "John" boat. He walked around to the front porch to be social.

Max jumped up with a start, and smoothed out the wrinkles in his orange polyester pants as Tom approached the porch. He stood and moved a little to his right, hoping Tom wouldn't see the half-empty wine bottle behind him on the ground. Tom pretended not to notice. "Tom Flowers, Mr. Bergeron. Pleased to meet you."

"Oh the honor is mine, sir" Bergeron replied in a stammering voice. They had been caught red-handed, if he saw the bottle, thought Max.

Tom just grinned and said, "I've got chores to do, just wanted to say hello and welcome." He walked around the corner and returned to the back yard, shaking his head. Karen was right he thought, must've been Ray Charles.

He'd have to tell Karen about the wine…but she was 75, what can you do?

Summer...2002

This was absolutely the best time of the year, for 17 year old girls. They would be Seniors next year, with all the uncertainty that followed. No worry, today, about life decisions such as college, a career, etc. Six months from these things would begin to intrude on their lives. Parents would try to help. Guidance councilors would invite them in. Next year was responsibility, and this summer was the last one, without the stress of adulthood.

Jess had gotten a retail job in a junior dress shop at Edgewater Plaza, named "Cutting Edge Fashion" The local shoppers just called it "The Edge." Connie was working part time at Bennies, to give the boys something to look at. She thought she was hot, and she was right. Jess was cute, Connie was sexy. Jess dressed young, but conservatively, especially at work. Connie wore tight jeans or shorts, usually with a tee shirt tied in a knot in front.

Josh called home, often, and had written almost every week. He was healthy, but homesick. It was debilitating, being around foreigners who didn't appreciate your help, and in fact, wanted you dead. All he could focus on was the mission, and being part of a team. He was good at his mission. In the 4 months there, he'd been promoted, now a full corporal. He'd received a couple of battlefield commendations, though he kept that to himself. His platoon had lost 3 Marines due to IED's, and he wouldn't mention that to those at home either. He was figuring on 12 more months in Afghanistan, tops.

Tom had received another promotion, he was the number 3 man at the Beau Rivage, now. He had begun to fish from his small boat on Back Bay. He liked to have a beer on Saturday, and fish for croaker, or red drum. He wasn't good at it, but it was good for him.

Jess's friend, Milo had come over the previous week. He was a wizard with computers.

In only a couple of hours he had doubled the RAM on both their home PCs, and had networked them with wireless internet connections.

When Tom wanted to pay, Milo just shrugged, "It's all just old stuff I had laying around." Tom wasn't sure, but he let it go. The girls had one computer, and there was another one in the kitchen.

Karen, was doing her usual juggling act. The library, house, the garden, cooking and shopping, and last, but not least, keeping her Mom from driving them crazy. She was doing well at that, especially now that Doris was spending 3 evenings a week at the Senior Center.

Goldie was caught up in all the activity. The house was always like a beehive. The girls coming and going two or three times a day. Grandma was always being extremely nice. She called me her four legged granddaughter.

One Saturday, they received a letter from Josh. Mom read it to the assembled family, including Goldie. It's dated June 3rd, she said.

"Hello all, from that friendly resort called Afghanistan. Having fun with the last batch of CDs you sent me, thanks. Most of the men don't have a lot of family support, so they have adopted you. Speaking of adoption, one of the men in my platoon, took in a stray dog last week. He was so thin you could count his ribs, but we found out he's the only one of us who likes MRE's, so he's got an unlimited supply of chow. He's put on 10 pounds. Not to worry Goldie (she looked around hearing her name), he can't replace you. I'm doing fine. I hope all of you are well, it's really boring here, to tell the truth.

Thirty minutes after writing the upbeat letter, Josh's platoon deployed for another 6 day mission into the northern hills. It was either his 11th or 12th mission, he'd lost count.

The next Saturday night, Tom was awakened at 11:30, by the telephone. Jess was home, but not Connie. "Calm down Connie," he said. "Where are you, honey? OK, I'll be right there. I know where it is." "Is it Connie?" Karen asked. "Yes, I'm going to get her, she's drunk, and scared. A boy tried to rape her."

"Oh, no," said Karen. "I'm going, too. She needs me." They jumped into Tom's car and raced down highway I-110, to a little nightclub called "Club Paradise." They burst through the door. Connie was sitting at the bar drinking coffee, with a coat over her bare shoulders. "This is my daughter, and she's a minor, screamed Tom."

"I know that," said the man behind the bar. "She ran in here asking for help. What was I supposed to do. I gave her a phone, and some coffee, and put a coat over her, she was shaking." "Sorry," said Tom, "parental overreaction." "Connie, are you OK, are you hurt?" Karen asked. "No, I'm just sort of beat up," she replied. I jumped out of the car at the light and ran here. Jimmy tried to force himself on me." "Let's take her to the hospital," Tom said. "No," Karen said. "If she says she's OK, she's OK. I know Connie. She wouldn't let anyone get away with anything. If she was hurt bad (meaning raped) she'd go after him herself."

"We'll see how she is tomorrow." Tom relented. "This isn't over." He turned to the bartender, and put his own jacket over Connie, and said, "Thanks, we owe you." "Hey, I got a daughter too." the man said. "If it was me, I'd want a piece of revenge."

Well, Tom's position wouldn't allow for personal revenge, but he had a plan. They got home, cleaned Connie up, who was now 99% sober, gave her one of Karen's Valium, and quietly put her in bed. Thank God, tomorrow was Sunday.

Early the next morning Karen overheard Tom on the phone. "Yes, I know what time it is, and that it's Sunday. Tell him it's Tom Flowers on the phone, and it's urgent." A couple of minutes later she heard, "Yes DeWayne, Connie was attacked last night by Jimmy Reese. Yes, Dr. Reese's son. Oh, this isn't the first time you've dealt with him. No, she's OK. No, I don't think we want to press charges, it's her word against his. I just want the hell scared out of him. I want him, and his family told that we might press charges. That would effectively cancel his Tulane acceptance, don't you think."

"Thanks DeWayne, sorry for the timing." Tom had helped DeWayne Holmes, the Biloxi Chief of Police, when his son had gotten into some trouble at the casino, nothing illegal, and he was 24, and responsible for himself. But in an election, it would have been used against DeWayne.

"I see you called in a marker," said Karen. "Only when it protects the family," he responded. "I'm proud of the way you've taken Connie in. She hasn't had a male influence since her father died. You never treat her any different than Jess. I appreciate that. Connie doesn't realize it, but she will one day…especially after last night."

In about an hour, Karen went upstairs to check on Connie. Jess was stirring, but Connie was deep in sleep. Then she saw Goldie's head look up to her from Connie's side.

Connie was sleeping with her arm around Goldie, something Karen had never seen before, not even with Jess. She approached the bed and said to the dog, "You could tell she needed a friend, couldn't you girl?" Goldie sighed, and put her head back on the bed. Karen walked quietly downstairs. Her husband was still at the kitchen table when she returned. "You know Tom, that dog's a miracle."

That afternoon, three of Biloxi's finest in blue, not to mention biggest and meanest, along with a female officer, paid a visit to the home of Dr. Samuel Reese.

Dr. Reese called Tom that afternoon. They had met. Around here, everyone had met. "Mr. Flowers, my son has made a big mistake. I'm humbly sorry. I'd appreciate you're not pressing charges. And you can be assured, he will have no leeway, zero tolerance, in the future. If there are any medical bills, just send them to me. It will come out of Jimmy's allowance times 10." Tom told the Doctor everything would be fine, but Jimmy was on notice.

This was a quiet Sunday. Connie slept late, but that was usual. Jess had an inkling that she had missed something. Doris was completely out of the loop, and acted normally, for Doris.

Goldie had come down when she smelled breakfast on the stove. "Can't I get some good Mexican food here?," Doris asked. "How about breakfast tacos or Huevos Rancheros, instead of this bland scrambled eggs and bacon?" Jess surprised everyone, "Grandma, I've been learning about Mexican dishes in my cooking class at school. Ever since San Antonio, I've been interested in it. I'm going to investigate, and if I can find the ingredients, we'll have Mexican food, at least once a week, maybe starting next weekend."

Everyone was stunned, especially Doris. Karen was encouraging, "I'll look for some cookbooks at the library." Jess came back, "I'm sure there is help on the internet." Tom was amazed how much of their life was made easier by the internet. "The best bait for Croaker, basic boat repair, changing a faucet," were all helpful things he had accessed, thanks to Milo. Karen used it to identify garden pests and diseases. They were becoming a modern family.

Around 11, Connie came downstairs. She was dressed much more conservatively than usual, just some jeans, flip-flops, and a blue chambray shirt, untucked. After a small breakfast, a few bites of egg, a piece of toast, and coffee, she looked at Tom and Karen. "Do you think we could go for a walk?"

Outside, she said, "Mom, Dad, I'm sorry about last night. I owe you better. I've never had anyone, treat me as nice as you two. You added me as part of your family, and I let you down. I'll do better, I promise, I really will."

Karen hugged the shaking, weeping girl. "It's just part of growing up. We all make mistakes. The important thing is to learn from them. The fact that you jumped out of that car, shows me a great deal about the type of daughter we have."

Tom interjected. "This is between us in the family. You're as important to me as my own birth daughter, and we respect your feelings. No one here is going to talk about last night. You can tell, or not tell, whoever you want. But, it's behind us. And I don't think you'll be seeing Jimmy Reese, again."

Connie looked at them with a question forming in her brain. Karen shook her head, "Don't go there, just focus on you. We'll give you all the support you'll need."

Later on, when it was just Tom and Karen, Tom said, " That shirt, long sleeves to cover up the bruises, I think." "Let it go," said Karen, "she's suffered and is going to have a tough time gaining back her own self respect. We have to be like the Rock of Gibraltar for her." "I know," he said, "it's just a father thing."

Jess left for her job at the clothing store at 11. They opened at noon, but everyone was expected to come in about 11:30, to get the store ready to open. It was a fairly busy time as the tourist season ran from May through August, which is why most of the "seasonal" type stores looked forward to the summer.

About 2 o'clock, Jess was in the front of the "Edge" when Milo, her "friend," stopped by. "Oh, I'm just on my way to the 'Gateway' computer store, I didn't know you were working today," said Milo. Jess said, "Milo, Gateway is a freestanding store in the parking lot outside the mall." "W..w..well," Milo stuttered, realizing he'd been caught, "I had to go get a new cd for my sister, and thought I'd walk through."

"Great to see you," Jess answered, but you know Ms. Parker, the owner, doesn't like us socializing while we're on the clock." "Right," Milo said, "see you at school, tomorrow," as he stumbled off.

Jeez, Jess thought, the one boy who pays attention to me, and I have to be a smartass and catch him in a fib. Would it hurt to play dumb once in a while?

Connie had quit the job at Bennies. Part of it was embarrassment, but she got lucky when a real estate broker friend of Tom's, Bobby Guilotte, called. His company needed an intern for the next couple of months (actually a glorified gopher). This was a busy time in real estate...lots of people bought or rented second homes during the summer.

He knew Tom had Jess and Connie. Were either of them available? Connie went for an interview, and was hired right away. While she was too young to have a real estate license, she could put up "For Sale" and "For Rent" signs, deliver documents, schedule cleanup between rentals, and lots more.

She couldn't be an agent, or give out the particulars of a property on the phone or in person. Sometimes, in a pinch, Bobby would let her open a property for a showing, but all she could do from there was to hand the prospect a copy of the MLS listing sheet. She loved it. It was a new world for her, and it was much more professional than "Bennies."

Jess was keeping her promise to her Grandmother. They had a Mexican breakfast about once a month, and a dinner every week. Jess was really started to enjoy cooking, and had signed up for advanced culinary skills as part of her senior curriculum.

It was difficult finding the proper ingredients and spices. She grew cilantro and jalapenos in the garden, but had to search for cumin, and particularly the proper meat. She searched for a cabrito recipe, but couldn't find goat meat anywhere. Finally she drove to the Greek area in the east end of Biloxi, commonly called "The Point," and bought some lamb. Who would know?

Her huevos rancheros were a big hit. She served them on a large corn tortilla, covered with homemade salsa.

She also started cooking Cajun food. No problem finding Cajun cuisine ingredients in Biloxi.

In the 40's and 50s, the Cajun population was probably a third of the people living here, and their way of life carried on. Their largest tradition, like the Italians, was great food.

She prepared etouffe, shrimp remoulade, red beans and rice, and famous Louisiana gumbo, all with warmly baked French bread.

Karen was amazed, and pleased, to have someone else cooking for her every now and then. It really took some of the daily pressure off her, and Jess was really getting good at her preparation.

A New Phase...Fall 2002

Summer had passed, the tourists gone. Tom's business at The Beau Rivage slowed at this time of year. They were now depending on the local population for 75% of their business. And people were into the back-to-school mode which almost consumes September. They would get a little busier after that, increasing to a hectic time at the Holidays. But, for now, he could spend a little extra time in his small fishing boat in the Bay.

The girls were in school, for that "pressure-packed" Senior season. The first couple of weeks was like a mating ritual. Everybody who was not in a "steady" relationship waited to see who had gotten together, or broken up during the summer break, before picking through the crop of remaining boys or girls. It was a sinister, sneaky, and awkward time. "Find out if I ask her for a date, if she'll go out with me or not," was a longstanding boy maneuver. Boys hated to be turned down, rejection spread through the "grapevine" like wildfire. Girls didn't like to be surprised either, put on the spot, with no where to hide. Despite the silliness of it all...it is a creation of our culture which has worked in free societies for centuries.

Karen was working about 35 hours a week. She enjoyed her work, and due to State funding, the De'Iberville library now had several computers. It was amazing how the world was growing smaller. Students no longer read volumes of books to research their work. Just put a few "key words" into a search engine, and "voila" your questions came back with hundreds of answers.

In order to help people utilize the library's resources, Karen had taken a 3-day course on computers at the adult education center, on "Practical Computer Usage." She was amazed at the number of people her age, and older, who were beginning to become "computer savvy." Looks like this invention was here to stay.

The girls were a lot closer, as different as they were, they played off the other's personality. Jess sometimes called it a "love-hate relationship," but they had very few fights. They had settled into their classes, both required and elective. Jess was a consistent B+ student. Surprisingly, Connie made mostly B's with the occasional C thrown in. Both were on track to graduate in the top half of their class this Spring. They both worked most Saturdays, Jess at "The Edge" and Connie, putting real estate flyers in the information boxes on the "For Sale" or "For Rent" signs. She was getting into this, now, and saw a future in it.

Jess worked at "The Edge" for three reasons, social status, to have a little extra spending money, and to get a nice discount on clothes. She didn't saw retail as a means to an end. She just wasn't sure what that "end" would be, but she was forming some ideas. Also, working at the store, waiting on friends, strangers, and tourists, had boosted her self confidence and removed the last bit of her natural shyness.

Doris was as happy as she had ever been. She was seeing a great deal of Max Bergeron. They were spending 3 nights a week at St. Helena's Senior Center, or going to a movie. Doris wasn't using a cane anymore. In the beginning it was vanity, she didn't want to seem old and infirm. Eventually, she weaned herself from using it at all, unless she wanted attention at home.

Goldie…was just Goldie. She was always helpful, ready to lift the spirits of anyone around, or console any member who needed a special friend in a down time. She was happy with the "extended family", more people to please, and more people to throw compliments at her. Of course she still missed Josh, but did get to hear his letters and telephone calls. She liked the phone calls best, she could recognize his voice coming out of the little phone.

Josh was on another mission, it could be the most intense, yet.

Baghlan...October 2002

Josh viewed the early morning sky from the troop transport helicopter. The sun had not yet risen, and the chopper was using night vision equipment to hug the rocky soil below. The bitter winter was closing in on them, which would make travel even more difficult. This mission was more complicated than most. There was one remaining Taliban stronghold north of Baghram. It was a few miles east of Baghlan, south of Kunduz. The Taliban strategy was to terrorize an area, and then when challenged, make an easy retreat into neighboring Pakistan.

This mission was designated "Operation Mouse Trap" intended to put an end to the guerilla attacks by the bearded ones. A force consisting of Marines, British army, and Northern Alliance fighters were to attack from the southwest of the enemy. Air and artillery would drive them out of their hideout, predictably toward the border.

Three platoons, including the one Josh was assigned to, were to land east, between the Taliban and their escape route across the Pakistan Border. There was one particular, less hidden, stretch of a hurried escape route which Command wanted to force the Taliban to utilize. This stretch was only about 500 meters long, and ended into large caves offering cover, so timing was critical. The three platoons consisted of 100 Marines, plus an unusually high number of 12 spotter/sniper teams. This entire group was to be inserted into two ridge tops overlooking the flatter plane. They would catch the enemy in a crossfire. What the Taliban wouldn't know was that near the end of this piece of the escape route would be two of the "Angels of Death," infamous AC-130 gunships. The latest model was armed with 2, 25mm, 5-barrel Gatling guns, a 40mm L/60 Bofors cannon, and a 105mm M102 howitzer. Josh had never seen these aircraft except as a demonstration and on training films.

The magnitude and ferocity of the AC-130 was world renowned, and justly so.

Josh's platoon, deployed on the south ridge. They made it to the top, and positioned themselves, ready to provide cover to the northern ridge assembling only a few minutes later. All was quiet. This part of the plan, the surprise, had been completed in almost total darkness. It was key to the operation, for this to be undetected. The spotter/snipers set their positions, two squads were sent 100 meters out to find any existing lookouts. They returned in about 10 minutes, both giving the "thumbs up" sign.

The leader of this operation was a Captain, named Hanks. He was only about 5 meters from Josh's position, so he overheard, "Victory, victory, this is X-ray, we are set, repeat we are a go."

About 10 minutes later, the skies to the west lit up like the 4th of July. They were pounding the enemy with a barrage of helicopters, drones, and artillery.

Ever so slowly the noise moved closer, and it seemed to be intensifying. In about 20 minutes, Josh heard, "X-Ray, sniper team 3 reporting. Hostiles approaching quickly, about 1000 meters out...estimate they will enter target area in 5 to 6 minutes." Josh heard Hanks answer, " All squads, hold your fire, I repeat, hold your fire. Wait for my order." Daylight was starting to light the field of battle, and they could see a over a hundred men on the plain below, retreating toward the safety of the caves.

"Gunships in two minutes." the Captain spoke into the mike, "Are they ready? Roger that, Command." and then he called all units."Open fire, fire at will. Open fire, fire at will." Josh and his fellow Marines shot with great accuracy, as their training dictated.

The valley below was drenched in a crossfire of bullets from both ridges. Taliban were firing wildly into the hills, no target in sight. The enemy who would stop behind a rock for cover would get zapped almost immediately by a sniper. Those who were running full out toward the caves, had a big surprise coming.

The two huge gunships appeared out of the rising sun, and with them came a fusillade of weaponry concentrated on a 300 x 200 meter space. The Gatling guns and the 40mm cannon turned the battlefield into something Josh had never seen. The thundering barrage continued on for another 5 minutes and the planes left to return to Baghram.

The field of battle resembled the surface of the moon, with hundreds of enemy casualties. Josh's platoon was involved in the clean up, attending to the wounded, and ID'ing the few Marines who were hit or worse, killed. Suddenly, Josh saw a Marine on his left flank, fighting with 4 enemy fighters. These 4 had missed the attack by holding back, and were now trying to surprise the squad from the rear.

Josh raced over to give cover, and saw that the Marine was down to his sidearm, an M9 Beretta 9mm, which was standard issue. Josh rushed to cover his fellow Marine, as several AK 47 rounds whizzed by him, and kicked dirt up at his feet.

He reached the safety of a nearby boulder, and shot one of the attackers with a 3-tap to the chest. He rolled to his right and squeezed off a couple more rounds, hitting a second man in the knee, taking the fight out of him.

The defending Marine was obviously hit, but managed to shoot the third Taliban fighter in his neck with a round from the Beretta, before he, himself fell to the ground. Josh squeezed the trigger, and heard the awful sound of an empty clip.

As he hurried to reload, the last warrior leapt at Josh, using his rifle as a club. Josh ducked, spun, and thrust his KA-BAR knife into the attacker's stomach, just as he was taught.

His adrenaline was pounding. He felt or rather sensed someone behind him. He whirled, only to see Captain Hanks about 3 meters away.

"Great job, Marine. I couldn't fire, he was too close to you. Let's go tend to our soldier who is down. Josh turned him over. He was wounded in several places. It was Chet Perry, but he had a pulse. "Get me a medic, and an evac, on the double," yelled the Captain into the radio. In 10 minutes, Chet was on a chopper, back to Baghram. The medic thought he would make it. "I'm writing a battlefield commendation for you, Flowers," said the Captain. "I saw the whole thing. It's young men like you who make the Marines what they are today."

"Thank you, Sir," replied Josh. "Permission to continue my assignment, Sir?"

"Permission granted," said Captain Hanks. That young man is going to make a hell of an NCO, thought Hanks.

Later, back at the Base, Josh heard that Chet was going to be OK. Some rest in a rear stationed hospital in Kabul, but no permanent damage. This was good news, indeed.

Holidays, Nov 02 , Jan 03

It was a wonderful time of the year in Biloxi, and it meant something similar, and things very different to every member of the extended Flower's family. For them all, it represented a time of family togetherness and time of sharing with decorations, cooking, and the season. But each one of them was presented with other things brought by this time of year:

For Tom, the casino was beginning it's Holiday boom time. Lot's of gamblers on junkets, husbands and wives taking in a famous entertainer, musical group or show. It was a lot to keep up with.

Karen, with the library not quite so busy, cut back to 3 days a week until mid-January and focused on the home front more, exhibiting her usual panache with decorations, tree trimming, and planning seasonal meals. This year she had Jess to help her with the cooking, and it turned out that many times Jess was the cook, and her Mom, playing the role of the sous chef.

Jess was caught up in the busiest time of the retail year Every day since Halloween, shipments of new merchandise arrived into "The Edge." The store had become a "hot spot" for the 13-18 year old crowd, so Jess was really enjoying it. "Oh, call me first, when you get new things in," some of her young customers would say.

Connie had learned a lot in the real estate business. And as the old pro agents always said, "Honey, this business is either feast, or famine." This was a famine time of the year in real estate. Almost no one wakes up Thanksgiving morning and says, "I think it's a good time to sell my house, and have strangers walking through it during the Holidays." So, Connie's hours were cut back a little, but she still loved the work, and was learning faster than ever.

Doris was spending more time at St. Helena's Senior Center. The people there elected her to be in charge of the Holiday Decorations.

So, when Max couldn't take her there, another family member drove there and picked her up. Most of the decorations and ornaments at the Center were old. Each year they would buy a few new ornaments, and add it to the collection. The only rule was that at least one of the decorations must have that year shown on it.

Doris was having a big time, making lists of items for people to bring in, once the tree was up. She assigned people to bring in mistletoe, gold streamers, bows, and the like. They had a fund for this every year by charging 25 cents per person for a night of Bingo.

Thanksgiving day came and went. The food was plentiful, mine was superb. Dark turkey meat is my favorite, and Jess had made a 22 pounder. The Cowboys were beating the Lions, again, and Dad was just into his nap when the phone rang. "Oh, great," screamed Mom. "Hold on Josh." She put him on the speakerphone which Dad had bought specifically for Josh's calls. Everyone crowded around the kitchen table except for Grandma, she was at the Senior Center.

"Happy Thanksgiving from Afghanistan," said Josh. Goldie was circling the table, looking everywhere for Josh, but couldn't find him. Finally she realized he was in the little box...so small, hmmmm.

"I'm great here, how is everybody?" "We're fabulous," Karen replied with excitement, " We're only missing one thing...YOU!"

"I know the girls are graduating soon. No more freeloading for you two." "No, they've both got jobs, and are working their butts off," laughed Tom.

But listen, if you could get home before the end of the NFL season, we might be able to push the Saints into the playoffs."

Josh had been reading the news and sports from Stateside, he knew the Saints were 7-4 but they almost always faded late in the season "They've still got a long way to go, Dad. They let one slip away last week." I have a feeling they're not going to make it, Dad. Hey, but tell Goldie to keep the faith. We'll get a Super Bowl yet."

Goldie looked around when her name was mentioned. Tom laughed heartily, he realized it was the best laugh he had in several months. He sorely missed his son, but didn't want to lay any guilt on Josh.

"Well, Dad, it's been so boring here that I've become quite a 'Texas Hold-Em' poker player. But don't worry, when I get back, I won't take all the casino's money. I wouldn't want to put you out of a job." "I'm not worried," Tom retorted, "you're not old enough to gamble at the tables yet. You have to be 21." His face froze. "Here, talk to your sister." Tom turned and walked away.

At that moment, Goldie saw a tear roll down Tom's cheek. Tom had realized too late what he had just said in jest. His son wasn't old enough to have a beer, or play blackjack…but he was old enough to die for his country. How his heart ached. Goldie followed him into the family room, where he was sitting in his favorite chair. He ignored the TV, and put his face into his hands. Goldie nuzzled up under his arm. "You understand, don't you girl? You're always around when someone needs help or love, thanks."

The phone conversation was medicine for the family, as well as for Josh. They laughed a little more, and then Josh had to say goodbye, and hand over the phone to the next Marine in line.

Karen and the girls were very excited, this call was just what the season was about. A family not all together in one place, but always together in spirit.

The day after Thanksgiving was called "Black Friday," in the retail world. It was traditionally the busiest day of the year in sales. It kicked off the Christmas shopping season, and put many businesses into the "black", as the accountants say. It was no different at "The Edge." Jess was working a 8 am to 8 pm shift, with 2-30 minute breaks. Now that she was 17, the child labor laws did not hinder her from working extra long hours.

Tom had an unusually huge crowd at the Casino, this could be a record day. Lots of people were in town, and there was a middleweight fight scheduled for Saturday night between two highly-ranked contenders.

Karen was working from 9 am to 1 pm at the library, mainly organizing, and allowing computer access. Her relief, only 1 person needed at this time of year, would work the 1 to 5 shift.

Doris was playing the crowd at the Senior Center. Max had picked her up at 9:30, and she planned to stay the whole day there with him. The Christmas tree would go up on the Monday after Thanksgiving. A longtime tradition at the Center.

Connie was alone wearing jeans and (secretly) working on her test to become a real estate agent. She wouldn't be old enough to take the test until April, when she became 18, but she could surely study until then. She really liked real estate. Connie heard a car pull up outside, wondered who it could be. She opened the door to a smirking Jimmy Reese, the boy who tried to rape her, standing on the front porch. He looked drunk, stoned, or both.

"You didn't think you could get away from me, did you, you little tramp?

Do you know how much trouble you got me into? I pass by this house every time I'm home, just hoping to see no cars, and catch you here alone. So now's a time for a little payback. She tried to slam the door, but he stuck an alligator skin cowboy boot between the door and the jamb, and pushed the door open, hitting her in the forehead. She tried to scramble to her feet. He pushed her down on the floor and said, "No, you stay down there, that's exactly where I want you."

Connie scuttled on her backside, toward her room. "I'll call the police on you, get out, get out now."

"It's going to be hard to call the cops, after I kick your teeth down your throat. I might throw you down the stairs, make it look like an accident. Who would know? But, I'm going to have me some fun with you first. You owe me that."

At that moment, a 90 pound furry yellow missile launched herself off the stairs, directly into Jimmy's head. Goldie knocked the surprised Jimmy back 6 feet, and his head snapped back, hitting the floor with a thud. He was out, cold.

Connie ran to her room with Goldie right behind. She locked the door and called the police. "I have an intruder in the house, he's trying to hurt me. I locked myself in the upstairs bedroom." She gave them the address, the dispatcher told her to stay on the line, the police were on the way. "Don't come out of your room until the police get there and identify themselves," the police dispatcher said. In less than 5 minutes a knock came on her door, "Officer Stewart, ma'm. You can open the door now, you're safe now. Are you OK?" Connie answered in the affirmative.

She came downstairs to witness 2 policemen escorting a handcuffed Jimmy Reese, to a squad car. There was blood running down the back of his head.

"How old are you?" The officer asked. "Seventeen," said Connie. "In that case where are your parents?," "officer Stewart asked. "At work," said Connie, "Mom's going to be home at 1:15." "Well, ma'm, I have to get a statement, and one of your parents has to be present. The forensic team will take about an hour, I have to stay with them, and it's almost 12 now you're sure you're alright?"

"Yes," Connie re-affirmed.

"Fine, give me her phone number, I'll tell her everything is under control. You sit over on the couch, and don't say anything until she gets here." Connie did as instructed.

Karen skidded into the driveway at 12:30 to the sight of 2 police cruisers and a van marked "Harrison County Crime Lab." She had called her replacement and asked her to come in to the Library ASAP, she would have closed the library, if need be, but it wasn't.

Connie filled her in on the details, during Officer Stewart's interview. The policeman, very smartly, wanted to hear it for the first time, not after counseling from a parent. But it was pretty straightforward. The Reese kid had done it again. And this time, Karen didn't think that his father could buy his way out.

After all the law enforcement personnel left, Karen was able to comfort Connie. "Goldie saved me," she said. "I understand," Karen answered. "And you're safe now."

Tom was the next to get home, but not until 5:30. They filled him in on the horrible events of the day. He blamed himself, for not pressing charges for the last incident.

"You can't do that honey." said Karen. "You were giving a young man, what you thought was a second chance. That's the type of people we are." "Who knew it was a pattern?"

That night at 8 pm, Dr. Reese was on the phone to Tom. "Please Mr. Flowers, he's a good boy at heart. It's my fault. I always spoiled him, so did his Mother. Please give him a chance to be someone in this world."

"If it were my decision," Tom said, "I would argue that I already gave him another chance. If what I've heard is true, so have several other people. But, it's not my decision, it's a family decision." "Well, factor this into your decision, Mr. Flowers. I will pay for the college education of your children, up to $100,000 apiece, in advance. If they don't want to go to college, they can keep the money."

"We'll make our decision tonight," Tom promised. That night, the family had a meeting. It lasted less than 30 minutes. At 11 am the next morning, Jimmy Reese, was charged with breaking and entering, destruction of property, trespassing, assault with intent to kill, and attempted rape of a minor. This was the family decision.

The family had agreed that the prospect of Jimmy Reese back on the streets, was chilling, and could eventually cost the life of an innocent person. This boy was a predator.

The next evening, after Jess got home from "The Edge" and dinner was completed, Goldie was treated to the leftovers and bones from the t-bone steaks. Lots of meat, and 1 bone. Mom had frozen the other 4. Earlier in the day Mom and Connie had gone to the pet store and bought a new dog collar to replace the old, ragged one she had. They bought one that had a small metal plate attached to it. On it they had inscribed, "For Goldie, our guardian angel, you make us feel safe." Life was good.

The Thanksgiving Weekend finished up on Sunday, with lots of leftovers, more desserts, and more Saints football for Tom and Goldie.

Life returned to some degree of normalcy for the next two weeks. The girls were in school, Tom and Karen working, and Doris decorating the Senior Center.

The "Tree" Party

The tree had arrived on Monday, Sammy Pantolino had a pickup truck he could still drive, so he brought it in with help from Max, and two others. "No fake tree for us," yelled Sammy. The men laid it on it's side and affixed the base, by screwing the supports tightly around the trunk. They sat it up, and had about a 10 degree lean to the side. "Listing to the portside," commented Ralph Hollister, a retired Navy seaman.

After about 10 minutes of men supporting the tree in an upright position while others loosened and tightened the screw supports, it was done. A beautiful 7 foot evergreen.

"You know," Sammy bragged, "Mr. Peters at the Methodist Church always saves his best tree on the lot for me." The group wasn't sure about that, but it was a fine looking specimen. And the decorating could now commence in full swing. Doris' goal was to be finished by Friday, and have a nice get-together of all the members on Saturday Night. Not that she wanted to show off or anything.

That Saturday evening the doorbell rung at 6. Tom opened it to the electric sight of Max Bergeron. He was expecting Max. What he wasn't expecting was the wardrobe. Mr. Bergeron had dressed "in season." Green double-knit pants, about 2 inches too short, a flaming red shirt, gold coat, white patent shoes and belt, and a flashing lapel pin which blinked with the message, "will make out for food." Doris hurried to the door in her finest plumage, accompanied by red sparkling shoes (think Dorothy!) and matching purse. They hurried to the car, "We can't be late," she was prattling on. "Dinner's at 7."

The party was well planned. Doris had ordered 2 roast beef sides, and a huge turkey from Mr. Shapiro's Deli.

He delivered them at 5, with warming lights, and had his sons there for the evening to do the actual carving. A perfect example of inter-faith harmony.

The tradition at this dinner was for each person or couple to bring a side dish, and Doris, of course, had first asked what each person thought was their own food specialty, and then she filled in around that list in order to have a balanced offering. She gave a pitiful dish, green beans, to Betty Malbon, who she really disliked. No reason for Betty to get any compliments. Jess had prepared her Grandmother's side dish, since Doris had said she was too busy.

Jess had produced a triple recipe of homemade stuffing with cubed bread, onion, and celery, it was a hit. Since Doris knew this in advance, she had asked Mr. Shapiro to loan them an extra large warming tray.

The Hall at the Senior Center had been set up with a long buffet table, plates, napkins and cutlery at the beginning. All the side dishes, including the stuffing were lined up as far as you could see.

Included was a large round table for the desserts, with more flatware, and a coffee pot with cups, sugar, cream, and their various substitutes, plus several large pitchers of water.

Then there were 2 carving tables manned by the sons of Mr. Shapiro. For beverages, Doris had planned 3 round tables throughout the room. One had a large punch bowl with a very zesty combination of flavors, surrounded by hard plastic cups. Max called this the "soft punch." The second was a bowl of homemade Sangria prepared by Ms. Cortez. It was the national drink of her home country, Spain. And in the middle of the room was the eggnog, spiked of course, and located right next to their beautifully decorated Christmas Tree, adorned with an angel on top.

By 7 o'clock there were at least 40 members present and the group began to form two lines around the long buffet table filled with side dishes. The cutting stations were kept busy for quite a long time, but they never ran out of food, that would be unpardonable.

Doris was feeling on top of the world, flitting from table to table saying hello to everyone and fishing for compliments. There were plenty of those to be had, deservedly so. The only downside was that she was doing so much talking, she wasn't eating. She was drinking lots of Sangria, though. At about 8:30 she switched to eggnog...not bad, she thought. Max was beside her almost the entire evening, but he was usually carrying a plate. She was doing all the talking, why not? The stuffing was his favorite.

At about 9, the party started thinning out, by 9:30 there were only about 15 people remaining. She looked at Max across the eggnog table, with one eye closed. "Max, she said, "the tree is leaning again, and the angel is waving at me..." Wham! Doris fell headfirst into the tree, it all came down, ornaments were broken, branches snapped, red and gold glass balls rolled around the room. Luckily the lights had become unplugged, when the tree fell.

She was right on top of the fallen tree, grasping the limbs. She looked up to see a laughing Betty Malbon. Oh no, anybody but her.

Max rushed to her side, and got her seated in a chair. Physically, she was fine, with the exception of a few scratches. Max brought her some coffee, and food, then more coffee and food. Finally a little assisted walking around, got her into a better, not sober, but better, state.

Max got her home about 10:45. She knew no one would know what time she got in.

Goldie's Garden 161

But what a mess they had left. Mr. Shapiro's sons "broke down" all the food stations, storing the leftovers in the refrigerator at the center, and tried their best to sweep up any dangerous pieces of glass. But there was still a lot to do. They stood in the front yard to finish the evening.

"I'll go in early tomorrow, Doris," Max said. "I'll have the chairs and tables folded up, the linens in the laundry, and the floor shining, before 9. No one will know any different. We were going to clean up today, anyway."

"Well, you can't handle the tree by yourself, and Betty Malbon already knows," said Doris.

Max replied, "Betty Malbon is an old crow who's badgering has killed off three husbands, and she's looking for a fourth victim right now. I wouldn't worry too much about her. Everyone at the Center knows she's a mean old hag." He continued, "I'll get Sammy and his son to help us with the tree. If we have to, we'll get a new one, a better one."

This seemed to placate Doris. "Come back and get me at noon," she said. "I think the girls are off, and they can help me redecorate the tree after you guys get it standing again."

The Dinner

The second week of December Karen was out in the yard one Sunday morning tending to the bushes, reviewing the garden, and throwing an old tennis ball for Goldie. Doris came out, with her cane. Karen knew that was trouble. Doris hadn't used it for weeks. The cane represented a request, or, at least, forgiveness for something small. The walker was used only for emergencies in Grandma's world.

"It's the Holiday season," Doris began. "A time of hope, charity and love." Now Karen was really worried. "You know, Max has no family. No one to have Christmas dinner with. He'll be eating alone, that prepared stuff they serve at the Center, but alone."

Karen pretended not to understand. "So you care about this man?" she asked. "Yes, very much," Doris said. "And you want to be with him at Christmas?," Karen asked. "Yes, more than anything," the old woman said. "Well, fine," said Karen. "If you want to eat with him at the Senior Center, I understand, and I'll explain it to the family. We'll miss you at dinner though," she said. Doris was flummoxed. Karen had turned the tables on her. Now what to say?

Karen let it lie for a few seconds, then decided to be generous, "Or you could invite Mr. Bergeron here for Christmas dinner. I know it would be a bother, the girls, the dog, the cat, but if he could be flexible...?" Doris bluffed, "That might work, I'll have to ask," and she turned and walked quickly back to the house, forgetting to use her cane.

Christmas day came, and at exactly noon, Mr. Bergeron rang the bell. Jess and Connie had it all planned out, as they both answered the door wearing sunglasses. Of course, Max didn't get the joke and the girls were biting their tongues to keep from laughing out loud.

Karen gave them the "death stare," and smiled at Max. "Welcome to our home, Mr. Bergeron. We're so happy you could join us on this special day. Please take a seat in the family room." She turned and said, pointedly, "Girls, I think you should both go to your room and get dressed for dinner. You're both been so involved with the preparation, you forgot to change. And off with the shades."

"I brought two bottles of wine," said Max. It's called "Scuttlebuck Hills." It was on sale at the Wal-Mart." "Oh, you shouldn't have," Karen said. "We already have our wine open and breathing (which was a "white lie"), I'll to save this for another special occasion." Right, Karen thought, like to keep the Japanese Beetles away from the garden in the spring. Tom got up from his chair, greeted Max and showed him where he could sit.

Yellow pants, thought Tom. Where are my sunglasses? Max was wearing a purple shirt, a cardigan adorned with reindeer, and "the Full Cleveland" which was white patent shoes and belt.

Tom decided to watch TV, and avoid the deadly mixture of pigmentation coming from Mr. Bergeron. In a minute, Doris strolled into the room. Tom could smell her coming. She was gussied up in a bright blue floral dress, a neckline that would have been fine for a woman 40 years younger, and loads of a sickly sweet perfume. The mixture of "moth ball" smell on the dress, and the overdone perfume, was ghastly.

Goldie thought "what's this?" and ran from the room. She started whining for Mom to open the door to the back yard. "Got to go girl?" she asked. "Ok, here you go. She must have to go badly, Karen said. She always loves having new people over."

Tom was relieved when Doris suggested "Let's go on the back screen porch, dear. I can enjoy a stogie out there." They headed outside, and Karen immediately, connected Goldie's fitful behavior with the malodorous wave passing through the kitchen.

Karen went into the family room. Her husband was sitting there staring at the floor and shaking his head. The girls came down, neatly dressed. "What's burning?", asked Jess, "Not my pumpkin pie, it's got another 30 minutes." "No," countered Connie, "I think there's a skunk under the house." Karen glared at them. "What?", the girls said in unison."

"Into the kitchen with you both. Aprons on. I don't want to ruin good dresses. You both look very nice, by the way."

They went to the kitchen, and when they got there, Jess offered, "Nothing's burning, I think it's something on the porch." Both girls peeked out the glass at the top half of the door, and then just looked at each other, laughing so hard they cried.

"Calm down girls. Today is a special day for your Grandmother, and you two are not going to ruin it for her," Karen warned.

"So, that's the dog who helped you," Max said. The door was open on the screen porch, because of the smoking. "Here girl, come on up here and visit," he called. No way, Goldie thought, and just woofed and paced around the yard. "Well, I'll come out to you then," Max conceded. After he got about 10 steps from the porch, Goldie ran over to him, playfully jumping and rubbing against him."I wanted to thank you for saving my girl over there," Max said looking at Doris. "She means a lot to me, and now, so do you."

About 1:30 it was dinnertime. Karen had put the "leaf" in the dining room table, extending it for the extra person. Sitting here, all together, was special. Most Sundays and Holidays they ate here, other meals were almost always at the small round kitchen table, due to differing school, work, and sleeping schedules, so this was very special.

Thankfully, the 90 minutes outside had had a positive effect on the combination of smells, and everyone could enjoy a great meal.

Jess had prepared the main dish. She wanted to be somewhat non-traditional, "After all," she thought, "how many turkeys can you eat?" She had selected Osso Bucco, which was lamb shanks cooked slowly in beef stock, diced tomatoes, and white wine for 2 hours. She added celery, onion, garlic, potato, and carrots about halfway through. She served the dish over linguini pasta.

There was bread, of course along with tossed salad, made by Connie, containing all fresh things from their garden. She had really pitched in, pulling carrots, digging potatoes, picking tomatoes, herbs and spices. Everything had turned out to be wonderful, and Karen was so proud of the girls. They had done 90% of the work, with her supervision.

They topped it off with a nice bottle of red wine (actually 2 bottles) with the girls enjoying their traditional one glass of wine. They didn't know how close they had come to "Scuttlebuck Hills."

Goldie was laying in her corner position of the room. "All those plates had bones on them," she noticed. "Why couldn't we have Holiday dinners, everyday?"

About 4:00, Mr. Bergeron, said his thankful goodbyes to everyone in the family, both two and four legged. Karen was happy that she had made her Mother's Christmas a little more special. As he was leaving, just on cue, the girls put their sunglasses back on and wished him a Merry Christmas. "Don't let that "Scuttlebuck" go to waste," he said to Karen. "It's great stuff, for a domestic wine." "Not to worry, Max, I've got plans for it already," said Karen, glaring at the girls.

Later that afternoon, Dad took his nap, with Goldie faithfully at his feet.

Christmas to the East

Ten and a half hours before Mr. Bergeron rang the doorbell in Biloxi, Josh and his fellow Marines were celebrating Christmas in Baghram, as best they could. They ate turkey, mashed potatoes, and gravy, in shifts. The enemy liked to stage attacks on Holidays in an effort to demoralize the troops and make them even more homesick, so they were on alert status.

Josh was enjoying his second bite of turkey, when "the fertilizer hit the ventilator", a little Marine humor. "Incoming," someone yelled into the mess hall as 107mm mortars and light rockets began falling on the north and east side of the base camp. Six "Black Hawks" and four MH-6 "Little Birds" were airborne in about 2 minutes, sweeping and strafing enemy positions. Josh and 3 pre-designated members of his squad went to their assigned point of defense, which in this case was a 3x3 meter elevated position containing a Browning 50 caliber machine gun, surrounded by sandbags. There were dozens of these emplacements around the camp's exterior, but only about half of them were manned during normal operations.

The pilots were very aware that they were being drawn into the open where RPGs or shoulder launched "heat seekers" could bring them down. Because of that, no helicopter operated alone, and none ventured more than 2 miles from the confines of Baghram. It took about an hour, but they rooted out the well-entrenched enemy, destroying several mortar positions and causing multiple casualties. A "Little Bird" had been hit and was struggling to make it back to base. Josh spotted it, coming straight for his position. It was smoking, and was about 2000 meters out. It's elevation was only 300 meters. It was being escorted by two larger Black Hawks. Josh knew the drill, get as close to camp as you can (before the chopper exploded), land, have the crew (only 2, in this case) and jump into the accompanying chopper furthest from the enemy.

In this case the enemy had been on both sides, so it didn't matter which one they used. "They better hurry," thought Josh. The Black Hawk to the left signaled by losing altitude, followed immediately by the smaller chopper.

They were about 1000 meters out, Josh estimated, when they landed the Little Bird and scrambled onto the Black Hawk. Together the two larger aircraft zoomed into the awaiting LZ at the base in no time. Josh was waiting for the explosion. After 10 minutes, there wasn't one. This wasn't good. Josh grabbed the radio which was standard for each emplacement, and called his platoon leader. "Defense Edward 6 (meaning position #6 on the eastern perimeter), to base, requesting permission to fire on Little Bird, Sir." His platoon leader came back, "Will advise, Edward 6."

The Marines didn't want the enemy coming in at night, stripping the helicopter of weapons, night vision equipment and the like. "Edward 6, this is Base Leader", aha, thought Josh. Platoon had to go further up the chain to get the OK to destroy a multi-million dollar helicopter. "That's a go, repeat, that's a go. Light it up." This was well within the range of the Browning. Josh fired multiple bursts, and the Little Bird exploded into a ball of flame. Cheers rang in his ears from Marines all around the camp. He was becoming a legend.

The camp returned to a semblance of normal activity. There was heightened awareness, and a dozen extra defensive emplacements were manned, but Josh finally got to eat his Christmas dinner. Maybe he'd get to call home later, he'd have to wait till at least 2300 to do this. He'd definitely write. Josh slept through the night, and was mad at himself when he woke up and realized he has missed his chance for a Christmas phone call. He promised himself he would call on New Years.

He didn't plan on having another mission the very next day, but orders were orders.

He and 7 other members of his squad were loaded into a Black Hawk at 0400. This was a recon mission, about 15 miles northeast. Their orders were to use their night vision and thermal imaging technology to locate Taliban supply lines. The squad would try to remain undetected during the shorter winter day, and ID the enemy the next evening and early morning, when they did most of their moving.

Once these co-ordinates were known, Base Command would develop a plan to eliminate the pathways, supplies, and the enemy combatants. The Black Hawk hovered about 10 meters from a hillside, and the Marines rappelled to the ground quickly. While this was more dangerous to the men than simply landing, they were able to begin the mission already half way up the hill, rather than start at the bottom, and climb all the way up. It saved at least an hour's time. The hilltop was to be their camp for the next 24 hours, when the Black Hawk would return.

The morning sun rose and thankfully, began to warm the mountaintop. Something was wrong! They heard Arabic voices close by. There was smoke from a fire. This was too close. Josh was the squad leader. He put his finger to his lips in a signal to be quiet. He pointed to Pvt. Lewis, and put his fingers under his eyes and pointed to a large rock, "See what's down there", he meant. It took Lewis about 5 minutes to get to the rock his appearance camouflaged by the "Ghillie" suit, they were all wearing.

He mouthed back to Josh "one hundred men, fifteen meters below." They were between a rock and a hard place. If they called in reinforcements, the radio would give their position away. An airstrike would be quicker, but his men would surely die as well from "friendly fire." Fifteen meters is nothing for a drone or F-14.

Josh decided to check all sides of the mountain, and found

that the enemy was not occupying the south or the west. Josh decided to chance it. He very carefully inched to the western edge of the butte and descended backward about 5 meters down. He pulled the radio, and plugged in the earphones he had been smart enough to include in his gear. "Base Camp, this is Alpha 1, come in." "Alpha 1 this is Base, you're breaking radio silence, this had better be good."

Josh explained the situation. The good news was that they had at least 100 Taliban and their mules loaded with weapons right below them. This was also the bad news.

Base Camp's plan was for Josh's unit to begin a descent in the same area he was now located, shielding them from the enemy and friendly fire. Base would dispatch 4 Black Hawks, which would fly directly over the squad toward the enemy, opening fire as they passed.

Josh confirmed, and ETA was 15 minutes. By the time he crept back to his squad and relayed the plan, 5 minutes had already passed. Josh pointed at Lewis, and held up one finger, then Peron, and held up two fingers, and so on. Josh would be last. One by one, his men began to inch toward the western rim of the mountain.

"Baaaaa." Josh looked up to see a scrawny black and white goat. The problem with goats was where their were goats, well you know the rest. Josh looked at Evans. Cpl. Evans had the only M40 A3 sniper rifle in the group, and it was fitted with a sound suppressor. Evans propped his rifle in the prone position and waited for someone to appear. He didn't have to wait long. In seconds a turban with a bearded face, appeared over the north edge of the mountain. He was focused on the goat. He didn't notice the soldiers until he was almost at the top. His eyes got wide, and Evans hit him, right between those eyes. The man rolled back down the hill, stirring up rocks and dust.

The others down below thought he had slipped, they heard no shot. Once they turned him over and saw the bullet wound in his head, they all began shouting and scurrying around.

Josh had called the squad back to the north and east side of the mountain's edge. No reason to be shot in the back as they tried to descend the other side. The Taliban would have the high ground. Josh wasn't going to give that up. Their best bet was to shoot down at the enemy and try to hold them off until the Cavalry arrived. Josh's squad had been equipped for stealth. They had no explosives, no M249 SAW, not even an M240, which would have evened the odds considerably.

The 8 Marines opened fire immediately, raining bullets down on the enemy below. The enemy was well equipped, however and just missed with 2 RPGs. "Lewis is hit," yelled Simms. Josh looked over. Lewis was hit in the leg and hand, but was still firing his M-16, one handed. Josh kept firing, "short controlled bursts," he yelled, but they all knew that. Figeroa, right beside him, stopped firing. He had a hole in the center of his helmet. Taliban were dropping like flies, but there were so many of them, and they kept coming. Josh was on his last clip of ammo. Then he would take Figeroa's. Josh didn't even look at his watch.

The Black Hawks would be here, when they got here, oh shit, the Blackhawks. He grabbed the radio, but kept firing. "Incoming Black Hawk leader, this is Alpha 1, do you copy?" "I copy, Alpha 1." "Black Hawk leader, Alpha 1 is trapped on he hilltop, not under cover, Tangos only 10 meters down the north and east slope, so far." "What are you asking, Alpha 1?" "It's my call Black Hawk leader, come on in, if you don't we're dead anyway. We'll take some of the Ghillies off to help you see us, but it's my call." "Roger that Alpha 1, rockets only as a last resort, ETA 2 minutes."

Josh yelled, "ETA 2 minutes, Ghillies off, repeat Ghillies off.

The squad ripped and cut at the camo suits with their KA-BARs, and kept firing. "Johns is down, yelled Simpson, "I think he bought it." "Grab his weapon and ammo," shouted Josh, as he kept firing with Figeroa's extra clip. The enemy was closing in, mainly from the north and east, but Evans spotted someone sneaking up from the west and fired a silent round right in his throat. "Keep watching our backs," Josh yelled, "good job." Josh ran dry in both M-16s, and pulled his Beretta.

The ground began to shake, Josh had hope. The Black Hawks, thanks to Josh's radio call, had developed a plan on the fly. Black Hawk leader positioned himself directly over the squad, firing its machine guns directly down on the enemy.

Two 7.62 mini guns and a 50 caliber Gatling created a formidable presence. His position, however was suicidal. The team leader, and Josh knew it couldn't last long.

Two of the other Black Hawks caught the enemy on the north and east slopes in a deadly crossfire. The 4th chopper had 3 Marines rappel down to the mountain top to bring extra ammunition with them.

As Josh's ranks and ammunition were replenished, team leader backed off from his untenable position, and along with chopper 4, joined the crossfire party. Samms, is down, yelled one of the replacements. Josh crawled over to him. He was the same comedian he had met at Boot Camp. He was gone. Fifteen minutes later quiet came over the battlefield. The occasional braying of a mule breaking the silence.

Cleanup was ahead. One hundred eighteen enemy dead. Over two hundred AK-47s, and other rifles, dozens of RPGs, several pounds of C-4, and loads of mortars. Add to that 24 mules (they stayed at the base of the hill, who said they were dumb?).

The sad news, four Marines were dead, five wounded, none of those were life-threatening. The news of the heroism displayed by Josh's squad, and the team of Black Hawks, was spreading quickly. Josh was promoted to Sergeant. A quick rise, but richly deserved. He'd been in-country for almost 11 months, now. How many missions? He had no idea.

New Years...2003

For New Years Eve, Connie and Jess had "double dated. Jess with Milo, and Connie on her first date with a boy named Carl Seasons. They went to the movies, out to eat, and then to Bennies. They didn't get in until 12:30, but that was the curfew for that night. Jess thought Connie was pretty forward with Carl, but she was also surprised at the lack of "come on" by Milo. Was it her, or him?

About 9:30 am New Years day the phone rang, and there was a mad rush to get to it. Jess leapt and pressed the speaker-phone. "Hi Josh," she gambled. "Hey sis, what's up?" They all gathered around. Jess said, "Glad you could make time out of your busy schedule to call home," she kidded. "If I'd known you were going to answer, I'd have waited," Josh said, he gave as good as he got.

"Son, we're all missing you," said Karen. "Me too," Mom. I'm still bored. "How's my four- legged girl friend?" Goldie's great, she's right here looking for your voice," Karen said. "She'll be 7 years old next month." "Man I feel old, why'd you have to remind me of that?"

"Hey Dad, I missed the Saints playoff games," he kidded. "How did we do?" "Well, you know the answer to that, Josh," he laughed, "but someday." "Absolutely," agreed Josh. "Well Dad, you can start calling me Sarge. They ran out of people to promote, and my name got pulled out of the hat." "That's fantastic son. The TV news said there was a lot of action around where you are. Is that true." "No way," replied Josh. "No enemies for miles around here," he said. "The town people bring us food and fruit almost every day, I'm getting fat."

"Hey Josh, its Connie. When you get back, I'll have my Real Estate license. I'll be able to sell you a house." "That's great little sister."

"I may be here a while longer, and then I'll have to save some money." "Not to worry," said Connie, "I can get you a house with a VA loan for only one dollar down payment, it's part of your veteran's benefits."

"Wow he said, we'll talk when I get back." (Josh had been directly depositing 95% of his pay, including the extra hazard/imminent danger bonus pay (not taxable), into a bank in Biloxi for a year now, only his Mom and Dad knew that).

Karen was happy that Connie was feeling like more a part of the family now. "And when will that be?" asked Karen. "Not sure Mom, I couldn't say on the phone if I knew, but probably another 6 months or so." Karen looked downcast, but wouldn't let it show in her voice, "Just stay safe, keep getting fat," she laughed.

"There's one more thing," Karen added. "Your Grandmother is thinking of getting married. She's right here, do you have anything to say to her?" "Hey Grandma, anybody married to you would be a lucky man." Be sure to enjoy the engagement. I hear it changes after that."

"He is the consummate politician," Karen thought, so did Dad, Jess, and Connie.

"But," Tom thought, "he's a Marine, and a good one. He knew the military. They don't just give many 20-year olds, the rank of Sergeant."

After Josh had his turn at the phone, and had to disconnect, the family sat together. "We'll see him soon," said Tom. "He'll be home for next Thanksgiving, that's the word I get from my military contacts." What he didn't tell them, was that those same sources, said he was in the hottest zone in all of Afghanistan. Tom could never tell the family.

New Years Day proceeded with Tom and Goldie watching 5 football games, or better described, with the remote control, parts of 5 football games.

Jess and Connie took over the kitchen. A ham, sweet potatoes, black eyed peas (a southern good luck tradition), followed with pumpkin pie for dessert.

Mr. Bergeron was invited, now that he was Doris' fiancée, He was sporting a pair of green checkered pants, a brown striped shirt, and yes, "the Full Cleveland."

Tom and Goldie decided to stay in the family room, watching the games, as long as possible.

At the dinner table, Doris made the announcement. "Max and I have been talking about marriage. But we've decided to delay any planning of a wedding. We care very much for each other, but we found out that if we marry, my Social Security will be cut in half. We're engaged, not going to see other people, but economics are what they are, and we need both retirement checks." Max was nodding all through the conversation, so they had planned this together.

Doris added, "But, we're going to be seeing a lot of each other, not just here. And I don't have a curfew."

Jess and Connie just looked at each other. Just what did that mean? Karen and Tom, were afraid that they knew.

Goldie's Chase...Spring 03

Goldie was in the prime of her life, and besides not having Josh with her, was also having the time of her life, as well. Whenever she was inside, due to rain, or whatever, she and Princess played chase throughout the house. The usual "track meet" began in the kitchen, then out to the family room, up the bonus room stairs, over Jess's bed, through the bathroom, over Connie's bed, down the stairs again, ending with Princess running under the dining room table. Where Goldie couldn't get to her because of all the chair and table legs.

One afternoon, after such and adventure, the rain had stopped and Grandma let Goldie outside for a while. As she lay under the Magnolia, Goldie saw some movement in the far corner of the yard. Goldie froze in an observing position as a small grey animal with big ears had crawled under the wooden fence, and started hopping towards the garden.

The little animal closed in on the garden gate. It hopped all around it, trying to figure a way to get to it's prize. It was on the far side of the garden again when Goldie thought, "Now! Go get it!," and she was off like a shot. The rabbit briefly hesitated, hearing, but not seeing the dog, then zip, it took off for the far reaches of the yard. The hunt was afoot.

"This thing is faster than Princess!" Goldie thought. They went round and round the yard and the garden. The rabbit never tried to escape back through the hole dug under the fence. "Why?" Goldie wondered. After about the 4th lap of the yard they were both tiring.

Suddenly the fence gate opened and Goldie heard Jess, "Goldie, we're home from school, where are you?" and at that very moment the rabbit ran right between Jess's feet, and out the fence gate. Jess jumped with a startled look on her face. She wondered, what was that?

Jess went to the hole and started walking away from the fence. Where did it go?

Jess closed the gate and walked around the outside corner of the fence, where the rabbit had disappeared, searching the yard outside the fence for any clues of the intruder. After walking about 30 feet, she saw a small hole dug under the fence where the rabbit could have entered. Presently, Goldie's nose was stuck through the hole, with just enough room to allow her to look out from the inside.

Jess knelt down in the overgrown area. About 10 more feet away was a scared, exhausted rabbit, frozen to a spot. Next to her were 5 little miniatures of her. Goldie could see too, now that she knew where to look. That's why mother rabbit hadn't used the tunnel under the fence for escape. She wanted to lead Goldie, or anything else, away from her precious babies. Just natural instinct.

Jess went inside and came out with Connie. She pointed out the "warren" so that she could see also, but not get too close. They both had gardening gloves on, and left a small dish of water, and a few vegetable scraps, like lettuce, carrot tops, and squash peelings in a pile beside the water. Then they left and filled in the hole beneath the fence.

She won't be using that anymore, too dangerous. They would check on Mrs. Rabbit from time to time. They didn't want to make her too dependent on the girls feeding her, but they wouldn't let her starve, either.

Then the girls came in the back yard, and congratulated Goldie for a job well done. They wrestled with her and kept telling her how good she was. Goldie was in Heaven...only missing Josh. She could feel a good nap approaching, with all the exertion from today.

Extra Crispy...March 03

It was a beautiful Saturday afternoon. There was a spring event planned at the Senior Center, for Sunday, and as usual, Doris was one of the key organizers. Max arrived at noon to pick her up, and deliver most of the supplies and props to the Center a day early. They were going to do (a very small production of) "South Pacific", including some songs by Rodgers and Hammerstein.

Doris was to perform "Some Enchanted Evening", while she assigned "I'm Going to Wash That Man Right Outta My Hair", to the three time widow, Betty Malbon. Betty wasn't very happy with her musical selection, but it was appropriate, and a good performance could land her husband #4.

They were having tropical stage settings of cardboard palm trees, a volcano in the background, crepe paper in Guava, Pineapple and Cherry, and about 200 floating balloons, of course, all tropical colors.

Max came to the door wearing pink pants and an orange shirt. Karen opened the front door and said, "I thought that South Pacific was tomorrow." Max replied, "It is, dear lady, it is."

Karen realized her 'faux pas', but, fortunately, Max did not. "I hate to impose on you ma'm," he began, "but we have so many props, and I have to bring many of them home for paint touch up and adjustment, plus the helium tank...we have to fill 200 balloons tonight. I was wondering if we might borrow your van, just for an hour or two today? Then to bring the props and balloons to the center tomorrow? Everything just won't fit in my car. I'm a very safe driver, no tickets, and it's just a short piece down the 2-lane road.

"Of course, Mr. Bergeron," Karen replied. "We're always eager to help the Senior Center however we can." "That's very nice of you, ma'm. We'll be extra careful, and won't be gone more than two hours."

Doris appeared, and Max told her the plan. Max and Doris thanked Karen and pretty quickly they went out to the "whale."

The Senior center at St. Helena was all abuzz in anticipation of tomorrow's big event. Men were already lining up folding chairs in front of the small "stage", and checking on the microphone and audio equipment borrowed from the High School auditorium. There was no school on the weekends, and the principal's mother and father were both active participants here, so he made the accommodation.

Max, Sammy, and Ralph loaded the van with crepe paper which would be attached to the cardboard props, several of the props which needed painting, the paint, paint thinner, and drop cloth. Also included were a box of tropical colored balloons which would be filled later that night (they just don't stay filled more than a day), and a cylinder of helium with a rubber valve which allowed for easy inflation.

After checking on the set up, Doris and Max hopped in the van, Doris had her 3rd glass of wine for the trip, out of a bottle Max had brought her. Max wouldn't join her, because he was driving. To top it off, Doris unwrapped one of her favorite "cheroot stogies."

They got home easily within the two hours Max had promised. Doris even had enough time to pour another glass of the wine, but she spilled almost all of it on the passenger side floor, when Max hit a bump. "Be careful," she said, "I know this stuff isn't cheap. And, now I'll be out here with Lysol to kill the smell." " The floor is black, just blame it on the paint thinner in the back floorboard," Max said quickly. "I knew I liked you for a reason," said the old woman. "You're smarter than you look"

They pulled into the shell driveway, Doris said "park over there, under that Oak tree. It will be cooler, and we can talk for a minute or two. "I think this engagement thing is perfect," said Doris. "We both get our full checks, I have free room and board, and get to see you all the time."

"I can't argue with that," said Max. "It works well for both of us, but, you can always move in with me, married or not. Remember that"

"You're such a sweetie," Doris said. "Let's go inside, and we'll visit some more, then you and Tom can unload the Van. They entered the house. And they both sat in the family room. Karen had gone to the store, she had left a note, Tom was at down by the dock, and the girls were upstairs.

In about five minutes.... "KaBoom!!!", the house shook like an earthquake tremor...it sounded like a bomb went off, outside. Doris, who had been nodding off, jumped out of her dream state. The girls ran downstairs to the front door and saw the whale engulfed in an inferno. They all looked at each other in shock, "My stogie," Doris said, "where's my stogie?" Jess ran to the phone and called 911 for the fire department. Tom ran inside, "Is everyone alright?" He saw everyone there, knew that Karen was at the store, and stared at the biggest fire he had ever seen.

"The fire department is on the way Dad," said Jess. Tom walked outside. Scattered on the yard were metal fragments, balloons, paint in tropical colors splattered everywhere, and at his feet was the front half of a bottle of "Scuttlebuck Hills".

Two fire trucks with sirens blaring, pulled into the front yard, and were able to contain the fire. The lower limbs of the old oak were scorched, but the damage was marginal, they may be saved. The grass was dead for a 20 yard radius.

The front shrubs were dead, the house was mottled with tropical paint colors, and had a 6-inch piece of shrapnel sticking through the roof. A couple of front windows had been blown inward, and the paint had blistered on the front door. Non-inflated balloons were everywhere, especially hanging from the trees. The van had it's windshield and all 4 side doors completely blown off. Pieces of glass and metal were everywhere, the tires were half melted, and smoldering, from the intensity of the heat. The mailbox had been blown out of the ground by the explosion.

"Let's see," said the fire marshal shaking his head while writing, "wine, paint, crepe paper, cardboard, a cigar, paint thinner, and yes, a canister of helium. That about it?" "A hell of a bomb. Sure glad you aren't with the terrorists, they could learn from you," he said to Grandma.

About that time Karen drove up. She stopped short of the "scene." Her face was a pale mixture of horror and bewilderment. She saw the whole family, so she knew no one was hurt.

A fireman came over to her and said, "Ma'm you can't stay here, we're still working a fire started by that old lady over there. Please go home."

"I am home," she mumbled, "I live here, that's my mother." "Oh, I'm sorry, I really am." Karen didn't know how to take that remark.

Doris was now going to have to face the music, times two. From Karen about her drinking, and from all the people at the Senior Center. The set of "South Pacific" was scattered everywhere in sight. Doris went back inside the house, and locked herself in her bedroom. She started making phone calls to people involved with the "production." Yes, there had been a terrible accident. No, she was unharmed. After 3 or 4 calls, she had morphed into the victim. People were feeling sorry for her, after telling her version of the "accident."

Mr. Bergeron said, "Mr. Flowers, I will be over tomorrow morning to help with the cleanup. I'll try to get a couple of the guys from the Center over to help, as well," he said. "Thanks Max," Tom said, we're going to need the help. "I'm sure the insurance adjuster will want to see, and photograph things as they are, before we start cleaning up." He went inside to call State Farm.

The adjuster was due tomorrow morning at 9 am. They didn't usually work on Sundays, but this was a special case, involving, auto, homeowners, and personal property.

The man from State Farm drove us at 9:00, sharp. Tom saw him through the window, and walked outside. He was a nice man, and introduced himself as Frank Browning.

"I thought I'd seen it all in 18 years at this," he said. "Hurricanes, tornados, floods, hailstorms. But, this tops it all," he said as he stood in the middle of the destruction. He started taking pictures of everything, and scribbling notes in the columns of the accident report on his clipboard. Tom said, "I'll get out of your way, just ring the bell, no it's melted too, knock if you need me. How about some coffee?"

No thanks Mr. Flowers. I need both hands for writing and handling the camera. It would be wasted on me, but thanks, anyway. After about an hour. Mr. Browning knocked on the door. "I'm finished," he said, "but I wanted to review my list with you to see if I have everything." Tom asked him in, and they sat in the family room.

"OK," the adjuster began, One 1997 Dodge Caravan, formerly blue, a hole in the roof of the house where shrapnel hit it, front door paint ruined, paint splattered on the front and roof of the house, possible six tree limbs which may need attention, two windows blown in, grass and landscaping dead. Does that about cover it?" he asked. "The mailbox," Tom said. "I didn't see it", replied Browning. Tom just stared at him. "We can't find it."

"Yeah, right," said the adjuster, "the explosion."

Max pulled into the driveway with two of his buddies, just as the man from State Farm, was leaving. "Hey, Max," shouted Tom from the front porch. "Come on in, we're good-to-go. I have a list for every one."

He turned to Karen. "I've called Mr. Ponder about the roof and the windows, and maybe power-washing the paint off the brick. We can do the clean up, painting, mailbox, and landscaping ourselves, but we need a professional for the roof and windows.

By the end of that Sunday, besides the roof and windows, things were almost back to normal, whatever that was.

A Big Job...March 2003

Tom was back at work Monday morning. He had given George Ponder a key to the house, so he could come and go as he pleased during the day. They had agreed on a $1,000 supervisory fee, and that was going to include putting a new mailbox in cement, at the end of the drive. Tom figured George would do most of the work himself, which was fine with Tom and Karen.

Tom was the Vice President of Human Resources, at the casino. This meant he was in charge of all the hiring done by the department heads, annual reviews for the employees, salary increases, promotions, discipline, and terminations.

Today, his meeting was with the VP of security, and the head "pit boss." There was a dealer who internal security suspected of collusion with outside agents, playing a "game" on the casino floor. Like many businesses, retail and the restaurant business were the worst, most of the casino stealing was from within. It was called "In-house shrinkage."

Casino security, and one of the pit bosses suspected that a blackjack dealer was "in cahoots" with a team who were involved in a old time scam. It went like this. Gambler "A" would be seated on the opposite side of the "pit" from his partner. He would be in a position to see the hole card of the dealer (one card was already dealt face up) if the dealer raised his card slightly higher than usual, while he was reviewing it. Gambler "B" was a player at the dealer's table. If the dealer had a combination adding up to twelve through sixteen, especially sixteen, then gambler "A" would signal his partner. If his partner was in a position to "double down, or split face cards, he knew the odds were with him. Blackjack has the best "player odds" of all casino games, about 44% with a "six deck shoe", but by knowing when to maximize your bets, a player could swing the game dollar winnings to 60%. Tom met with the casino professionals. They had videos of a short man with a ruddy complexion playing several different times at a blackjack table, almost always with the same dealer.

Every time, a certain Latino man would be on the other side of the "pit" at an angle to observe the dealer's hole card. The gambler, and his suspected cohort wore a number of disguises including fake mustaches, beards, and hats, to disguise their appearance. They saw that the dealer pulled his "hole card" higher and reviewed it longer than he did when the ruddy faced man wasn't playing.

The tapes were "damning evidence." The change of how the dealer reviewed the hole card was the killer. They had a cheat!

That afternoon, when the dealer in question, John Gabriel, checked in for work, security escorted him to the conference room on the fourth floor, When he saw the head of security, the head of the pit bosses, and Tom waiting for him, he broke down in tears.

"I needed the money," he cried. "If I didn't do it, someone else would." Security, and Tom saw a pot of gold at the end of the rainbow, with this remark. If he could name people involved in other scams, they had hit the jackpot.

After reviewing the video, the dealer just hung his head. "There's a way out of this for you," Tom said. Help us with others who you know are in a similar situation, and I won't recommend jail time. You can't work in another casino, ever, but you can avoid incarceration, and get on with your life, how does that sound, John?"

John liked that idea, and they all huddled for the rest of the afternoon. He gave them lots of information.

"Tom concluded, "OK, you have to check in for work. We'll say you called in late today. If the others get a hint of this, they will scatter into the wind. Just remember, we'll be watching you as closely…no make that more closely, than the others.

Do you have a signal, which tells them security is tighter than usual?" Tom asked. The dealer just nodded, keeping his head down. Most gamblers knew that on each day several random tables were selected for extra scrutiny. Therefore, the "not tonight" signal would be given. Tom continued, "Then give them the signal, but don't act any different. Act positive and friendly. You should be happy we're giving you a chance to avoid jail."

In the next 30 days, casino security was able to clean house, either firing or arresting 8 other dealers, and 1 pit boss, about 10% of the floor staff. They also arrested the cheating gamblers and made sure the other casinos got all the photos and information. It was a "close knit" community. If nothing else, it let the employees know that they were all being watched.

Net revenues at the Beau Rivage went up 3%, without changing a thing. Casino security, and Tom were heroes in the corporate offices. One of the dealers threatened to file a discrimination suit, which was Tom's bailiwick, but several ethnic groups and both genders had been involved, so it would never amount to anything.

Tom was smart enough to know, from his personnel training in the military, that when you disciplined a female, you had another female in the room as a witness to what was said, and not said. He made sure that he, and his subordinates worked that way with all the "protected classes" of employees.

April-May 2003, Decisions

Graduation for Jess and Connie was just around the corner. Tom and Karen told the girls that they wanted to have a discussion with each of them, individually, regarding their future plans.

They all agreed to meet on Saturday, April 19th. Connie in the morning, before she went to the real estate office, and Jess at 5:30 when she came home from "The Edge."

Karen looked at Tom and said "I wonder if we're pushing them too hard? I can't even remember when I was eighteen, and had to think about the future." Tom responded, " We have to get them thinking about their lives. And we need to know what their higher education plans entail."

Both girls had been accepted by USM, in Hattiesburg, and also Mississippi State, in Starkville. But neither had followed up with a campus visit, or more correspondence. Were they just stalling?

Tom and Karen had many discussions about this in the ensuing days. They couldn't figure out what the girl's plans might be, if they even had any plans. Tom, with his military background, hated surprises, and this was important.

Saturday finally came, and that early that morning Connie, Karen, and Tom walked down to the water (with Goldie, tagging along). Tom noticed a good sign during the walk. Connie had a manila envelope with her. After they made a little small talk, Karen, who had noticed by now, asked "What's in the envelope, Connie?"

A big smile crossed Connie's face as she said, "It's my real estate license. I passed the test the day after I turned 18."

Connie excitedly continued, "I want to be a real estate agent, I love it. I've been around it for awhile now, I think it's in my blood. And Mr. Guilotte said he would take me on as an agent in his mentor program."

"It's like, he'll put me with one of his best agents, and I'll shadow them on all their appointments for six months. Then I'll be on my own".

"The only problem is, I have a favor to ask of both of you," she said. "What's that," asked a smiling Karen. She had never seen the girl so happy. Connie began, "Mr. Guilotte, and the agents I spoke with, all say that you don't make much money in this job for the first couple of years. So even though I'm 18, I was wondering…"

Karen cut her off, "You don't have to wonder, you're family. Besides that, we already have money put aside for your education, per our promise to Vicky. So this is your education. We respect that."

Tom added, "You stay here just as you have in the past. I still think we need a curfew, but it will be later than it is now. And I know it's expensive to get started, license fees, real estate dues, you'll need your own car, and probably a laptop computer. We'll take the start-up money from your fund, and then give you a monthly allowance from it. But, your allowance will not be for food or housing, that stays free, as long as you want. And I think I can speak for Karen, we're both very proud of you and support your decision 100%."

Connie was glowing with excitement. Goldie could sense the positive conversation, and added to the happy occasion by jumping around and running in circles around the three of them.

"I have one favor to ask," said Karen, "Don't keep us guessing for so long in the future," she laughed.

Connie walked back to the house to get dressed for work. Tom looked at Karen and said, "Wow, she did all that without telling us?" "She did a great job," Karen replied. "One down, one to go. I hope it turns out as well as this one."

When Jess arrived home, she was changing into some jeans and yelled downstairs. "Mom, Dad, I'll be right out. She arrived at the dock, Goldie was trailing behind. Jess had familiar, manila envelope. This time it was Tom's turn to ask, "What's in the envelope, Jess?"

"It's my future," she said matter of factly. And I hope you'll approve. I've given this a lot of thought the last couple of years. Ever since we went to that Mexican Restaurant in San Antonio, I've been hooked on cooking, you've seen that."

"I've been accepted into the School of Hotel & Culinary Arts, at The University of Southern Mississippi, Gulf Coast Campus, in Gulfport," she said. "Since I'd already been accepted to USM in Hattiesburg, this was an automatic OK." Jess added, "It's a 2-year course, and when I graduate, I'll have no problem finding a job here or anywhere else in the country, the world for that matter. I love cooking, you know that, and I can learn the hotel business."

"There are some things we'll have to work out, but..." "Stop," Karen interrupted her, just as she had Connie. "There's nothing to work out," she said. "You're family. You'll live here, eat here and sleep here, just like now. There will be a reasonable curfew. We'll pay the tuition (which would be much less than at USM), out of the college fund we've saved for you, and be able to give you a small allowance each month."

Tom added, "You can keep driving the Accord, until Josh returns. When he does get back, we kept the insurance money from the "whale", and we'll get you a car of your own."

Karen said, "It's your decision, but you can keep working at 'The Edge' on weekends and holidays if you wish, but we want you to focus on your schoolwork. We can't have an 18-year old burn out."

"There's just one thing," Karen continued. Uh-Oh, Jess thought. Karen said, "You're going to have a roommate." Jess blinked, not understanding. "It will be Connie," Karen explained. "She's going into real estate, and is going to be here at home for a couple of more years."

Jess was ecstatic. "So she told you, this morning, right," said Jess, as Goldie was doing her running in circles act again. Tom and Karen looked at each other. The last to know, except for Doris, who didn't enter into this picture.

"One thing I just thought of," added Tom. "The Beau Rivage has a great management training program. Once you graduate, I think you should give it, us, some consideration."

"You couldn't work in the casino area until you turned 21, but we could start you in the hotel and restaurant areas for the first few months, and save the casino till last." He added, "But, you'll have to earn any job interviews there with your grades, no favoritism allowed. And, your interviews would be with my boss, who will be especially tough on you. Just something to keep in the back of your mind." Jess, gave them a big hug, and ran off to the house, Goldie close behind.

Karen looked at Tom and said, "I think we did OK, but man, am I tired." I feel like I've been through the mill, " answered Tom. "I'm beat, and I'm happy it's over."

"It's never over," stated Karen, "never. How about a glass of wine?" They went back to the house, hand in hand. Graduation was right around the corner, and the girls both had wind in their sails.

Connie's Car, Summer 03

The girls graduation from De'Iberville High School was typically middle America, apple pie, only with Grandma thrown in. The senior graduating class had grown to 276 students. Jess and Connie were both in the top one third, and had almost perfect attendance. Connie was going to take a couple of weeks off getting things together for her new real estate career. Tom was helping her shop for a car, reading the classified ads, checking the internet, etc. After about a week, they hit pay dirt. There was an ad Sunday, in the local *Sun Herald* for a 1999 Jeep Cherokee. The ad read "1999 Jeep Cherokee, only 22,000 miles, well cared for. $7,800, OBO (or best offer). Tom liked the sound of this, so did Connie.

From Tom's perspective, it was a car with a great reputation for quality, it was in the price range they had agreed on, and it had lower than expected mileage for it's age. Connie liked it because it was a "cool" car, and she needed something which she could show houses in, and store her paraphernalia, as well.

Tom called on the ad, and spoke to the owner. His name was Joey Pinella. He was in the merchant marines, and had only driven it about 3 months a year. With the Gulf War going on, the shipping companies were operating at near 100% capacity. His father had died, about a month ago, and had left his Dodge Ram pickup to his son. He liked that better than the Jeep, so he was selling. He was barely using 1 vehicle, 2 was a real waste.

He gave Tom directions to his house, which was in Ocean Springs, adjacent to Biloxi, just east across the Highway 90 bridge. Tom made an appointment for 1:00 that afternoon, and asked the man if he could bring his friend from the motor pool with him to examine the car. Joey said, "No problem, it runs great, but if it was my daughter, I'd do the same thing." Tom got on the phone with his friend, and luckily he was available.

At 1:00, Tom, Connie, and Tom's friend, Lanny, pulled in front of a house which had a silver Dodge Ram, and a red Jeep Cherokee, parked in the driveway. Connie loved it at first sight. Obviously, the man was expecting them.

Joey Pinella walked out the front door wearing an Atlanta Braves baseball hat, jeans, and a t-shirt that said, "Grateful Dead 2000 Tour."

He introduced himself, to the others. And asked, "You want to take it for a spin?" There was nothing Connie wanted more. Frankly I know nothing about cars, except how to drive one.

Tom turned and said "Connie, you and Lanny take it out for five minutes, I'll stay here with Mr. Pinella. After talking with Joey, for a few minutes, it turned out that Joey's aunt worked at the Beau Rivage as head cage teller. "I knew that name sounded familiar," Joey said." My aunt Esther, speaks very highly of you."

"Glad to hear it," said Tom, "she's one of our best." When Connie and Lanny returned, Lanny gave Tom a big nod. They had stopped at the Exxon station down the road, which allowed Lanny to check out the belts, listen to the engine run, look for any oil leaks…everything checked out fine. Then he drove it about a half mile down the road to check the suspension and brakes. Lanny was satisfied. They returned to the Exxon and Connie drove back to her father, and Mr. Pinella.

"Connie, what do you think?" Tom asked. "It's a dream, I like it a lot!" said Connie. Tom turned to Joey and said, "We'll give you $7500 cash, what do you think?"

Joey stuck his hand out and they shook on it. Tom said, "I can give you a personal check today, for a $500 deposit, and bring you a cashier's check for the remainder, tomorrow.

"Mr. Flowers, I don't need to have a cashier's check from you. Just give me a personal check for the entire amount, and if you need time to move funds, I'll hold it a day or two."

Tom thought about the logistics and replied, "That's most gracious Mr. Pinella, the check will be good, Tuesday, after 2 pm. He wrote the check, Joey signed a "bill of sale" Tom had brought with him, they shook hands again, and they drove away, Connie in her new, awesome Jeep.

Tom took Lanny home and returned home to find the family reviewing Connie's new car. "We need to talk about plates and registration," Tom told Connie. "No," Dad, said Connie, "I went online last week, and have all the blank paperwork needed for DMV." All I have to do is fill in the make, model, and VIN number, and I'm set." Tom looked at Karen. They were impressed.

Jess

Jess knew that she would really have to focus on the hotel side of her education. It also involved a great deal of math calculations, which was not her strength. Profit and loss statements, cash flow charts, inventory turn rates, payroll expense percentages, occupancy forecasts, and more.

A soufflé was easy for her. But, in order to graduate near the top of her class, she would have to "get" the hotel operations.

She had seen that the keys to room bookings were nearby attractions, quality of room for the dollar, and cleanliness with regular updating of the rooms, and public areas.

The lobby and front desk appearance were also a big factor. This was fairly straightforward, theoretically speaking, that is without knowing the budget for capital improvements, renovations, and so forth.

Conventions were another matter, entirely. There were plenty of "sharks" swimming in the same tank, and it was all about sales. You had to call on corporations, sell your hotel and it's amenities, the surrounding area attractions, the hotel's convention halls and "break out rooms", and the always important, "Great place to bring the family to for an extended long weekend." Guest speakers had to be "comped" and you had to have special lighting, a dais, microphones, and backups for everything. A dead mike, with the CEO speaking, and this Corporation would never return your phone call again.

Food and beverage, i.e. the restaurants and bars in the hotel itself, had to be very diverse and accommodating. Most large hotels today had at least 3 restaurants, and 2 bars. For the restaurants, there was usually the breakfast buffet/lunch eatery, and then a very nice place, with steaks to seafood.

Better places usually had a "theme" dinner place with an ethnic setting, such as Chinese, Italian, or Mexican, depending on what area of the country you were in.

The bars, at a minimum, usually consisted of a "meat market" where the swingers from out of town could feel young again, and an "off the lobby" bar, complete with working and meeting areas for the "Yuppies", where they could gather, dissect the day's activities, then go to dinner with a group.

The F&B business was very specialized. Many hotels leased the space to specialists, who paid a percentage of their gross as rent. There were arguments for and against that. The prevailing theory at the time was that if you were a large entity, such as the Beau Rivage, then you had the wherewithal, and structure, to do it yourself. If you were a smaller, single entity, you tried to lease out the business to professionals.

Special events were much like conventions. These were usually large corporations holding their regional sales meetings, complete with charts, graphs, and "Power Point" presentations.

You needed lots of rooms with twin beds, as some businesses were making their junior staff share, but full mini-bars, which enjoyed excessive mark-ups, partly to pay for the shrinkage. An executive making $125,000 per year, thought it clever to drink the vodka or gin, and spend an hour replacing it with water, and super-gluing the bottle cap to make it appear unopened.

This was all in addition to the millions of dollars lost every year with guests taking toiletries, towels, robes, clothes hangers, lamps, TV remote controls, light bulbs, sheets, toilet paper, pillows...the list was endless. A guest from Atlanta, who kept their home thermostat at 79 degrees in the summer, thought nothing of cranking the hotel's AC down to 65.

Open House, Summer 03

Connie attacked the real estate business, with her typical aggressive style. She knocked on doors of "For Sale By Owners" offering her Broker's marketing strategies, calling "Expired Listings" and holding "Open Houses" hoping to capture clients who were in the market to buy, and didn't have an agent representing them.

Since she didn't have any of her own "listings" yet, she was holding houses open for other agents. It was good for the other agents, because they got the extra exposure for their Sellers.

Connie had heard that very seldom did you actually sell the house you were holding open. New agents used "Open Houses" to try to meet people who were in the market to buy, and weren't working with another agent. She would offer to email them listings from the MLS which met their criteria. Then, she would set up appointments for the homes they showed interest in.

Email was far less intrusive than a phone call. No dinner interruptions, no child wailing in the background. They could study the listings from work or home at their convenience. Many older agents in Connie's office weren't tech-savvy. They didn't know about emails, or the technology they were missing. And, Connie wasn't going to tell them.

This Sunday she was looking forward to her open house. It was on the south side of the 110 bridge in a subdivision called "Cedar Point" The homes there were $200-$275,000, depending on size. It was a popular neighborhood. It was near Keesler and a fairly new elementary school was less than a half mile away.

She had done her homework. She had printed out the MLS listings for all the other homes for sale in the community. She also had a list of all the homes sold here in the past 12 months.

She could talk about the area like an expert, which is what Buyers wanted in an agent.

She put up three "Open House" signs…one at the entrance to the community from the main street, with 2 balloons attached, one at the right hand turn you had to make to get there, and one in front of the house. She got there at 1:50, used her lockbox key to get in, and went through turning on lights, plumping pillows, setting out flyers for the house, and a stack of her business cards. All done and ready for business.

Three hours later, she turned out the lights and locked the door on the way out. No one had come. Well, nothing ventured, nothing gained. You just have to keep trying.

Bad Trip, September 2003

Sergeant Josh Flowers, was leading his squad into the northeastern hills for another mission. This was a longer trip than usual, taking about an hour's flight time from Baghram. He still had Evans and Simpson, his 2 most experienced men, who had been with him during the hilltop attack in December. The others ranged from Pvt. Fields, who had joined the squad 3 months ago and seen plenty of action, to a new man, Pvt. Swanson, who was going into his 1st operation. He had fearful eyes, Josh had seen it before. Had he been like that in the beginning, he asked himself? Probably so, he let out a smile.

There were 3 squads, and 3 Black Hawks. The overall platoon leader, was the same Captain Hanks whom Josh had worked with in numerous battlefields over the past months. They worked well together, and had mutual respect for each other's ability.

They had been sent to relieve a platoon who had observation duty near the Pakistani border. They had been in position for a week, and it was time to rotate out. Just like the platoon they were replacing, they would have 3 observation camps about 500 meters apart, almost a mile of distance, on a hilltop, facing east. They were to report back to Baghram on the radio, on all Taliban movement. If needed, they could call in drones or heavier fire power, but that wasn't the mission. The military was looking to see just who was supplying the enemy from Pakistan, but the "brass" were very cautious about upsetting our Pakistani "allies", and wanted no border incidents to shake that fragile friendship, if at all possible.

The Black Hawks landed on the west side of the hill, like the squads, about 500 meters apart, and shielded from the border. The incoming squads deployed, the relieved squads boarded, total time on the ground for the aircraft, less than 45 seconds.

Josh's squad was the furthest north of the three, with Captain Hanks taking the traditional, commanding, middle position.

In less than an hour, all 3 squads reported as being in place. Then, Hanks reported to base, that the platoon position was set. All they had to do was watch and wait. It didn't take long.

After about 30 minutes, mortars and rockets started dropping from the sky onto all 3 positions. AK-47 fire was everywhere. It had been a well conceived trap. Someone must have tipped off the enemy about the platoon rotation, and they used the time between one platoon going down the west side of the hill, and the replacements getting up the hill to set up attack positions in close proximity.

The men took what little cover they had, while Hanks radioed the base. Base Command, Niner-3 calling in. "Heavy incoming mortar and rocket fire sir. We need aerial assistance ASAP. The base answered, "Niner-3, Niner-3. Can you tell which side of the border the enemy fire is coming from? Repeat can you see the origin of the attack?"

Hanks answered, "That's a negative sir, too much smoke and confusion, my men are getting pummeled, request wings with eyes, ASAP, sir." He wanted F-14s who could see the attack. He couldn't direct drones under this heavy fire. "I don't care where the attackers are, we need help."

After about 30 seconds of a heated discussion back at Baghram Control, he heard, "Request denied, Niner-3, repeat, request denied, can't fire at the border, can't take that chance." Hanks was stunned. He had heard stories of troops being abandoned due to politics, in Viet Nam, he just never thought it would happen again. Hanks bellowed, "Then request immediate extraction, Base command, repeat, request immediate extraction at previous drop off point., about 500 meters west of current position."

"Birds will be in the air in 5, ETA 1-hour, repeat ETA 1-hour." One hour, Hanks thought, they weren't going to last 10 more minutes. His squad already had casualties, probably the other squads did as well.

"Flowers and Nash, we are leaving to the drop zone for extraction," Hanks said into the radio. "Fall back, repeat, fall back." Hanks elaborated, "One half of each squad at a time with covering fire. Spotter-sniper teams, remain just over the ridge, and cut down as many as you can if they decide to advance."

Josh sent 5 of his squad over the ridge, he stayed behind with 4 others to provide cover, emptying clips of ammunition toward where the enemy was located. In about 10 more minutes, the first to retreat had secured positions, so Josh and the 4 others scrambled over the ridge.

He looked at his men. Only 2 flesh wounds which he could see, they had been lucky...so far. It only took the enemy a couple of minutes to recalibrate their mortars, now landing closer. They regretted giving up the high ground, but it was their only chance to survive.

It was a deadly retreat, Marines dragging other, wounded or dying Marines behind them. In another 30 minutes, the entire platoon had set up defensive positions in 3 places at the bottom of the hill. There was a small gully, about 3 feet deep, with some rocks on the edge which provided some cover. The spotter-sniper teams had been the last to join them.

"Casualty report," Hanks screamed into the Radio. Josh came back, "1 gone, two injured, one seriously." Then Nash's squad, "2 gone, 1 minor wound," said Nash. Hanks had 2 dead as well, plus one bad injury, a gut wound. "Evac in 15," Hanks reported to the squad leaders.

Hanks screamed, "Enemy advancing down the hillside, slow them down," Hanks knew they weren't going to make it for 15 minutes. And then a beautiful sight appeared.

An AC-130 gunship came in, fast and low, between the Marines and the enemy. It shredded the enemy with a hellacious fire. The Taliban tried to hide behind rocks, and take cover in small outcroppings. This "Angel of Death" was the one thing they feared over everything else.

The gunship made a tight turn and came back for another pass. Spraying the mountainside with it's 25mm Gatling guns. Thank God for the Air Force, Josh thought, and he turned to the welcome sight of incoming Black Hawks. His squad scrambled on the one nearest them. They were still under fire, but it was less than before the AC-130 had arrived. They carried the dead and wounded onto the chopper. Josh was the last to get on. Wait, where was Swanson, the new man. Josh scanned the area, every second on the ground endangered everyone. There he was, behind a rock, too scared to move.

"Come on, Marine," Josh yelled. Swanson didn't move. "Thirty seconds, cover me, I going to get him." Josh leapt off the chopper and raced to the frozen Marine. Josh grabbed him and pulled and pushed until he got him on board. Josh jumped on the chopper. His men extending their hands, pulling him on board as the Black Hawk zoomed away.

"I'm hit," Josh couldn't believe those words came from his mouth. A searing flame ran up his leg. He was racked with pain. One of the flight crew had a battlefield morphine injector and administered it to Josh. It still hurt like hell, but he was going to make it.

Ninety minutes later, Josh was sitting in the field hospital at Baghram. The pain was intense, but was on a morphine drip, so it was becoming more manageable with every minute.

Deutschland

Josh had been hit at the top of his right femur. It wasn't life-threatening, but it needed attention. One quick look at the injury from a doctor back at Baghram was all it took. "You're going to Germany, Sgt. Flowers. Next flight to Ramstein Air Base is at 09:00 tomorrow, I'm writing the orders now.

Josh complained," It doesn't feel that bad. I think a good night's sleep and I'd be OK." "You're heavily sedated right now Sergeant, if I removed that drip, after an hour, you'd be begging to get on that plane." Josh didn't think so, but orders were orders. He'd be back soon.

Josh was loaded onto a C-130 Hercules the next morning, with about 30 or 40 others. The flight time was to be 6 hours and 30 minutes, to the base in southwest Germany. When they landed he noticed 2 things instantly. There were trees, flowers, and grass. Things he hadn't seen in a long time. And secondly, the air was rich. His lungs devoured the fresh, crisp air.

After about a half hour he was loaded onto an ambulance for the 15 minute drive to Landsthuhl Regional Medical Center. This is operated by the U.S. Military as the primary medical facility serving injured troops from the middle east. LRMC, as it is called, has been in operation since 1953, and has several updates and expansions since then.

On Josh's first afternoon there he was examined by a internist and then an orthopedist. The intern treated the wound, dressed it better than it had been at Baghram, and started Josh on a course of antibiotics via the drip he was already on for pain and fluids.

The orthopedic wanted to get X-Rays and an MRI on the right hip. He thought he knew the status of Josh's injury, but a piece of shrapnel or bullet lodged into the joint would complicate things.

After those procedures, Josh was scheduled to see the orthopedic doctor the next morning at 09:00. He was sent back to his ward, for the evening. He could get a good night's sleep. Josh was happy with that. He was tired, it wasn't just the drugs, but he had been through a great deal that day. He was beat.

But he was also hungry. He hadn't eaten since a little coffee and toast that morning…a world away in Afghanistan. They must have known, because in about 5 minutes a young German orderly came to his bed with a huge steak and fries. "Hier est ihr abend essen, bitte." Josh couldn't speak German, but he knew what the young man was saying (here is your dinner.)

Josh awoke with a start, halfway through the evening. No, there wasn't an alarm, no mortars, no gunfire. Then he remembered where he was, and what he was doing. And his hip was screaming with pain. The nurse had given him a button to push if he needed a quick shot of extra morphine. He had laughed, then. Not so funny, now. He finally located the device and squeezed the soft button. In about 5 seconds, the pain lessened, considerably. Josh was glad he didn't have to ring the "call bell", there were about 30 other soldiers in his ward, some far worse off than he.

After breakfast the next morning, he waited until the doctor called for him, and he was loaded into a wheelchair, and rolled, along with his drip, to an examining room. The doctor was looking at his tests, and reading the radiologist's reports on them when Josh was wheeled in.

"Well, sir, when can I go back," Josh asked. The doctor answered, "We're going to keep you here for a week or so and make sure there are no complications or infections, then we'll send you on your way. The wound has no foreign matter in it, so it shouldn't be any problems, but I'd rather be on the safe side of things." Great, thought Josh. Back to the squad!

The doctor saw that Josh didn't understand. "Sergeant Flowers, I've contacted your CO, already," Josh was still smiling. "No, sergeant, you're going to need a new hip. You're going stateside. I'm setting up a referral, right now. I hate to be the one to tell you, but your fighting days are over."

Josh felt like a cement block had landed on his head. Did Josh hear him correctly? "Are you sure, Sir? Can't you be mistaken?" he asked. The doctor replied in a very concise tone, "I've been through years of school and, now 8 years of medical practice. I couldn't be more sure...the top of your right femur is shattered...it's 100%."

"But sir," he begged, "if I can't fight, then I can't be a Marine. The past 2 years, I've been a Marine."

"I understand that soldier," he said. "Total hip replacement is a safe, well-proven procedure. In a young man like you, it won't even slow you down much. But in certain situations, it could get dislocated. You, and those around you, would be at a greater risk. I'm sorry to be the bearer of bad tidings."

Josh was still in denial. There must be a way around this, he thought. I'll sleep on it.

That night, he woke again, with pain. He pushed the button, and fell back asleep. The dreams were disturbing, but so were his thoughts when he was awake. What would he do? How would he live? So many questions. He had not had to worry about making life decisions for the last 2 years, just followed orders, and made combat decisions based on his training.

His fourth day at LRMC was one he'd never forget. A young lieutenant opened the door to the ward and shouted "Commanding Officer in the ward, all men at ease," which was good, because most of them couldn't stand if they wanted to.

A two-star Army General named Jacobs marched into the ward, followed by a Marine Colonel.

They strode to the foot of Josh's bed. Josh gave a crisp salute which they returned. The General said, "Colonel Lee is the ranking Marine here at Ramstein, where I am the CO." He then deferred to the Colonel.

"Sergeant Flowers," he spoke. "Sir, yes Sir", Josh answered.

"For exceptional valor in the face of enemy fire, Afghanistan,12 September, 2003, you have been chosen to receive this honor." The colonel opened a 3x5 walnut colored box, and said, "This is the Navy and Marine Corps Commendation Medal with "V" device. This is the highest honor the Marine Corps can issue. I am proud to be the one to bestow the thanks of a forever grateful Corps." Then he, and the General snapped a salute, which Josh answered with a shaking hand.

"Thank you Sirs," Josh responded. Immediately, the General said, softly, "No, son," like the Colonel here said, "Our thanks is to you." They turned "right face" and left the ward.

It was then, the ward erupted with yells, shrieks, whistles and applause. Some of the men took to banging the ends of their crutches on the floor. The hospital staff came in and gave him a standing "O", since most of the men couldn't.

Josh looked at the medal. It was hexagonal, embossed with a gold eagle, and hung on a green ribbon. He thought, yeah, I had decorations and ribbons before, lately the Purple Heart, but this is something else, indeed.

Josh slept better that night, but still woke up with the same questions of the future. And a new one started creeping into his head…"Why Me?"

Josh was examined again by both of his doctors on day six. "I think you're about ready," the internist said, "I see no problems here." The orthopedic added, "We have your surgery cleared. The medal didn't hurt." he smiled, "Just kidding. I think you can call home, now. We didn't want to worry your family until the situation was stable, but now you're right on track."

"You can tell them you're being sent to the Kelsey-Seybold clinic in Houston in a few days. They specialize in joint replacement. The time from surgery to full recovery is 8-10 weeks." The Doctor added, "You'll be able to walk in about 4, but give them the longer estimate to be able to feel like yourself again. You'll have the surgery, and be able to go home in 5-7 days. Do they live close to Houston?" Josh was still in a fog, with very conflicting emotions.

Luckily, today was Sunday. Josh waited until 15:00 to make the call, allowing for the 7-hour time difference. Back in Biloxi, Tom was the only one of the family already out of bed. He heard some stirrings…and then the phone rang. Who could be calling this early? Tom wondered.

"Hi Dad," Josh said. "Good Sunday morning," he continued, trying to stay in good spirits. Tom responded, "Good morning yourself, hold on, I'll get the rest of the 'wild bunch' out of bed," as he rose from his chair.

"No, not yet, Dad. I need to talk to you first, and I don't have a time limit, today." Tom sat back down in his chair and listened to his son's story. After about 10 minutes, Tom said very positively, "Son, you're coming home. That's all that matters to me, and that's all the family will care about as well. We're excited. You're injured, but it's not permanent."

"But, Dad," Josh began…Tom immediately interrupted, "No buts, allowed, Josh, your family will be ecstatic. And your Mother and I will meet you in Houston."

Once you know your travel plans, let me know. We'll come back here after you are out of the hospital. I know the Military can set up your PT here, at Biloxi's VA Hospital. Now that we're past that, I'm getting the family out of bed, I'll fill them in on the details later."

In about 30 seconds, the family had surrounded the speaker-phone. The girls were squealing, Karen was yelling, and Goldie was barking. She didn't know why, but she felt electricity on the air, and wanted to show her support.

The call lasted about 5 more minutes, with Josh mainly saying a (falsely upbeat) "Hey, I'll see you soon," or "Dad will explain later." They disconnected, and Tom had everyone sit down around the table to tell them the circumstances of Josh's return. Afterward, everyone was still excited, but just a little anxious. "I know plenty of people who had hip replacement surgery," he said. "Two of which, Henry Choi, and Mandy Brown, I work with."

"They get along great. I wouldn't even know about it, but they were swapping stories in the employee 'break room' one day when I was there. Josh will be fine," he promised.

A couple of days later, Josh had been processed out of LRMC, with paperwork routing him to the Clinic in Houston. The same young orderly, had helped him gather his gear, flight and hospital paperwork, MRI and X-Ray films, and helped dress him in the sweats and sneakers they had provided for him. It was the first time in 20 months he wasn't wearing his Marine Corps BDUs...it was uncomfortable, emotionally. He still had the drip attached. He didn't like that either, but it was needed.

The orderly wheeled him out to a waiting ambulance. From there a few minutes to Ramstein, and a Military transport to Houston.

Two airmen helped him into the back of the vehicle.

The German orderly shook his hand and said, "Gehen sie mit Gott," he said, (Go with God). Josh smiled back at him, and said something he had been practicing, "Danke fir alles", (Thanks for everything), and the orderly broke out into a big smile.

Josh was going home. Well, first to Houston, then home.

Biloxi...September 2003

After Josh's phone call and Tom's explaining the details, the family settled into it's standard Sunday rhythm. They had started having the family meal at noon, rather than one, which allowed Connie to have her "Open Houses" between 2 and 5. They were almost always finished with the meal by 1 or 1:15, at the latest.

Tom had explained that the next Sunday he and Karen would be in Houston, they would probably leave on Tuesday and be gone about a week, returning with Josh in tow, reclaiming his old room. It was good that it was on the 1st floor. Houston was just a little more than 400 miles to the west, Interstate 10, all the way, so no more than a 7-hour drive.

Jess would be in control of next week's meal, but she was already doing most of the preparation, anyway. Jess would be in her classes during the week, so 2 or 3 days next week, Connie would work from home, doing her MLS searches and emails from her laptop. Her busiest times were the weekend, when Jess was not in school. It would work out well.

Max arrived exactly at noon. He was resplendent, in bluish paisley slacks, a chartreuse sweater vest over a pink striped shirt, and of course, the white shoes and belt. Doris came out of her room when she heard the doorbell, and escorted Max into the family room.

Tom told Max the news of Josh's return, but not the details. "I look forward to meeting the young man," Max said. "We could swap war stories together."

Jess and Connie looked at each other and smiled. Jess whispered to Connie, "Yep, when he was in a battle, they were still riding horses."

Connie stifled a laugh and whispered back to Jess, "Has he looked at himself in the mirror? Those clothes, you could get blinded looking at colors like that." "Girls," Karen snapped. "Manners please. No whispering at the table." Of course, Max was oblivious.

After lunch, everyone had something to do. Doris and Max went to the Senior Center. Connie had an open house, gathered her signs, and put them in her Jeep.

Karen went to the store to stock up on supplies, and toiletries for Josh. Tom took his car in to have it serviced in advance of their trip. Jess went upstairs to the computer to study for school on Monday. About an hour into her study, the downstairs phone rang.

She ran down the stairs, 3 at a time. "Hey, sis," Josh said with false cheer, "how're you doing.""Great now that we'll see you soon." She continued, "Are you OK? You don't seem like yourself?" "I'm great," he answered. "I'm just a little tired," he explained." Even to himself, he sounded different. He decided to keep it short, he felt a little "down" and knew he couldn't fool her forever, they were too close.

"Jess, can you relay a message to Mom and Dad for me? Tell them I'll be flying into Houston early Wednesday morning, and go directly to the Clinic. Dad has the address."

"Sure," she replied. "They were planning on leaving here on Tuesday or Wednesday, depending on your schedule. It's an easy drive to Houston."

"Thanks, a bunch, Jess. I've got to go now, but I sure look forward to seeing you all, real soon. And take care of my 4-legged girl friend, I miss her too." "No problemo," Jess smarted back. "She's going to be so excited."

Houston...October 2003

Josh landed at Elllington Field in Houston, Wednesday morning, October 1, 2003. A military ambulance was again his transportation, to the Kelsey-Seybold Clinic. He had been pre-registered, and was brought to an examining room to wait for his doctor.

About 5 minutes later a distinguished gentleman walked in, and greeted Josh. "Hello Mr. Flowers. I'm Dan Wright. I'll be the surgeon who performs your procedure. I've reviewed the films which were emailed to me. They did a good job in Germany getting you ready. I foresee no problems. Do you have any questions or concerns you want me to address?"

"Mister Flowers", Josh thought, that sure sounds strange, but that's who he was, now. He asked Dr. Wright about hospital and recovery times, and he got basically the same answers he received at LRMC.

"Recovery time is 4-6 weeks before you can walk without a walker or cane. After that you should be 95% in 6 months. At your age you'll do very well. In 9 months, you won't even know you've had surgery, except for the banana shaped scar on your hip. Forgetting the surgery is the only thing you have to worry about."

"What do you mean," asked Josh. The Doctor answered, "After this surgery, people get careless and forget their rules. "Here they are, (1) We don't want you picking things up off the floor, bending from the waist. (2) We always want to maintain a 45-degree angle between your chest and your thigh, so no crunches, or sit-ups (3) no crossing your legs, at night, sleep with a pillow beneath your legs."

"You follow those rules, and you'll never have a problem," he said. Your surgery is scheduled for 1st thing in the morning. Do you have any questions about the surgery? "Yes," Josh said, "I have no idea what this operation does. Can you explain it to me?"

Dr. Wright smiled. "Most people don't want to know, but I've heard you're not like most people. And, with the background you have, you can probably handle it. Here it is" he said. "We open up your leg to reveal the hip area. In your particular case, there has been some muscle damage as well."

"I'll evaluate that. We pull the muscle and connective tissue out of the way to get to the hip socket. Your hip area is probably a mess, which I will repair, on the way out, after implanting the prosthetic." "Prosthetic," Josh said in a panicked voice.

Dr. Wright smiled. "No, young man, not a 'peg-leg' or anything like that. We in the medical field use that term to describe anything we implant in a load bearing area. Let me continue, and you'll understand."

Josh nodded, and the doctor continued. "We remove the hip bone from the socket. Your socket looks like it's undamaged, that's a real bonus. A shot 3 inches higher would have led to severe problems. Then we screw a smaller ceramic hip socket into the existing one. We formerly used glue, but a small number of patients were allergic to it, so we stopped that. We then take your damaged femur and cut off the top portion of it. We have that calibrated down to the millimeter, utilizing the films taken in Germany. Now, the prosthesis itself is titanium. It looks like a fine-toothed saw with a golf ball sized knob on the top. The knob is your new hipbone. This saw end of the device is hammered into the marrow of your femur. The knob placed into the new hip socket, I repair the muscles on the way out, and we close. About 3 hours, start to finish."

Josh looked pale. The Taliban with their AK-47s he could handle. This was different. And he wasn't in control. Doctor Wright came over and put his hand on Josh's shoulder. "That's why most people don't want to know. It sounds brutal, and it is. But, it's a very safe procedure, and I've done over 200 of these."

He added, "If it's of any comfort, you're in the best shape of any patient I've had. Most people come to me after years of a sedentary lifestyle, due to the pain, and 50 pounds overweight is the average, for a man or woman. Do you know how much that hinders their recovery?" The best news is that after the initial discomfort, you will have no pain, and after recovery, you can swim, play golf, basketball, just about everything but skiing. We're going to take you to your room now. I know your parents are due in about 1:00. I'll make sure they get in to see you this afternoon. They can stay as long as they want, up till 8:00 that is.

Tom and Karen got into Houston about noon, they had left at 5 am. This place was monstrous, thought Karen. At least twice as large as Atlanta. Tom used his pre-written directions, and reached the clinic at 12:45. they checked in at the visitors desk, and were shown back to Josh's room.

After a lot of tears of joy from his Mom, and "I'm proud of you," statements from his Dad, his parents stepped back. A boy had left them 2 years ago. Here sat a young man. Much more filled out. Much more focused. Injured, yes. Permanent, no. They made sure to keep mentioning that fact. They talked about the girls, Doris, and crazy Max. They saved the best for last.

Karen said, "We set up Goldie's bed in your room. We knew you'd both want that." They talked, non-stop through Josh's 6 pm dinner, and were still at it at 8:00 when the nurse came in and told them it was time. He needed his sleep. Josh would have a big day tomorrow, she said. They said their goodbyes and left for the Holiday Inn where they had reservations.

It was going to be a long night for everyone in Houston.

The Procedure

At 8 am the next morning, Josh was put on a gurney, and wheeled into a pre-op room. He was asked several times what the last four digits of his Social security number was, which hip was being operated on (once he said, "you'll figure it out"), what was his DOB, was he allergic to anything, etc., etc.

Then the anesthesiologist came in and had questions regarding general anesthesia, wanted to look down his throat, and other questions regarding allergies. The Physician's Assistant, came next. And he answered her questions as well, for the fourth and fifth times.

Then the head OR nurse entered. She and another nurse removed the drip Josh had been wearing for days now, and inserted a new one in the other hand.

Finally, Dr. Wright came in and told Josh not to worry, he was the lead-off man today. Josh wasn't worried. He was starting to feel sleepy.

Three hours and twenty minutes later, Dr. Wright walked out to the waiting room and sat down with Tom and Karen. "He's fine, he did great," he said. "There was a little more muscle damage than I expected, but we handled it. A boy, I'm sorry, a young man, like him won't have any problems. He's healthy, strong, and in good shape. The mental part will be the toughest."

"What do you mean," Karen asked. The doctor explained, "I've seen several of these military men. Especially combat veterans. One moment they are protecting us from harm, part of a fighting unit, bonded by blood. Then, bam! They have no identity. They have to form a new one. Mentally, it's tough. You should have seen his face when I called him <u>Mr</u>. Flowers. It was probably the first time he'd ever heard that."

"He'll need help and family support, and I can see he'll get plenty of that. But, it will still be a challenge. If he needs help, someone to talk to, get it for him, whether he wants it or not." Dr. Wright added, "He'll sleep the next couple of hours. Why don't you two get some lunch, and come back later this afternoon. Even tonight, he'll still be loopy. He'll come around completely by tomorrow morning."

"Based on what I saw, I would expect to release him next Monday or Tuesday. I'll get you all the material regarding his recovery. We set up his Post OP home care through the VA in Biloxi, as requested. He'll see a nurse a few times, at home, for coumadin, a blood thinner, staples removed in about a week or so, PT, etc. It's all in there."

Josh awoke, wondering where he was, then remembered. He had a large elastic "girdle around his hips, was a bit woozy, but had no pain at all. Maybe he'd take a little nap, he thought. The next time he woke, a nurse was wanting to give him a sleeping pill. He took that, and dozed off again.

A bright light was coming in through the window. Was he in heaven? No, it was just morning. MORNING...he had slept all night. He looked at a chair in the corner. His Dad was slumped down in it with his feet propped up on a stool. Someone had placed a sheet over him from the chest down. "Dad, Dad," he whispered. Tom's feet fell off the stool, as he opened his eyes.

"Hey son, I thought I'd be up before you. Guess I didn't make it. How are you feeling?"

"I'm not feeling anything," Josh said. "Which is great, I guess." His Dad offered, "The Doc said you did great. Said you'd be outrunning me in 90 days...we'll just see about that," he challenged. "I left your Mom at the hotel, promised her I'd call her cell as soon as you were awake. It's not quite six, but I keep my promises."

Karen must have been up and dressed already, because in less than 15 minutes she walked through the doorway, and planted a big, but careful hug on her strapping son. "Your color's back," she said. "You look good."

An orderly entered and delivered Josh's breakfast. "You don't have to eat the first morning, if you're not hungry. "Bring it on," said Josh, "I'll probably want two." "Just let me know," the orderly said, "there's plenty."

Next the supervising nurse came in. "You'll be up for PT at 2:00. I'm letting you slide this morning. Now that you're awake, someone will be in with your meds in a minute." and she walked away. Josh looked at his Dad. "Did I wake up back in boot camp?" he asked. They both got a good laugh out of that.

The nurse with his medications arrived. "First thing," she asked, "what is your pain level from 1 to 10, 1 being very little, and 10 extreme, which I can tell by the comedy, it's not a 10."

"I'm at zero," Josh answered. The nurse said "You won't impress me with any Macho act. What is it, really?" "Zero," Josh said again. "Listen ma'm, I spent a week with a broken femur, on a drip. I know pain. Right now, mine is zero. I'll let you know if that changes, believe me."

"OK, she said, but I have to ask 6 times a day, so please be truthful." Josh said he would, and she left.

Physical therapy the first afternoon, was not as simple as Josh had imagined. They wheeled him down to the therapy room. He was shown the proper way to rise from the wheelchair to the walker. He had to walk across the room in the walker, and they showed him how to handle steps.

Good foot leads when climbing, injured foot leads when descending.

He also had to perform "range of motion exercises" on a workout table to increase his flexibility. He returned to his room as tired as he used to be after a 3-mile run.

They brought his afternoon medications, where he was introduced to little shots in the stomach with a drug thinner called heparin. This was used to prevent blood clots from forming.

That night, his parents performed an undercover mission for their son. Something Josh had wanted for 2 years, now. He had refused his 6:00 dinner. Tom and Karen arrived at 6:15. Inside Karen's "Hobo" purse was a "Whopper" with cheese, large fries, and a partially melted chocolate shake. Josh wolfed it all down. As good a meal as he had been served in two years. High on carbs, fat, and protein…he needed it.

Every day, he saw progress. Pain was minimal at worst. By the end of the 4th day, he was using the walker to go to PT. The next morning at 10 am, he was released. With his prescriptions, films, and follow-up schedule, Tom and Karen pulled out of the Clinic portico, and headed home. It was Tuesday, October 7.

Josh felt relieved, and worried. The past had been comforting. The future was full of uncertainty and filled with worry.

Homecoming, Oct. 2003

Seven hours later, oyster shells crackled under Tom's tires as he pulled into his drive. Josh said, "Dad, just sit here for a second." And they did. Josh soaked it in. He had never known if he would see this again. In his mind's eye, he had belonged to the Corps. But this was home.

In about 10 seconds, the house erupted. Two girls and a 4-legged flash of gold surrounded the car.

"We have to be careful for a little while," Karen warned. They seemed not to hear. Josh, who had been propped against the passenger door, opened the window, and Goldie tried to crawl through it to get to him. "Easy girl," he said. "We've got plenty of time." Everyone relaxed and backed off a little. The girls watched as Josh sort of hobbled inside. Oyster shells and walkers were not really compatible. But, he got inside, and sat at the kitchen table, so he could soak up the attention.

That first night, Josh slept with the angels, including a very gentle Goldie. She knew he was injured. She took extra care in sleeping beside him on his bed, not hers. They both enjoyed the warmth, and the caring.

The next morning was like a family reunion. Everyone had taken off work, or school, or whatever. They had breakfast as a family. Josh felt the closeness of having loved ones around him. However, he still really missed the Corps, and his responsibilities to his squad and platoon.

The nurse came over that afternoon to measure his blood viscosity, and whether to increase or decrease his coumadin. It checked out OK today and she left.

The physical therapist came over later, and they went through the range of motion and stretching exercises. This would all be repeated for the next few days, then he was on his own.

Sunday came, and all were there, including Josh's newest friend Max Bergeron. Josh though that Max was the evil twin to Mr. Camouflage, and told that to the giggling girls.

He said, "In case of alien, or any other attack, flee the area Max is in. he'll be the first one targeted."

Karen looked up to correct the unruly girls, again, but once she saw the instigator was Josh, she let it go. No reason to spoil the camaraderie, not now.

Things went as per schedule. In just a few days, a nurse came over and used a wire cutter to remove the staples in his hip. Josh realized that there were two liberating moments in this process . First, when the IV was finally disconnected, and second, when the staples were removed. Now he was Josh again. Not hooked to a bag connected to his wrist, and now free of the staples which had held him together for over a week. He was rejoining the human race.

Unexpectedly, a few days later, a U.S. military car pulled up in front of the house. A U.S. Marine Major got out, his aide opening the door. Karen answered the bell. "Ma'm, is Sergeant Flowers available?" Karen was puzzled, but led him into Josh's room.

She stood there as the Major handed Josh a piece of paper. Sergeant Flowers, this documentation, shows that in addition to the "Navy and Marine Corps, Commendation Medal, you have been nominated by the CO, Afghanistan Theatre, for the CMH. I've been instructed by the CO to advise you that it may not get approval, with the political climate being what it is, but the nomination, itself, is a real honor. It is a pleasure to bring this news to you." Josh saluted, out of habit, and the Major responded, with an equally crisp salute. The Major, and his aide said, "Ma'm, we can see our way out. Thank you for your time."

Karen asked, "Josh, what is the CMH?" Josh said sheepishly, "The Congressional Medal of Honor, Mom. The big magilla. Probably won't happen, as the Afghanistan struggle has taken on a political life all it's own. But, it's nice to be nominated."

"What did you do to deserve this award?" Karen asked. Josh answered, "My job, Mom, I just did my job."

Later, when Tom got home, Karen told him of the visit from the Marines, and the CMH nomination.

Tom went into Josh's room. He said, "Son, I'm not being nosey, but this nomination isn't something they pass out like good conduct awards. Do you want to talk about it?" "No, Dad, I don't. That's in the past. I've been thinking too much about it, anyway."

"OK, son. Just remember, I'm here if you need me."

Josh seemed to go into a different zone after that. In the days ahead, he became more distant, more frustrated. His recovery was going very well. He was off the walker, using a cane in three weeks. Week four, he abandoned the cane. He started slowly, walking around the yard, and down to the dock. Goldie was his constant companion, running around him in circles, her tail going 90 miles an hour. She would bring him the old tennis ball for him to throw. Sometimes he would play the game, sometimes not.

Josh was having a bad case of "identity crisis." He was no longer a Marine. What was he?

What was he going to do in the future? His old friend, Chase, had been to see him. They talked some, but they didn't have much in common, any more.

Chase was entering his Junior year at U.S.M. Josh had considered going back to school, the military would pay for it, but it seemed a step backward, after all he had seen and done.

It wasn't money worries which plagued him. He had saved almost all his money, which was tax free while in Afghanistan, and now received a small disability payment every month. Josh just felt worthless, not contributing to anything. He was drowning in self-pity. "Why Me?" It kept coming back to him.

He was sitting on his bed one afternoon. Everyone was at work, school, or the Senior Center. Tears were running down his face. "I'm just useless," he said out loud. He opened his night stand drawer, and removed a bottle of pain reliever. "Percocet 7.5/500." He hadn't needed these during his recovery. Maybe he did now. This could be his way out. After all, he had no status, no job, no future. He was "dead wood."

"Bang, bang, bang", the silence was broken. "What the heck," Josh exclaimed, looking outside his door. It was his old basketball, followed by Goldie. She had found it in a corner of the bonus room upstairs and rolled it down the steps to Josh's room. She looked expectantly at him, tail wagging furiously. "Hoops girl?" he asked, wiping the tears away with the back of his hand. She remembered that word, and ran to the back door. Josh made free throws for about an hour, Goldie being the faithful ball retriever. He still didn't feel confident enough with his hip to try jump shots, but he was getting there.

The next couple of weeks slowly brightened for Josh. He challenged himself to get a direction, some goals for himself.

He could accomplish anything. He had become somewhat "computer savvy" during his time in the Middle East. When they weren't on an "OP", the men played video games, surfed the net, and read up on the news from home.

He decided to use the downstairs computer, to bring up ideas for his future. After a couple of days, of hit and miss, he really hadn't seen anything which stuck out for him. But, he was trying, that was important. The basics, he thought. What are the basics? he went to "Google" and typed in "Career for ex-Military", and hit enter. He got over 200,000 responses in less than 1 second. After eliminating those groups hiring "para-military" mercenaries, airplane and helicopter pilots, nuclear power positions, and others. He came across a listing which said, "Gain your degree in law enforcement with your GI benefits. Pell Grant assistance offered. Learn at your own speed, online."

This is something worth looking into, Josh thought. No, he didn't want to become a policeman, but something was beginning to take shape in his mind.

An Idea...November 2003

By mid-November, Josh had a pretty good idea of where he was headed. He needed to talk. That Saturday, after breakfast, he looked at his Dad. "Have you got a few minutes?", he asked. "Sure," said Tom, "You want to take a walk?"

They went out to the yard, and down to the dock, followed by Goldie, as excited as ever. She seemed to be slowing down a little, but that was to be expected, Josh thought. "Dad," he began, "there are two things, I'll start with the little one. It's about the Accord, I want Jess to have it, I'm going to get something else. It has low mileage. I haven't needed a car, because I couldn't drive until now, but now I'm ready. I saved all my money for two years."

Tom waited for him to finish, then replied, "Josh, I've already promised Jess she could pick out her own car when you returned. We had an "accident, with your aunt Vicky's old van, and we saved the insurance money, for Jess. You know how it is Josh, Connie picked out her Jeep, Jess should have the same opportunity. I think she wants a Toyota Corolla. Beside that, you can use the Accord for a trade-in, and spend less of your savings."

"That sounds fair, Dad." Josh said. "What's the second thing, son? Asked his Dad."

"I've been looking into a line of work that interests me," said Josh. "It will take some preparation, some studying, but I wanted to bounce the idea off you. With my background, and some on-line college courses in law enforcement, I have an idea it could be a hit." Josh continued, "There seems to be a growing demand for personal protection companies. One with a discreet profile, and high tech capabilities. I took the chance and called several companies, you know, to pick their brain."

"All of them were co-operative, but one guy in Atlantic City, was a 15-year Marine veteran, Mike Force. He said I could come up there for a couple of weeks, and see how his company operated, as long as I promised not to open my business in Atlantic City," he laughed.

Tom loved to see his son laugh, again. He was sure Josh didn't recognize how different he sounded, just in the past 5 minutes. Positive, eyes sparkling, and purposeful. And he was proud that Josh thought enough to ask his opinion.

"Josh, I think that's a great idea," Tom agreed. "You wouldn't believe how many requests we get at the casino for just that."

"Some of the big entertainers have their own people, but most do not. For the majority of the performers, the fighters, and the celebrities, I usually tell them to call Dewayne Holmes, who checks with his officers who want some off-duty pay."

Tom continued, "So you can take these courses on-line, wow! Will the government pay for this education, not that it matters?"

"All checked out, Dad. I can start the courses next week. The school has already pre-qualified me for a Pell Grant. So, I'm good to go."

Tom put his arm around Josh as they began to walk back to the house. "So the most important thing, son, is what kind of car are you interested in?"

Tom went to the store and bought steaks and baked potatoes for dinner that night. He would cook both on the "Weber." He added two bottles of decent wine as well. He felt like celebrating, for the first time in quite a while.

Jess and Karen basically had the night off, just fixing a tossed salad for the beginning. Josh's favorite, pecan pie, was made that morning.

Dinner was wonderful. Everyone's steak was made to order, the potatoes were perfect, and the wine was very good. After dinner, Tom stood and said, "Josh has asked me to let the family in on his future plans." He gave them an overview of what Josh was planning. He also added that Jess and Josh would be car shopping in the next couple of weeks.

After his speech, he poured Josh, Connie, and Jess, a small glass of wine and toasted, "To the family," he said. After a sip, he went to the kitchen, grabbed a paper plate, put his steak bone on it and placed it on the floor. "To the whole family," he said to Goldie.

Sunday dinner was the usual, with Max attending. After dinner, Doris said, "Max and I want to tell you something, also. I'm going to move in with Max. It's nothing personal, but we're getting up there in years. We want to see more of each other. And I'm getting tired of having sex in the back seat of his car."

Karen's head hit the table, and Josh snorted iced tea out of his nose, almost choking. We'll still be coming for Sunday dinner. "Thank God for that." Tom commented.

The Move

After leaving the Flower's Sunday Dinner, they had made the same (without the sex comment) announcement to their friends at the Senior Center. They had hinted at some announcement to their friends during the previous week, so there was a full house.

Congratulations had been given by all. Everyone knew of the "marriage penalty" involved with Social Security, and understood that the couple would lose income if the married. So at this age, unless you were wealthy, you "lived in sin" as the Church was fond of saying.

On Monday, Josh signed up for on-line school, Jess went to class, Tom, Connie, and Karen went to work. Sammy Pantolino brought Max, and his pickup truck to the house to move Doris and her belongings.

Doris didn't have a lot to pack, no real furniture. Max had two TV's, and they had bought a new bedroom suite together the previous week. It had been delivered on Thursday, and included a King-sized bed. Doris had claimed the left night stand, because it was the furthest from the window. Max had hired "Molly Maids" to come in and clean up the place last week.

Max owned a small home about 2 miles from the Flowers' house. It was in an "adult community" meaning you had to be a minimum of 55 years old, to maintain ownership here. The community offered tennis, a recreation room, fitness classes, and a 9-hole golf course. The house, itself, was only about 6 years old. It was a single story, only around 1800 square feet, plus a front-loading 1-car garage. The three bedrooms included the master, with bath, and a walk-in closet, the other two were a "Jack and Jill" with a bath in between. The kitchen and great room made up the rest of the interior.

There was a covered patio outside, facing east, which offered respite from the sun. Doris immediately took over most of the walk-in closet. Max, even with his sartorial splendor, only used about a fourth of it's space. The bathroom was another matter.

As they had agreed, when the decision was made to move in, Doris would use the master bath.

Max had already moved into the bath between the "Jack and Jill." "Women need more space," Doris had said. Max had agreed. They made it work. Later that night, Max saw Doris without her false teeth for the first time. They were in a glass, by her night stand, soaking.

Thanksgiving Week, 2003

Josh was really enjoying his on-line schooling. It was the first time since Parris Island, that he was in an actual "study" mode. No, he wasn't required to have any "law enforcement " training, but it would help him get his "Private Investigator's" license, and a gun permit, both of which he would need for his company, not to mention a business license.

He particularly appreciated the "learn at you own pace" commitment that the school offered. He knew, that if he applied himself, he would get his 2-year degree in 9 months. That was his goal. He liked goals.

Connie would be pretty slow in real estate, at holiday time. Jess would be the exact opposite, "Black Friday" was tomorrow, at "The Edge."

Thanksgiving day was the best time of the year. The weather was cooler. The family was all together, for the first time in years. The food was great. Jess had made a huge turkey, plus all the trimmings. This was Goldie's favorite day of the year. Her food bowl was filled several times. Life was good. On Thanksgiving day, the Lions finally beat the Packers.

Friday and Saturday were more football (college). On Saturday, USM beat Eastern Carolina 38-21, to finish a fine season at 9 wins, 3 losses. They would play in a bowl game sometime around New Year's Day.

The Saints were on TV, Sunday this year, so Tom, Josh, and Goldie were excited. This year, it was against The Washington Redskins. The Saints held on to beat the Redskins 24-20. Tom, Josh, and Goldie ran around the family room like crazy people. The women looked on in amused interest. What was this all about, the girls wondered.

Doris gave the details of the move and how she and Max were enjoying each other's company. Thankfully, she left it at that.

Dessert was pumpkin pie, made possible by the garden, with real whipped cream on top, which they all really loved.

The men and Goldie were beginning to look like footballs, Karen thought. After 8 or 9 games in 4 days, how could they keep it up? Then she looked in on them and understood the secret...naps, they were all 3, snoring.

Josh thought that one of the best things about his classes was that if he wanted to take an hour to review or study, it was right there, on the computer. He took advantage of that opportunity several times during the holiday weekend.

He now had his own computer, which Jess's "boy friend" Milo, had added to the home network. He could study anytime he wanted, and anywhere there was a computer with internet access.

Josh's courses were divided into 2 types, general law enforcement, and specific laws. General courses focused on the basics of law enforcement, criminal law, apprehension, surveillance, crime scene investigation, etc. The specifics changed according to your state. A good portion of the course was State of Mississippi oriented.

Josh was absorbed with his education. He now had a goal and wasn't going to be stopped. In six weeks, the middle of December, he had completed 6 months of his courses and on-line tests. At this pace, he would be able to start his company right after he turned 21, in February.

Christmas   2003

Somehow I knew that this was going to be the best Christmas of my life, Goldie thought. She had heard the parents discussing big plans. Plans for a 4-day holiday. Christmas and the following New Years Day were on Thursday, so many people, Dad included, were taking Friday off as well, to extend the Holiday.

Thursday morning at 8 am the family gathered beside the tree and began to open their presents. The girls were at the age when they were anticipating things they needed for business.

Connie was first. She opened a box which said "Palm Pilot" on it. She was excited. "Another step into the 21st Century," she said. The "Pilot" was a PDA (personal digital assistant) which would replace the old paper notebook "Day Timer" and allow her to store her (small) client and resource list, and appointment book. Plus, she could "synch" it between her home and laptop computers. "Goodbye Mr. Gutenberg," she said. "It was nice knowing you. For 550 years, we have depended on printed paper for everything, not anymore."

Jess was next. She had been shaking her gift for several days, trying to ascertain the contents. No luck. Upon opening the box, she found a card. The card said "I'm outside." she rushed to the front door in her sweats, and saw the 2000 Toyota Corolla she had test-driven last week. Her Dad had said it was a little "out of their budget," but now she knew he just wanted to surprise her. She ran over to him and started hitting him on the arms, playfully. "You tried to trick me," she said. "As usual, it worked", he kidded back. "I'm glad we could get you what you wanted."

Josh had a similar predicament. His box was light as a feather. He opened it and found only an envelope. Inside the envelope were two things.

An "open-ended" round trip airline ticket to Atlantic City, and a coupon for five nights stay at the "Resorts International Hotel" there, (the same owner as the Beau Rivage and the Mirage in Las Vegas). "Wow," Josh exhaled.

"Son, you said you had a former Marine in the personal security business there who was going to help you break in," Tom said. "Think of this as an investment in education for your new endeavor."

Josh was excited, but then came Goldie's turn. As usual, she had the largest sized box. "I got this for you girl, let me open it." he said. He pulled a huge wad of material and stuffing out of the gift-wrapped box. Goldie was puzzled by it's appearance. "You've needed a new bed for a long time," he added. "This bed is made from camouflage material."

Josh continued, "Best of all, it has the name and logo of my new company inscribed on it. It's not registered yet, but for you and the family, I wanted to announce it in a special way."

There was a bald eagle emblem. Below the eagle were the words "Special Corps...Personal Security." "That's what I'm planning on naming it," he declared.

He placed Goldie's new bed in his room and took the old one to the trash, but before he put in the can, he held it to his face, and took a deep breath through his nose. Appreciating the scent his dog had left. Impulsively, he removed the stuffing from the bed, threw it away, and kept the old cover. He put the old cover inside the new bed.

That evening, Goldie proudly slept on her new, Josh Flowers customized, one of a kind, bed. She was starting to feel a little bit older, but that was OK.

New Years 2004

Eating, football, more eating, more football. This was the typical New Years Day. It actually started New Years Eve, for Josh. USM played in the Liberty Bowl against Utah. Unfortunately, they were overmatched. They kept it close in the first half, but the "Utes" pulled away to win 17-0. The Saints missed the playoffs, again, coming close with an 8-8 performance. "Just enough to get our hopes up for next year," Dad said, with Josh nodding. "I'm certain they'll win it all someday, Josh said." "That will be a wild party." Dad wasn't so sure.

It rained almost the entire weekend. That was OK, Goldie could "hold it" longer now, and besides it was starting to be uncomfortable, using the stairs. That was OK, too. Dad was saying the same thing about himself.

Karen asked Tom, "Have you noticed Goldie limping?" she asked. "Yes she seems like her leg is bothering her a little," he answered, "but she's getting older, and it's been so cold and damp. That's never good for your joints."

But Goldie was happy, Josh was studying every chance he got, Jess was out of school for the weekend, Connie's business was dead until January 15th or so, and they were all home. Goldie got all the attention she wanted, extra food, extra bones.

On Sunday Max and Doris came for Dinner. Max had on some iridescent pants, a black and gold striped shirt, a yellow sports jacket and the usual shoes and belt. The combination was frightening, but the family was getting used to it.

Doris had obviously been drinking before noon. Her face was more red than usual, not just where the makeup had been overly applied, and, she was smoking her stogie, Karen immediately escorted her to the screen porch.

She swayed through the house with her red frilly dress looking like she was going to a square dance.

For dinner, Jess had decided on shrimp gumbo, served over rice. She had prepared her own roux, whisking flour into the oil when it reached 500 degrees. Of course, she used a cast iron skillet. Then she added okra, celery, bell pepper, garlic, and other vegetables all from the garden. Then a little gumbo file, which thickened the mixture, lastly the shrimp, and highly spicy andouille sausage. A loaf of french bread, and "perfection." She had pecan pie, with vanilla bean ice cream, in Josh's honor.

Doris, came in, and ate, had 2 glasses of wine that Tom had learned to stock for Sundays. Halfway through dessert, Doris passed out, falling face first, into the pie.

The table was silent. Then, "I think she likes the pie," Connie said. "No doubt," Mom agreed.

Atlantic City, Spring 04

Josh landed in Atlantic City and was met at baggage claim by Mike Force, the former Marine. "I spotted you the moment you got into the unsecured area," Force said, "You walk like a Marine."

"Well, thanks, I think," replied Josh. "That was a compliment," Mike said, one Marine to another. "I hope I can help you not get spotted during the next few days," Force added. Josh finally grabbed his bag, and they headed to the parking garage. There he saw a black "Hummer" with a logo, "Force Security" emblazoned on each side. They got out of the garage and drove toward the Force Security office, which Josh had learned was only 3 miles from the airport.

"This is the high profile vehicle we use mainly for advertising at big events, like fights, concerts, sporting events, things like that. The people we protect never ride in this. The first key is low profile. The second key is being alert to threats, the third is overwhelming response," he chronicled. Force continued, "The 1st two are self explanatory. 1, Don't take the obvious route, no matter what your client wants, 2, Stay alert, threats are everywhere. The third key is reality. I don't want one of my guys getting in a fight with some nut job who has a knife. I want four of my guys, kicking his butt and discouraging others."

"Backup and redundancy are important. I insist on it, and I insist my clients pay for it. If they want some goon with a 38 Smith & Wesson watching over them, fine. If they want to feel secure, they use me. They can afford it."

They pulled into the parking lot of Force's office and an old model Jeep wrangler pulled in beside them.

"Josh, I want you to meet my #1 guy, Randy Pierce. He's been tailing us since the baggage claim. Lesson learned?" he said.

"Don't feel bad, you were in your comfort zone.," said Force That's OK," Josh said, "Randy, turn around." Randy turned around, and one of Josh's baggage claim stickers was on his back. "Saw him at baggage claim, tagged him," Josh said.

"Man, this is going to be fun," Force laughed, so did Randy.

Later that night, Josh accompanied Mike and Randy on a job. They had been hired by a rap star who didn't trust his "posse." His real name was Demetrius Jones. His performing name was "Gangsta King Killa."

"All these clowns in the posse are carrying," Mike said, "and most, illegally. I told Mr. Jones, that they couldn't get in the way. If we had a problem, he had to do what I said, immediately. That's tough in this culture. The group doesn't trust outsiders moving in on their meal ticket."

"I reminded him of Tupac Shakur, being killed in Las Vegas, while surrounded with his armed homeboys. That brings it into reality. This guy is just starting to make it to the big time. The money is rolling in. Twenty grand for a worry-free weekend, is cheap. Paid in advance, as always."

Twenty grand, Josh thought, wow!

The next day Josh went with Mike and Randy to interview for a job. This was for a singer named Julia Wonder, who had been booked for 2 weeks, at one of the larger hotels on the boardwalk. Before they entered the hotel suite, Mike asked, "Josh, mind if I use you to help get the job?" "Of course not," Josh replied.

They entered and found Julia and her "manager / boyfriend" on the large sofa in the middle of the 12th floor suite.

Julia and her manager stood, as the 3 security people entered the room.

"We came in to town 2 days early to finalize these plans. Julia is under enough stress, we don't need to worry about her security," said the manager. "But," he added "I'm not sure you are the people we need. We have some people who travel with us. They came in earlier, and can provide the same security for less."

"Then I guess this is a wasted trip," Force said, and turned to leave, then paused. "These people who travel with you, are they licensed to carry firearms in New Jersey? Do they know the ins and outs of the hotel exits so they can have a plan B and C?" he asked.

"Do they work regularly with the heads of security of this hotel? Will they be recognized as 'friendlies,' if the worst happens?"

"I think the answer to all those questions is no, but that's just a guess," Force said, "And the answer to the same questions with my company is yes."

The manager narrowed his eyes and said, "Your proposal quoted $75,000, for the two weeks. Can you do better than that?" "Yes I can," Force replied. "Which part of my protection would you like me to not do? You see that man there, my associate?" He pointed to Josh. "He's been nominated to receive the Congressional Medal of Honor, for extraordinary valor under fire. He doesn't need the practice."

The manager signed the contract, complete with a 100% payment by certified check, five minutes later.

The next day, Force and Josh talked a great deal about the organization, methodology, employee relations, client recruitment and retention, etc.

This was becoming a real education for Josh. He knew how to be alert, to assess threats, to handle himself in a "situation." Now he was learning how to run a business. You could be the best security company in the world. If you couldn't make a profit, it would never matter.

A couple of things Josh had noticed were critical. First, surround yourself with the best people possible. Second, negotiate like you don't need the business, and Third, don't compromise. Your way or the highway. One client injured, one oversight, would get around to all other potential clients, and the competition, like wildfire. And it was always your fault.

Josh would return to Biloxi as a smarter businessman, who just happened to be a highly-decorated former Marine.

Spring 04…Goldie

While Josh was in Atlantic City, I started to feel older, more creaky, my leg was bothering me. "Tom, I'm worried about Goldie. She seems to be limping more," Karen sounded concerned.

"I'll take her in to Dr. Yung," Karen said. "I'm off tomorrow." She went to the phone and managed to get an appointment for the next morning.

Cool breezes swept my ears back as Mom had left my window about half-way open. I loved car rides. We pulled up in front of the Vet's office, and I looked at Karen with concern. "Just a check-up, girl. This time you'll be leaving with me." I felt the comfort in her voice, and that satisfied me.

Dr. Yung came into the examining room and saw me for the first time in years. "Boy, she's grown quite nicely." she said I saw that Dr. Yung had grown too, but not in height, oh well.

Karen described Goldie's limping, and the doctor started rubbing my front leg, it hurt a little, but not too bad. "I don't feel anything loose in there, no tendon or bone crackling. Have you tried glucosamine?" she asked. "It can provide some relief for joint tenderness, I'll also give you a bottle of anti-inflammatory pills you can give her twice a day as treats."

"Treats" was one of the words I knew, so I was excited. Dr. Yung said, "I'll do a blood work-up on her and send it out to the internal medicine vet in Gulfport, just to make sure everything's OK, but I think it's just part of the aging process."

Mom and a cute young helper snuggled me while the doctor drew some blood for the tests.

"We're done," she said, as she put a band aid on my leg. "Here's a treat for being so co-operative," Dr. Yung said, and I gently took it from her hand.

"I'll call you when we get the results in a couple of days. I think the pills will have some effect by then as well."

As promised Mom and I rode home together. The window was still there for me, and I took full advantage of it. Life was good.

Mom relayed the visit to Dad when he got home from work. He was relieved that things seemed to be normal. I was happy to get more treats. I knew that Josh would be home in a day or two because I had overheard the family talking about his trip to Atlantic City."

Sure enough, the next day, Josh drove home from the airport. He was bursting with new ideas, and things he had learned from Mike Force. I've never seen him so excited.

Mom told Josh that she had taken me to see Dr. Yung, and that we had some pills / treats which would make me feel better. Some tests had been sent to another doctor as a precaution.

After all, I was eating and drinking fine, not having any "accidents" and it really hurt just a little when I went up and down the steps. I could still "shoot hoops," and then, like he was reading my mind, Josh said "shoot hoops, Goldie?" And I ran for the door. Not as fast as a couple of years ago, but pretty good.

We got outside, and I noticed Josh was paying more attention to watching me, than making the baskets. I think he wanted to see for himself, how I was. I did good, chasing down errant shots, "heading" the ball back, and waiting for more. After a few minutes, Josh said, "OK girl, back inside." And we went inside through the screen porch and rested. "She seems a little sore," said Josh to his parents.

"We just started her on the pills yesterday," Mom replied. "Let's see how she responds in the next couple of days."

Josh had decided to get a Range Rover as his company vehicle. They were reliable, rugged, and safe. It was a good security SUV with the combination of toughness and power.

He had 3 dealers who carried the brand and were trying to outbid each other. He finally narrowed his search down to a dealer in Biloxi, and one in Mobile, less than an hour away. It just came down to the lowest net price, considering the trade-in for the Accord.

That afternoon Josh and Dad drove up in a shiny silver Range Rover. Everybody came outside to see it, making silly noises about how it was perfect for Josh. He then looked at me and said, "Goldie, ride?" And I scrambled over to my door. Josh had to help me get in, the Range Rover was a lot taller than the Accord, but I didn't mind. He dropped the height of my window, and off we went. So this is how the world looks from up here, I thought. A new angle on life. The weekend was one of the best, ever. After dinner with Doris and Max on Sunday, Josh took me to the beach.

Monday came, Dad, Connie, and Mom at work. Jess was studying, Josh was filling out some on-line business information. Jess answered the phone. "No, but I can give you her number at work, she won't mind, here it is." said Jess.

"Who was that?", Josh asked his sister. "Dr. Yung," she said, and then it hit her.

About 20 minutes later, Josh called his Mom. She told him, "Dr. Yung said there were some different things in the blood test, markers of some type. They want Goldie to come in for an x-ray. Can you take her in today?"

"I'll go right now," Josh said. "I'll call her back and tell her you are on the way. You won't have to wait," his Mom replied. "I wasn't planning on it," declared Josh, the Marine in him coming to the surface. He hung up the phone.

"Goldie, ride?" he said, a little differently than usual. "I'm going with you," Jess said, not asking a question.

They got into the Range Rover. Goldie was in the back, but her window was down, her ears flapping in the breeze.

They took the X-Rays, and the two siblings waited for Dr. Yung to review them. She came out and said, "There's a growth on her left foreleg near the shoulder."

She continued, "I called the internal medicine vet. who analyzed the blood work, he wants to do a biopsy on her leg, and send it to the lab. His name is Dr. Richards. He's on Pass Road in Gulfport. I called in a favor, he will see her when you get there, if you can take her now."

Two minutes later, the three of them were headed west on Pass Road. This is a road that runs parallel to highway 90, all the way from Keesler A.F.B., to Gulfport. It's full of strip malls, fast food, and offices, so as they got nearer the address, Josh had to slow down so as not to miss it. Jess had called her mother's cell, to give her updates.

They found it, and walked in with Goldie. It wasn't very busy, but this was a specialist, who worked by referral from other vets only...no walk-ins, however they would never turn away an emergency. They gave the receptionist the X-Rays, and she directed them to a small room to wait.

Dr. Richards came into the examining room and immediately fell for Goldie. "What a beautiful girl you are," he said to Goldie, ignoring the two young people, which was fine with them.

He looked at Josh and said. "Today, I'm going to give her a local anesthetic, and a light injection for some overall sedation. Then about 20 minutes later, I'll take a small sample of the mass... "mass?" Jess interrupted.

"Yes I'm sorry, she has a growth on her upper leg, we call that a mass. It's not huge. I didn't mean it to come out like that. This growth could be something, and it could be nothing, but that's what we're going to determine. I'll send the tissue sample to a pathologist. These are people who look at this kind of thing through a microscope, all day long, every day.

Now, if you'll both wait outside, I'll bring her out in about an hour. "I'll stay with her," Josh said. "Me too," Jess chimed in. No," Doctor Richards said, "we can't allow that for her sake. We want to keep her in a sterile environment, with no visual stimulation, like seeing one of you two. She would try to come out of the anesthesia."

Dr. Richards said, "The pathologists will tell us what it is or is not. It takes a few days, probably a week, and you can't hurry them. However, I'll send it Fed Ex overnight, and they will fax me the results when they know."

Brother and sister dejectedly waited in the lobby, not talking, staring at the floor. Jess reached out to take Josh's hand, he squeezed it. "I love her too," she said with tears running down her face." "I know," Josh responded, "I know."

In another 30 minutes, Goldie walked out, a little tipsy like Doris, led by an assistant. Goldie brightened when she saw them her tail wagging back and forth. She may be a little groggy until this evening. And give her very little to eat, until she seems hungry, sedation can cause upset stomach.

They loaded back into the "Rover" and headed home... to wait.

Goldie slept most of the way, but managed to catch a little air before they reached the house.

They unloaded, and by this time Mom, Dad, and Connie, were all home. Josh looked at his watch, 5:30, where had the day gone?. He had coffee for breakfast, Jess only a piece of toast. Jess tore into the kitchen, planning an early dinner.

The week continued, as everyone tried not to worry about things they couldn't control. Goldie was acting fine, playing outside, a slight limp, but nothing much. As human nature dictates, the tension grew with every passing day. Still no news. But, he had said a week, hadn't he?

Friday came and went, still no news. It was looking like a long weekend. Saturday morning at 9 am, the phone rang and Karen answered it. She had forgotten, the vet was open a half day on Saturday. Yes doctor, I see, she said. "Can you set it up for me," she asked. "Thank you."

No one was around at the time except Karen and Goldie. "You'll be OK sweetie. We'll take care of you." She called out to the back yard, her husband already working on a project. "Tom, can you come inside for a minute?"

"An oncologist," he muttered. "What does Dr. Yung think?" "It's not her field, so she doesn't want to speculate. We have an appointment on Monday," said Karen. They talked a little more, and Tom said, "Call your Mother, Sunday dinner is off, until further notice, nothing against her or Max. Then call the kids, as soon as they can all be here, we're having a meeting."

At 11:00 everyone was at the dining room table, Goldie happily nearby, her tail wagging. "The doctors say that Goldie has cancer." Tom said.

He let that soak in for a while before continuing. "We don't know how bad it is, or isn't, and won't know until Monday. What we do know is the special place she holds in this family."

He continued, "So, I've made a decision. Tomorrow will not be dinner as usual. You ladies are in charge of preparing a family picnic, at the beach, in Goldie's honor. We're going to act like tourists."

There was that word again, "beach", Goldie thought, with excitement. The next day they piled into Josh's new "Rover", it was the largest, and headed south, over Back Bay, towards the beach.

Josh drove, his Dad rode "shotgun", the three women in the back passenger seat, and Goldie, on her special bed in the very back cargo area, with the window rolled down a ways.

It was a perfect Spring day. They staked their claim to a large section of the beach, with towels, an umbrella, a small tent, an ice chest, two picnic baskets, and a tennis ball. Wow, Goldie thought, this is terrific, we've never done this as a family.

They stayed at the beach for three hours, running with Goldie, letting her get into the water, chasing the ball, and eating, and eating. Fried chicken (without the bone for Goldie), potato salad, beans, bread, and apple cobbler. Even Goldie had cobbler.

It was a great time to be in the Flowers family. Monday would present a new challenge, whatever that may be.

The Verdict

Karen, Josh, Connie, and Jess, along with Goldie, met with Dr. Spence, Monday at 11, in his office.

Dr. Spence said, "Osteosarcoma is bone cancer. Let me give you the basics. I'll be blunt, then you can ask me questions. Usually by the time physical symptoms show up, the cancer has metastasized, that means spread, to other parts of the body, especially the lungs and lymph glands. There is no cure. There is only comfort, and end of life planning. The usual thing we do is to amputate the leg. Then we try to deal with the disease in the rest of the body. The prognosis is that she has 2-4 months. Now I will answer questions. Please excuse my manner, but I never give false hope."

"Thank you," said Karen. "We just want the best for our girl. She's a special part of our family." "They are all special," said Dr. Spence. "No," said Karen, "you weren't listening, she's special." Josh had not seen this side of his Mom before. "Sorry," said Dr. Spence. "Here are my questions," said Karen, and she enumerated them:

"One, will amputating her leg, extend her life?" "No said the doctor, it could reduce pain, but it's spread too far. Even without X-Rays, I know that."

"OK," she continued, What treatments options will extend her life?" "Chemotherapy, mam, could give her an extra 2 months. Please, I know the visions that word brings to mind, but I want you to know that canines, don't have the horrific side effects that humans endure. You bring them in, they get the treatment, a couple of hours later they go home, take a nap, and they're fine. No hair loss, no vomiting, nothing.

Karen asked, "Alright, when will we know it's over, it's time?" Dr.

Spence answered, "You'll know, mam, you'll know when she is in great pain, that it's time."

"Anyone else," Karen asked. They all shook their heads. "Not that it matters, but how much does this chemotherapy cost?" Dr. Spence, said, "$1200 a shot, ma'm, once a month."

Karen huddled with the others. Josh was adamant, "We're not going to amputate her leg, if it won't prolong her life. She has too much pride for that." everyone nodded.

"We'll be here tomorrow for her shot, but no amputation." Karen declared. Josh took Goldie in for her shot on Tuesday. Josh never thought about the fact that there were specialists in the animal world, just like the human one.

He returned to pick up Goldie, and she was ready as promised. $1200 was a lot to pay, but it was only $40 a day to keep her as pain free as possible, he didn't care what it cost.

Dr. Spence had also given them some "pain pills", which he said they would eventually need. Goldie was hanging her head out of the half-opened window, and then taking a nap in the same position. She wasn't hurting, yet.

The next weekend the family drove about 40 miles north, through Kiln, home of Brett Favre, where the land was not so flat. Tom had rented a campsite, and Josh had used his Marine skills to set up a tent where they could all eat and sleep for 2 days. Goldie loved being outside, new smells, new ground, a real experience. They, had too much to eat and spoiled Goldie. Life was good, she thought.

Weekends went like this for a long time. Each weekend being special and different. Goldie walked a little more slowly every week.

After the third monthly shot, things were still good for a couple of weeks. Then, one night, Josh heard her crying. This was it. He wasn't going to let her live in pain for his benefit.

She could barely get around, at this point, and the pills no longer helped.

The next morning, they had a family meeting. After a lot of tears, it was decided. It wouldn't get any better. Karen called Dr. Yung, "It's Goldie's time," she said and hung up. Josh and his Dad, put Goldie into the back of the "Rover", and started off.

Josh stopped after about 30 feet, and said "Wait." he got out, and put Goldie into the passenger seat, had the window halfway down and rested her head out the window. "Now we're ready, he told his Dad, so is she." They drove away, with the wind in Goldie's face, her ears flapping in the wind.

Josh and Tom returned in about an hour, alone. Both of them had red eyes. They all sat at the table as a family. Everyone was in shock. "She went peacefully, Tom said. "I was there, but Josh was holding Goldie when she got the shot. He kept telling her that she was a good girl…that she was his hero."

That day, they all realized how much she had meant to the family. Goldie had been the "glue" which held them together.

Two days later, Josh came home from the mortuary with an urn, filled with Goldie's ashes. He handed them to his Mom, and said "These ashes are for the garden. That's where she'd want to be."

An Awakening

I slowly opened my eyes to a brilliant, sunlit day. The sky was remarkably blue, with a few, puffy white clouds. I was in a beautiful meadow, a waterfall was to my left, a stream of clear water flowed from it. The weather was warm, but not hot. It was like one of those days in October in Mississippi. My belly felt warm, and full. I looked ahead, and was surprised to see familiar faces running playfully toward me.

I saw Daisy, my first Mom, with little "Green" running beside her, struggling to keep up. And there was Vicky, the carbon-copy of her sister, Karen.

"We've been waiting for you Goldie," Vicky said as they nearly reached me. I got up, I could walk, it didn't hurt anymore. I ran to meet them. Sweet kisses, and hugs from all of them. They all seemed and felt so alive. But, where was I?

"We can hear you," said Vicky, but her mouth didn't move. "Yes," Daisy agreed. I could hear their thoughts, and they could hear mine. "Why am I here, and where is here?" I asked. "You are in the Spirit World now," the little Green one said. Vicky continued, "When your body dies in the World of the Present, your spirit comes here. You get to see and learn from the ones you bonded with while you were in the World of the Living."

She continued, "We have come to explain, and help you through this process. In a little while, you will have a session with the Guide of the Spirit World. She decides your fate. And if you are very lucky, you may be given some choices. We'll be beside you during the assembly."

"How do you like it here?",asked Goldie. Daisy spoke up, "Here, all is perfect. You never get hungry, tired, sick, or cold. You are always with beings who you love, and who love you. You live forever, and no one ever dies."

"Wow," said Goldie, with her thoughts. "Does everyone who leaves the World of the Living stay here?"

"Oh no." said Vicky, "The Guide decides. Her decision is final. In he past few years, I've heard that fewer and fewer get to stay here."

"If they don't stay here, where do they go?" wondered Goldie. Goldie forgot that her thoughts were the same as speaking, when "Green" startled her by saying, "You must tell her, Vicky."

"Yes," Vicky explained. "There are three worlds, The World of the Living, which you just left, The World of the Spirits, where you are now, and another, The World of the Dead, where many spirits are sent."

Daisy added, "I can feel you want to ask about this third region, but no one here knows. A spirit who has been banished to the Dead World, has never returned." The others nodded in agreement.

At just that time, Goldie noticed a mist forming near the waterfall. "It's beginning," said Vicky."

A shape began to form in the mist. It was a shape which began as a unformed veil, and settled into that of a woman seated in a tall chair, with another, chair by her side. She was smiling as she looked at me. "It's my Mom, Karen," I thought.

The woman replied softly, "No, Goldie, I take this shape so as not to frighten you. I always assume the temporal appearance of someone who the newly arrived spirit loved or trusted in the world of the Living. I searched your memories, and appeared thusly. Is this acceptable?"

"Of course, I love her," Goldie thought…or said.

"Perfect then," said the Guide.

"We always have witnesses, I see you have three of them." Goldie looked over her shoulder at her long departed loved ones.

"Let me explain how this works," she continued, "have you ever had dreams Goldie?" "Of course," she thought back. The woman said, "Dreams are deeply intertwined with the Spirit World."

"One time, when you thought you had a dream about these three witnesses behind you, it was in response to me, asking for your testament for them."

"You don't remember, but I do, and so do they. Your testimony, and others like you, allowed them to stay here." Goldie looked back, and the three were respectfully nodding.

"So now, I will ask those who live in the World of the Present, to speak about you. You will see their Spirits here, briefly. They will be having what they think is a dream. They will not be able to see you, and in some cases will, or will not remember any part of their 'dream.' The Guide closed her eyes and asked, "Let those Spirits who would speak for this little one, bring their testaments here, and be heard. "

A mist began to form in the chair beside the Guide. It was more transparent than the Guide, but Goldie recognized it easily, as the appearance of Jess. She had her eyes closed, but everyone could hear her thoughts, "Goldie saved my life from the hurricane. I had treated her badly. I tried to make her look negligent, tried to shame her, but she saved me anyway. I will always love her. She was very special to me."

Jess slowly dissolved away. The Guide looked at Goldie, "It's one thing to do a good deed for someone who has shown kindness toward you, it's quite exceptional to save someone who has tried to hurt you."

She looked back to the chair, as another form was developing. The spirit of Doris coalesced into a thin veil of a spirit. "This one is weak, I see," said the Guide. Doris reached out with her thoughts, "I ignored the dog, never had anything to do with her. I wanted all the attention for myself."

"I was selfish, I always have been. But one day I fell, and hurt myself badly. Goldie brought others to help me, because she couldn't do it alone. Yes, if she had been 5 minutes later I would have died, but she saved me. I'll never forget her."
As Grandma faded away, the form of Connie began to take shape.

Connie said. "Goldie was not my dog. For quite a while, I was not a good person. I did things I shouldn't have. I took risks and showed bad behavior. One day a bad man had me trapped alone in my house. He was going to do bad things to me, even kill me."

"Goldie protected me from this bad man. She leapt on him and knocked him to the floor. I had time to go to my room, lock the door and call for help. Today, this bad man in in a place where he can no longer harm people like me. There would have been others hurt by him later, but Goldie stopped him." Connie faded away. The Guide again looked at Goldie, "to save someone is special. To keep them from hurting others in the future is extraordinary!"

Lastly, Josh appeared. She loved seeing his shape take form. Even when he had been away at war, she loved him most…he had picked her. Josh's eyes were closed, but she heard him thinking, "I came back from a terrible place. I had been injured, and was only 20 years old. I felt sorry for myself, and thought 'Why Me?' I was on rock bottom, with no self esteem. I was in pain, not from the outside, but from the inside. I wanted to quit living, but Goldie never gave up on me."

"Eventually I realized, that I shouldn't give up on me either. She saved me…not from dangerous men or awful disasters, but she saved me from myself. She helped me get off of the bottom." And then, sadly for Goldie, he too, dissolved into the mist.

"I think I've heard enough," the dog heard from the Guide. "You've helped nurture this family. You've protected them and helped them grow, just like the garden you once watched over." Goldie gave a puzzled look to the Guide. "Yes," the guide thought, looking at the dog, "I saw that garden in their thoughts, as well, you were an excellent tender of your gardens. On garden of vegetables, and one garden of people."

"Goldie, you are certainly not going to The World of the Dead. But, because of your past goodness, I will give you two choices, and you must make your decision now.

You have done so much good, that I can see you are badly needed in The World of the Living. They have far too few spirits like you, my little friend."

Yes, you can stay here with your loved ones. You will never be hungry and you will never die. You will live in bliss, forever. Or you can go back, and do more good.

"What is your choice, Goldie," came from the Guide. Goldie thought about it. She loved Vicky, Daisy, and "Green." She loved the tranquility.

Goldie turned and directed a question to the Guide. "I think I can arrange that," communicated the lovely image of Karen. "Go kiss your friends goodbye, I know you will be seeing them again."

Home Again?

Tom Flowers was heading home from the Beau Rivage. It had been a long, busy week at the casino. He had just turned off the 110 bridge toward home. He was dwelling on the events of the previous work week. Business was picking up, and he was thinking that if things continued…Tom stood on his brakes to stop short of something in the road. What the heck was that? He got out of the car, and there huddled in front of the vehicle was a little yellow dog, unhurt, but scared.

Tom picked it up for a closer look. No tags, no collar, nothing. He examined it closely, then had a thought. "You're going for a ride with me, girl." He put the dog on his lap, and closed the door. But, the puppy crawled over him to stick it's head out of a barely cracked driver's side window. "You like that girl, let's lower it a bit." She stuck her head out and felt the wind in her face, her tiny ears flapping. Tom pulled into the oyster shell driveway, and took the pup inside. "Look what I found," he exclaimed. The family poured into the kitchen, all in amazement. "It looks just like Goldie," Josh said, "she has the same eyes, and everything."

"And only a week after she died," Jess added. Connie piped in, "I had a dream about Goldie, just last night, it seemed so real."

All together, the family looked at Tom pleading, "Can we keep her, please, please." Before he could answer, Karen picked the puppy up and looked her right in the eyes. "I say it would be bad luck to ignore a gift from heaven, like this. Let's make her our new family member. All in favor, say Aye." Everyone said "Aye."

"Tom," said, Karen, "let's put her in the back yard for just a little while. I'm sure she is excited, and puzzled," although she didn't look it. "Lets make sure we start her training the right way, just like Goldie."

Josh volunteered, and took her from Karen, letting her out to the yard through the screened door. He put her on the ground beside the garden.

The whole family watched from the screen porch. The pup search the yard with her eyes, and sniffed around the garden. Then she stopped, looked back at the assembled family, and walked directly toward the Magnolia tree, and laid down right under it.

They all looked at each other. Karen, with eyebrows raised, finished everyone's thought.

"Yes, truly a gift from heaven."

To Be Continued.

Ken Olive is currently working on sequels focused on members of the Flowers family, and the new Goldie.

Look for Josh Flowers in "Special Corps" coming soon.

Biloxi...A Special Place

During Biloxi's long history, eight flags have flown over her. These flags included the flags of six countries: France, England, Spain, the Republic of West Florida, The Confederate States of America, and the United States stars and stripes. The other two flags were state flags: the Magnolia State Flag and the current Mississippi State Flag.

Pierre Le Moyne, Sieur d'Iberville (after whom the Biloxi's Back Bay region is named) founded Biloxi. Landing onto what is a group of barrier islands collectively known as the Mississippi sound, on February 10, 1699. On February 13, De'Iberville and 14 men landed at present-day Biloxi. After several days the French became friends with the Biloxi Indians, which is still the name of the Biloxi High School athletic teams today.

The Spanish and French influence survive throughout the region. They still celebrate Mardi Gras, and the other Christian holidays. The predominant religion of the local, non-military, population is Catholic. But the community is truly multi-denominational, with a large Jewish population.

Biloxi was the retirement home of Jefferson Davis, President of the Confederacy. Mr. Davis' home, still existing along the beach on highway 90, is named "Beauvoir" or beautiful view, in French. He lived there from 1877 – 1889, along with his dog "Traveler", named after the famous horse of Robert E. Lee.

The evolution of Biloxi involved the warm Gulf waters, abundant with life. Around the turn of the 20th century, Biloxi was widely regarded as the seafood capital of the world. Dozens of shrimp and fishing boats found sea life plentiful. In the 1920's Biloxi had over 50 active seafood factories and processing plants.

Some of the first fishermen were Austrians from the Dalmatia Coast.

From 1890 to 1910, Bohemians, Czechs, Greeks, and Croatians were some of the first foreign laborers.

Cajun families had been a strong base in the region for decades, arriving from Louisiana. Today, Vietnamese make up a large portion of the seafood industry.

Keesler Air Force Base was activated in 1941. It has served many functions, but has always focused on training. From B-24s to Aerospace Projects.

The tourist industry boomed in the 1950s when Biloxi and adjacent cities imported white sand and created it's "largest in the world" (at that time) man made beach, which stretched for 27 miles. Illegal gambling was also pervasive in the 50's and 60's. Of course, bars and night clubs had flourished in Biloxi for decades before, serving liquor, and live entertainment (in fact, in 1967, Jayne Mansfield died the night of an appearance at a local night club in Biloxi), and you could buy beer and wine in many convenience stores. All you had to do was to pay a fee to the state to look the other way, and they did. With the legalization of casino gaming in the early 1990s, Biloxi was suddenly transformed into a destination spot for short or long vacations. Casinos and their peripheral supports of hotels and restaurants grew almost overnight.

Biloxi has been hit by numerous hurricanes, the largest and most intense, was Camille, in August 1969. It remains the most powerful storm to make landfall in the U.S., with winds of up to 220 m.p.h. But, they rebuilt.

On August 29, 2005, Hurricane Katrina hit the Mississippi Gulf Coast with high winds, heavy rains and a 27-foot storm surge, causing massive damage to the area. Katrina came ashore during the high tide of +2.3 feet at 6:56AM,

Two days later, in an interview on MSNBC, Governor Barbour stated that 90% of the buildings along the coast in Biloxi and neighboring Gulfport had been destroyed by the hurricane.

Several of the casinos, including the "Beau Rivage", and "Hard Rock" were devastated, some torn off their foundations and thrown into the coastal buildings, contributing to the damage.

The local population rebuilt again. With New Orleans getting all the attention, the people of the Mississippi Gulf Coast had 95% of the infrastructure and businesses restored within 3 years. Schools, libraries, and churches got priority. Roadways were redone, bridges repaired, "Beauvoir" restored. The casinos and hotels were quickly rebuilt, over 40 casinos exist today. Anyone who wanted a job, had 2 or 3 to choose from, and many people on the coast were taking more than 1. Just as after Camille in 69, the spirit of this diverse community was a shining example of American pride.

They did it themselves, again. And they will the next time too, as well. This is a proud part of the our country.

www.ingramcontent.com/pod-product-compliance
Lightning Source LLC
Chambersburg PA
CBHW070219030726
47505CB00006B/1734